MW00586475

JANIE CROUCH

CRITICAL

instinct

DEDICATION

This book is dedicated my husband, Kevin. If I could go back in time twenty years to our wedding day, the only thing I would tell my younger self is that I was making the greatest decision I could possible make by marrying you.

For all the times I've looked at you in the middle of a book and said, "this is the worst book ever" and you've told me how to fix it.

And how your advice on fixing it always involves adding alien drug runners and space ships. Because, you're right, those things always make books better.

I loved you 20 years ago. I love you now.

I will love you forever.

CHAPTER 1

H E SAT WITH THE PICTURES *of the women in a perfect circle surrounding him. How innocent they all looked. As if they would never betray a man in the worst way possible. Abandon him then continue to take —to purloin— month after month after month.*

Betray. Abandon. Steal.

Their pattern was unmistakable and brutal. So he had created his own, just as brutal.

Strangle. Stab. Burn.

Each woman surrounding him now had a pre-determined place in the pattern. But regardless of where they fell in it, the lesson was the same: a woman would not be allowed to betray, to abandon, to steal from a man.

He was saving future men from these women. The men would never thank him, of course, because they would never know that he'd preemptively destroyed those who would no doubt attempt to destroy them.

But he didn't need thanks.

He touched every picture gently, running his fingers across each face from left to right at the same angle. He touched all ten photos except one, the one that had broken his pattern.

But he would not think about her tonight. Her time was coming. He flipped that picture over and slid it back from him.

He turned to the eighth picture instead. This was the next one. The one he must focus on.

He ignored the voice in the back of his head that said the pattern was ruined. That until he took care of the one he pushed away, none of the others would have meaning. But that would have to wait. He couldn't get to her now.

So he focused harder on the other picture. Memorized the lines of her face as she stared back at him in the photo. Touched the picture again as if he could stroke the strand of auburn hair that had fallen over her forehead as she stared out, no idea he was taking her photograph.

He studied the picture all night until it was all he could see in his mind. Would be all he would see in his dreams. Would be all he would think about until he made sure she would never betray, abandon, steal from another man.

Across town, in the deepest darkness of night, an artist stood in front of an easel, a colored pencil clutched in her fingers. Eyes staring unfocused in front of her, her hand drew the image of a woman. Beginning with a strand of auburn hair that had fallen over a forehead.

She drew —unable to stop, unable to see, unable to feel the blood dripping down from her nose and the agony of clenched muscles within her own body— until she finally finished and collapsed to the ground, exhausted.

CHAPTER 2

DAMN IT WAS GOOD TO be home.

Brett Wagner brushed the last of the cold rain from his head as he sat down at his desk in the homicide division of the Portland PD and turned on his computer. He'd never thought he'd miss the gloom of early spring in the Pacific Northwest, but he had.

South Florida, for all its bikinis, really only had two seasons: hot and melt-your-face-off hot. But it had served his purposes for the last fifteen years, since at eighteen he'd accepted a football scholarship at a mid-sized university there. It had gone on to give him a place to live, and a police force to join, and ranks to move up. Brett had loved it in South Florida, had thrived there.

Yet the 305 had never really been home.

But it had been as far from Portland as he could get and still be in the United States. A distance he'd needed when his parents and two younger sisters had been killed in a car accident and his life had pretty much imploded a few months before he'd finished high school.

Who would've thought he would end up back here where it all started? Brett took in the organized chaos around him. Phones ringing. People walking, talking. The constant click of keyboards, printers, doors opening and closing. Some things didn't change much. Law enforcement stations were one of them.

"Here you go, QB. A gift from Captain Ameling." A uniformed officer dumped a load of files, at least half a dozen deep, off on Brett's desk.

"Seriously, Randal? More?" Brett rolled his eyes at both the high school nickname that still followed him even though he hadn't played ball in nearly a decade and the files that had been piling on his desk all week. Captain Ameling was making his displeasure at Brett's hiring known.

"That's what happens when the Chief of Police is your uncle and you get hired despite the Captain's wishes. Cold cases."

"Chief Pickett isn't my uncle," Brett muttered, grabbing the uppermost file before it slid off the top. But he had been Brett's father's best friend and in Brett's life so long that the title was more true than honorary.

"Look, man." Randal's grin was just as big as it had been in high school. "You don't have to sell me. We're all glad to have our beloved QB back in town. Terri says hearts, and certain lady lingerie parts, are already melting."

More eye rolls. "Randal, you do know that leading a high school team to a state championship doesn't actually have any bearing on real life all these years later, right? And definitely isn't why I got the job here."

"Your success record from Miami was impressive from what I've heard so nobody doubts you're qualified for the homicide detective position." Randal shrugged, still grinning. "I say take your passion and make it happen."

Brett could practically feel his eyebrows finding a new home in his hairline, but he couldn't keep from chuckling. "Did you just quote *Flashdance* to me as life advice?"

"Hey, I'm just saying don't let it get you down. Captain Ameling's just a little pissed that Pickett went over his head. Who knows, maybe Ameling thinks you're gunning for his job."

Because Brett's dad had been police captain before his untimely death.

"Trust me, I have no desire to be captain. Hell, I'll be lucky if I ever get to any current homicide cases the way I'm getting loaded with cold cases."

"Well, Chief Pickett did mention you had a knack." Randal clapped him on the shoulder. "I'll leave you to them.

Terri wants me to invite you over for dinner. Says there's a number of *old friends* that would love to get reacquainted."

Randal waggled his eyes and Brett had no doubt Terri meant some of her cheerleader besties from back in the day. Tall and blond like Terri herself.

But Brett had already done that. Had married a high-maintenance ex-cheerleader only to be divorced by her a couple years later when she realized how much attention Brett couldn't pay her because of his job. He had no interest in someone who needed his attention all the time.

Brett waved Randal off. "We'll see." The other man chuckled and took off down the hall. Brett hoped Randal wouldn't be back with more cases. Or dinner invitations.

Brett would ease into those when he was ready. Maybe in about three or four years.

He opened and glanced down at the file that kept threatening to slip off the top. He grimaced; an aggravated assault and battery of a young woman from two years ago. The bruises that covered her face and body were difficult to look at, no matter how long he'd worked violent crime. But unfortunately, there was nothing particularly unusual about the case. It was just something terrible that happened to yet another person.

Brett closed the file and tossed it into a mesh organizing tray on his desk. Really, this case wasn't even his problem. Assault and battery, even as horrific as this, wasn't a homicide, so it wasn't one of the unsolved cases Brett would be looking into.

With a population of nearly two and a half million in the greater Portland area, there were plenty enough homicide cases –hot and cold– to go around. He didn't need to pick up any others.

Brett looked at his desk and sighed. It was already buried under paperwork, from HR forms he needed to fill out to all the cases that were being dumped on his desk. It was beginning to eerily resemble his new townhouse; buried in stuff Brett needed to sort through.

"Ah, the weary detective sigh. Well-known in departments all over the country." Brett heard the familiar, friendly voice behind him and turned.

"Chief Pickett." He stood up and held out his hand, glancing around to see if the chief's presence was disturbing the workflow of the area. Evidently not since none of the other detectives or officers were paying much attention to the other man. It meant Adam Pickett spent enough time in this area that it wasn't unusual for him to be here. Brett wasn't surprised.

Brett smiled. "You down here to see where the real police work gets done?"

Adam shook Brett's outstretched hand before slapping him on the shoulder good-naturedly. "Yeah, I can see all the police work right there." He pointed at the multiple files littering Brett's desk.

The chief sat in the chair next to the desk. Brett sat back down in his own seat and attempted to make some sort of organization of the mess on his desk. Not easy since he didn't have a bulldozer.

"Yeah, I think Captain Ameling wants to make sure I feel welcome."

Chief Pickett chuckled. "I may have mentioned that you had a good knack with unsolved cases."

Brett shook his head. "Don't do me any favors. I'm going to have to find my way with Ameling on my own."

"Forrest is a good man. He'll come around. At the end of the day we're all on the same side. And, this will give you a chance to test your mettle. Prove you're more than just the return of QB."

"Jesus." Brett laughed and rubbed a hand across his face. "You knew my parents before I was born. Please tell me naming me Quentin Brett wasn't my dad's way of basically assuring I would one day play football."

The older man chuckled. "I can make no such assurances, sorry."

"I would love for you to hang around and chat, Chief, but as you can see I have a pile of cases to get to." Brett picked up the assault and battery file that had most recently been given to him. "Some of them aren't even homicides. Like this one." He passed the file to Adam. "Nasty Aggravated A&B, but I don't think this belongs on my desk, unless someone was killed and I don't know about it."

The chief took the file but didn't open it. That wasn't a good sign. "This case isn't a homicide. You're right."

"But you wanted the file in my hands."

Chief Pickett –very much the Chief now and not Brett's "uncle" Adam– sighed. "Yeah, I did ask for this one to be given to you." He held out the file.

Brett took it and looked through it again. The case was two years old. The victim, Caucasian female Paige Jeffries, age 28, attacked by unidentified assailant. Had been abducted and severely beaten, but had escaped when the abandoned warehouse the perp had taken her to had caught fire.

"Pretty brutal assault," Brett commented, looking at the photo of the woman in the hospital again. In it both her eyes were swollen shut, her nose, and possibly jaw, broken, if Brett had to guess.

"Yeah, she was lucky to have survived. I thought you might remember her. The two of you went to high school together."

"Name rings the smallest of bells." Brett couldn't picture her in his mind. "And with our age differences, she would've been a freshman when I was a senior. And a lot of my senior year…"

Brett shrugged. The whole end of his senior year was a blur because of the loss of his entire family.

Adam knew that. Brett had moved in with his family. "I know. Just didn't know if maybe you knew her."

"Not that I remember. So what's special about this case, if you want a homicide detective to take it?" Brett looked through the investigative report. "At a cursory glance, the police work seems solid. Two years makes it pretty cold. Although, I hate that this happened to someone from the school."

"You into art at all?"

That wasn't the question Brett was expecting. "Um, no. Not at all."

"Paige Jeffries is a painter. Famous."

"Wow." He'd still never heard of her.

"World-renowned, as in, dining in the White House on more than one occasion. She's very highly respected."

Brett looked at the picture again. With all the bruising it was difficult to get a true idea of what she really looked like. In Brett's mind all world-renowned painters looked like Van Gogh or da Vinci — some old guy with a beard and part of an ear missing. Definitely not this young woman.

"So it's a celebrity case." Great. High maintenance. His least favorite trait. "What is she, putting pressure on the department to find who did this to her?"

Not that Brett could blame Paige Jeffries for wanting to find the sicko who'd hurt her so badly. But still, celebrity cases often got ugly.

"Actually, no it's not so much Jeffries herself who's putting pressure on us. It's the governor. His wife is a good friend and patron of Ms. Jeffries."

Outside pressure from way up high to stay on the case. Even worse. Like it or not, politics were part of police work. Brett didn't embrace it, but he accepted it.

"What do you need me to do?"

"Interview her again. I have a meeting with the governor soon and I want to be able to provide an updated report. Be able to say we are still actively investigating the case."

Brett shook his head. "Adam, you know I'll do anything for you. But I just don't think this is a good use of my time. Why can't you just send a uniform to get her statement? I doubt anything has changed at this point."

"We've done that before and it blew up in our faces."

Now Brett was definitely confused. "How?"

Adam shook his head. "Look at the hospital pictures again."

Brett opened the file to study the photo of Paige Jeffries' battered face and torso. He flipped that one over to look at the second picture, but it was just a duplicate of the first one.

"Yeah, it's bad," Brett told the chief, closing the file. "But I still don't get what you want from me."

"Look again, Brett. At both pictures carefully."

Brett's jaw clenched and he forced himself not to sigh. Adam didn't waste time without a reason.

Brett slowly and deliberately opened the file again, scrutinizing the first picture then the second copy. He took the second photo out of its protective plastic sleeve. He grabbed it by the corner to set on his desk, but realized when he moved his hand that it had left a smudge mark on the photo.

Except this wasn't a photo at all. It had been drawn, not taken with a camera.

Now Brett understood. The amount of detail in the drawing was amazing. Holding it up side by side to the hospital photo, he marveled at the similarity. As if the artist had studied the photograph for every detail then copied it line by line.

"It's a drawing," Brett whispered, mesmerized by its horrific detail.

"Yeah, pretty impressive, isn't it? She did it. Paige Jeffries."

"The victim drew an exact replica of her own hospital trauma documentation photograph?" Brett shook his head in distaste. "That's kind of messed up."

Chief Pickett stood up and leaned over Brett's desk to look more closely at the photo. "Well, this is where you come in and why I need you personally to talk to her."

"Okay?" Brett still wasn't clear.

"Ms. Jeffries claims she drew that picture *before* the attack. *Weeks* before."

"What?" Brett leaned back in his chair, scoffing. "That's impossible."

"That's what I'm pretty sure we told her at the time. And what every officer we've sent out to talk to her since has said. But she's held firm." The chief shook his head. "Artists. Go figure. Always looking for attention."

Brett couldn't think of any other reason why someone would claim to have drawn a picture so similar to the hospital photograph weeks beforehand.

He shrugged. "It's just sort of sick if you ask me – no matter when she drew it." Not that he believed she'd drawn it before the photograph had been taken, because that would be impossible.

"Like I said, the governor is going to ask about her at our meeting; he always does. This time I'd like to have something to tell him."

Brett traced the picture with his finger. "With drawing abilities like that, no wonder she's famous. That's amazing."

"Crazy thing is, she's not famous for drawing. Evidently, that's not really her talent. She paints. Something about 'complex color combinations.'" The chief snorted. "Whatever. I fully admit I know nothing about art."

"Trust me. I know even less." The only artwork Brett had ever owned, outside what had been left to him from his parents, was two small paintings someone had given him right before he left Portland after graduating high school. He didn't know who'd left them on his doorstep, just knew that something about them had always made him feel better even after losing his family.

Adam stood. "I'd appreciate it, as both the chief and your Uncle Adam, if you'd make time to talk to Paige Jeffries. See if there's possibly anything that was missed in her case. Talk her down from whatever ledge she gets herself on with the governor's wife and then makes everyone's life here more difficult."

In other words go talk to someone whose drama level was off the charts. An artist, no less. Second only to cheerleaders for their high-maintenance temperaments.

"And see if I can use our old high school memories to help."

Adam smiled. "From what I understand, the QB always gets his girl."

"That was a long time ago, Adam."

"You do this and I'll get Ameling off your case."

Brett shook his head. "I do this and you just leave Ameling and me to work out our own issues."

"Deal." They shook on it. "I'll expect your report by EOB tomorrow."

Brett nodded as the chief walked away and picked up the file again. He didn't know what the hell was going on with Paige Jeffries' claim that she had drawn herself before the picture had even been taken. Obviously there had been some miscommunication. Or whoever interviewed her had talked to her while she was still in some sort of traumatized state.

Or... she was really looking for any attention she could get. Brett grimaced.

Damn it was good to be home.

CHAPTER 3

B RETT HAD WANTED TO RESEARCH Paige Jeffries
before the interview, had wanted to know everything
there was about her. He had even planned to call
Randal and Terri to see if they remembered any details about
her from high school.

Captain Ameling had other ideas, bringing Brett on four
current homicide cases. Brett was glad the man wasn't going
to keep Brett in cold cases the rest of his career, but getting up
to speed had taken all day yesterday and today.

When Brett told Ameling that he had to step out from the
station to interview Paige Jeffries, it had actually been their
first time seeing eye to eye.

"You don't have time to be looking into an A&B cold case just
because the vic happens to be a famous artist demanding attention."

Brett nodded. "I couldn't agree more. This is a one-time
favor, then I'm out."

Ameling didn't have to ask who the favor was for, just
pursed his lips and nodded.

So Brett was on his way to Paige Jeffries' house with
only the file he'd looked over with Adam yesterday and was
attempting to glance at again when he got to red lights. The
further he had to drive out of the city to get to her house, the
more pissed off he became. Her house was beyond the city
limits of Portland, past even the suburbs, up on an overlook.

Obviously privacy was important to Jeffries given the length of the private road leading to her house. Finally he pulled up to a guard house that controlled a massive gate leading into the main drive. A security guard checked his identification and badge, then allowed him through.

While the house was nice, it wasn't ostentatious. There was a warmth to it. And the view of the Willamette River and overlook of the city was worth the miles of windy driveway. Given the location, size, and view of her home —not to mention full-time security— Brett had to assume that a career as a world-renowned painter provided a pretty hefty paycheck. Definitely no starving artist here.

Brett parked his car to the side of the house and knocked on the front door. He waited so long for a response he would've assumed no one was home if a guard hadn't just let him through the gate. Brett raised his hand to bang on the door again when it opened.

Paige Jeffries. Brett recognized her immediately from high school. If he'd been able to research her case even the slightest bit —one regular photograph where her face hadn't been covered in vicious bruises— he would've recognized her.

He hadn't known anything about her then. He'd been a senior to her freshman. But they'd had one class together… an art class, ironically. He'd needed it for some sort of elective credit and it had been in the middle of football season so the coach had worked something out with the teacher. Brett had been absent more than he'd been present.

But every time he'd been there, Paige had been too. With those eyes as crystal blue then as they were now. Like the sea off the coast of an uninhabited island or something. That clear of a blue.

He might not have remembered anything about her, but he remembered those eyes. Gorgeous.

And they were becoming more wary by the second. She backed up from Brett's intense gaze, looking at him like she couldn't quite place him.

Guess not everyone recognized the great high school QB. Randal would laugh his ass off.

Brett took a step back also, not wanting to cause her any alarm, but couldn't force himself to look away. It wasn't that she was so striking a beauty. Or even that she was his usual type. Confident, casual, busty and/or leggy blonds were Brett's normal poison.

The woman in front of him was none of those things. She was tiny, no more than 5'3 to Brett's 6'1. Soft, golden brown hair that flowed past her shoulders and down her back. But damn if he could look away from her, and vaguely recognizing her from high school had nothing to do with it.

"Paige Jeffries?"

She nodded. "You're Brett Wagner. I didn't really pay attention to the name when I got the message that someone was coming to question me again. I didn't realize you worked for the police department."

So she did recognize him.

Paige opened the door far enough to allow him to enter. "Please come in, Officer Wagner."

"Detective." He decided to try charm. "But please call me Brett. We went to high school together, right?"

Paige nodded, wariness not leaving her eyes, as she stepped back and allowed him to enter. Brett walked through, giving her a wide berth. She didn't look like she wanted him coming anywhere close to her. "Yes. But I doubt you remember me."

He smiled. "Actually, I do." He hadn't remembered the name, but definitely remembered those eyes. "Art class."

"You weren't there often enough for you to call it a class." Paige closed the door behind him, and on the reminiscing. "The chief of police must have a meeting with the governor soon."

"Actually, he does. What makes you say that?"

The corner of her lips turned up in the barest hint of a smile. "I'm the governor's wife's pet project." She shook her head. "I shouldn't say that. Melissa is my friend. She feels bad about what happened to me and wants the person who did it to be caught. So every time the chief and governor are meeting, someone like you shows up to see if there's anything new to be found with my case."

Paige turned and gestured down the hallway. "Kitchen, okay?"

"Sure."

Brett followed Paige through the hall, noticing the huge windows that seemed to dominate every wall on the first floor. It was almost as if the house completely opened up to the forest behind it. Natural light flooded the entire house. Brett stopped, transfixed by the beauty.

"Wow. That's pretty amazing. The windows and light."

Paige stopped and turned back. "We don't have an overabundance of sunny days here in the Pacific Northwest, so I like to allow as much natural light in as I can."

"Because you're an artist?"

Paige looked at Brett for a moment before answering in her soft voice. "I guess so. But mostly because I'm just a person who likes light. Those windows were the main reason I bought the house."

Brett followed her into the kitchen. "I don't blame you. How long have you lived here?"

"Since my art career took off nearly five years ago."

Brett tried to remember where she lived in high school but couldn't. He really hadn't known much about the quiet, shy girl she'd been.

Paige walked to a bar stool at the massive granite island situated in the middle of her kitchen and gestured to the other one for him. "Can I offer you something to drink?"

"Sure, just some water if that's okay."

Paige looked almost surprised at his acceptance of her offer. Brett had found over the years that taking whatever food or beverage a witness offered helped them to open up. Made him seem like more of a guest, less like someone to be nervous around.

Paige walked to the refrigerator and removed a couple bottles of water. "You're not like the other officers that have been here." She handed him one of the bottles.

"How so?"

"They were always trying to get in and out as quickly as possible. Ask their questions so they could check them off their list and be able to report back there was nothing new with my case. They never took water. Never mentioned the lighting."

Brett frowned. "Do you think the other officers were ignoring facts pertinent to your case?"

"No. I just think they didn't want to be here. It was always like they had drawn the short straw or something." Paige shrugged. "Did they send you because we knew each other in high school?"

She was definitely smart. Or wary enough of the department to know their tricks. Brett side-stepped. "I don't think the couple of sentences we spoke in art class would constitute knowing each other." And honestly, after his family died, he'd never thought of Paige Jeffries or her blue eyes again until today.

Blue eyes that held shadows. She looked like someone chased by demons. Bone-weary exhaustion from trying to outrun or fight them. Maybe he and the chief had been wrong. She certainly didn't seem like she was some sort of attention seeker.

"I'm sorry if you feel like anyone at the Portland PD was not putting their best effort into the case." And that was the honest truth. No matter what anyone felt about Paige, whether she was putting undue demands on the department or not, she was still the victim. Everyone should be trying to do whatever was in their power to catch her attacker.

Brett didn't even let himself focus on the fury building inside him at the thought of what had happened to Paige. At what she had suffered. That jaw poking out at him had been broken, her face hit so hard one of her eye sockets had collapsed. Her nose shattered.

So if she wanted to stand outside the department with a bullhorn and picket signs demanding they do more to catch her attacker, Brett wasn't sure he'd blame her.

"It's not that I don't feel like they've tried their best," Paige said softly. "I think I made them uncomfortable. Like they didn't know exactly what to do with me. Go ahead and ask your questions," Paige said, sitting on a barstool across from him. "Or... actually I can probably answer your questions without you even asking them."

"You think?"

She took a sip of her water, then continued, holding up her fingers as she ticked off the questions. "No, I have never remembered anything about my assailant. Even though I must have seen him at some point, I can't remember anything about his features at all. How am I doing so far?"

Despite her slightly defiant tone, Brett could tell these were still hard statements for her to make. "Yes, definitely questions that were on my list."

Paige stared down at her water bottle, all of the fight seeming to suddenly leave her. Her voice was much softer as she shrugged. "I've never remembered anything more that would help. It would almost make you think some part of me doesn't want to catch him."

Brett could read her frustration with herself. His hand itched to reach out and touch hers, to comfort her in any way he could. He ruthlessly tamped the feeling down. This was not the time or the situation. Plus, the questions were only going to get harder.

But the desire to touch her, to comfort her, was almost overwhelming. She looked so little and lost sitting on that barstool, clutching her water bottle.

"It's okay not to remember," Brett offered, feeling it was the least he could do. "It's your mind protecting itself. No one would ever blame you for that."

Paige nodded shortly, but Brett could tell she wasn't convinced. It didn't seem to matter if others blamed her. Paige blamed herself.

"And you want to know about my picture," she continued, her voice even more quiet, if possible. "The one I drew."

"Yes," Brett responded gently. "It's in your file, directly behind the photograph taken of you at the hospital."

"That picture is the reason why nobody wants to come up and talk to me, you know." Paige stood and walked over to the counter by the sink, as if she needed to put distance between them. She turned and leaned against it. "It's never the same person twice. How did you get so lucky to be the one chosen if it wasn't because we went to high school together?"

"I volunteered." Brett shrugged, not elaborating.

One dainty eyebrow raised. "You volunteered to take my case?"

"Yeah. Plus Chief Pickett is my friend."

"Ah, so he had to play the friend card to get someone up here."

Brett shook his head. "No, it's not like that. I'm pretty good at cold cases so the chief wanted my opinion. I didn't mind coming here, even when I didn't think we knew each other at all in high school. Maybe I can find something other people might have missed. Fresh eyes."

She shoved her hands into the pockets of her jeans. "But that's right now. In a few minutes you'll get to your questions about the drawing of myself. Then your fresh eyes theory won't be so viable."

Brett could feel his eyebrow raise at her quiet skepticism. "Is that so?"

If possible, Paige's smile was even more sad. "You'll be the latest one who has to tell the poor woman who was attacked and almost beaten to death that she's a liar or just plain crazy. So, congratulations: short straw."

CHAPTER 4

MIC DROP. PAIGE OUT.

Neither of them actually left, but he probably wished he could. Probably wished they'd never had that art class together in high school.

She remembered him from school, of course. She doubted there was anyone who wouldn't remember the charming, handsome quarterback with a quick smile for almost everyone. He was older now, his brown eyes more jaded, his smile not as quick. But he was still ridiculously handsome, tall and fit, with a strong jaw and cheekbones, a slight dimple in his chin. Not to mention a lock of black hair that still fell over his forehead like it had in high school.

All the girls had had a crush on Brett Wagner —*QB* to his friends and teammates— back in the day. Heck, probably a lot of the guys too.

Paige hadn't.

Or, more accurately, she'd known there was so little a possibility that the senior football star would ever even notice her that she'd never even thought of him in that way. Paige had been closer to Brett's younger sisters, twins, who had been a year younger than Paige. Lydia and Audrey had been so friendly and outgoing —like miniature, non-athletic versions of their brother— people couldn't help but be drawn to them, shy Paige included.

She'd even painted them after their deaths. Left the paintings for Brett outside his door. She doubted he still had them now if he remembered them at all.

And she doubted he wanted to be here, despite the fact that his friendly QB smile remained on his face.

Paige had been through interviews with the police enough times to know that the next question Brett would ask would be about her drawing. She would insist she drew it weeks before her attack, which she had, and things would rapidly go downhill from there.

Liar or crazy. Those two options were always what it came down to for the investigating officers. Paige was either lying to get attention or suffering from a form of traumatic delusion, thinking she'd drawn the picture weeks before the attack, could be possible.

Paige wished she had never shown the drawing to the police in the first place. And she darn well wished she'd never actually drawn it. Actually, *them*.

All of them. All the dozens and dozens of pictures she'd drawn over the last two years.

Paige sighed to herself. She was tired. Last night had been yet another night of haphazard sleep. Every night was. Even the nights where she didn't awake huddled on the floor so exhausted she could barely move, like she'd been beaten.

Today she hadn't woken up with sunken eyes and blood dripping out of her nose, fingers cramping and head pounding from drawing something she couldn't remember.

But that didn't mean she'd gotten a good night's sleep. Just because the crazy hadn't happened didn't mean the normal nightmares had taken a break. She had plenty to fear in the dark.

So Paige didn't really want to do this. Didn't want to be called a liar or crazy —however dressed up the terms were— by Brett Wagner, charming hometown hero.

Who was still so attractive it sent little flutters through her stomach.

The thought caught Paige off guard. She hadn't thought of anyone as handsome in a long time. Two years to be exact.

"Crazy or liar, huh?"

Brett's question brought Paige's attention back to their conversation. "That's usually how it goes once the questions start about the drawing."

"Because of when you claim to have drawn that picture that is remarkably similar to the one taken of you in the hospital?" Paige could tell he was trying to keep his voice neutral and eliminate any trace of incredulity. She appreciated the effort.

"Yes. I still claim to have drawn the picture three weeks before the photograph was taken." Although she didn't know why she still kept claiming that when no one was ever going to believe her.

Hell, she'd drawn the picture herself and still didn't believe it.

Paige could see that Brett didn't know what to do with that information. He tried a different tactic.

"You make your living as an artist now right? So you draw for a living?"

"No, I paint. Believe it or not, I'm not really very good at drawing. Colored pencils are definitely not my specialty." She preferred bold oils.

"I'm no expert, as we both know from how often I missed our art class, but the drawing in this file seemed pretty damn good to me."

Paige shook her head. "That is the exception, not the norm."

"But you paint?"

"Yes."

"Realistic figures? Similar to the ones in the file, but with paint?"

"No, my paintings tend to be much more abstract. Although they do involve people, mostly they center around colors."

Paige didn't mention that the colors she painted, the ones that allowed her to make a very lucrative living from her art, were based on the auras of color she caught from people. To Paige, people were surrounded by colors. Her talent was capturing those colors on canvas. The ones she'd done of his sisters were the first ones she'd ever made public in any way.

But she was sure that telling Brett about auras would just land them right back in the "crazy or liar" conversation. Although he hadn't gotten to that point just yet.

But standing there, watching him, she realized she couldn't wait to paint him. Not him as a person, but the colors she so very clearly saw surrounding him. Was almost desperate to immerse herself in his colors and paint him.

The thought once again caught Paige off guard. She hadn't been interested in painting the colors of someone she actually knew in a while, had mostly stuck to the soothing colors of children and older people the last couple of years.

But something about Brett Wagner pulled her in.

"Would it be possible for me to see some of your paintings?" he asked, once again drawing her back from her thoughts.

"Unfortunately, I don't have any of my artwork here right now." That wasn't the complete truth, given all the drawings of the women she'd done over the past two years, but it was as close as she was going to tell him.

"Isn't your house also your studio?"

Paige smiled slightly at the disappointment in his tone. Evidently he really wanted to see her paintings, although she didn't know if it was for personal or professional reasons. "Yes, but I'm having a show next week at a gallery downtown. All my pieces are there."

"I see."

"You should come to the opening of the show. It's sold out but I could get you a ticket." The words were out of her mouth before she could stop them.

They both stared at each other, neither seeming to know what to say. Had she just asked him out?

"I mean, whatever," she backtracked quickly. "I just meant if you need to see my work for the case, that's probably the best way to do it."

Paige got up and walked to the refrigerator and opened its door. She didn't really need anything from it, but couldn't stay sitting at the island with him any longer.

"That would be great. Maybe I'll do that, thanks." Paige heard him say, but didn't take her head out of the fridge. "So you don't really draw normally, you paint?"

"That's right." Paige knew she had to pick something out of the refrigerator. She couldn't stay in here forever.

"Why did you draw the picture of your attack rather than paint it, if that's your normal medium?"

Surprised, Paige turned from the refrigerator to look back

at Brett, her quest for food she didn't really want forgotten. "None of your police buddies have ever asked me that before."

Brett gave a slight shrug. "Why not?"

"They probably just lumped all art in together. Assumed if you could paint then you could draw and vice versa. Or they just never got past the part where I mentioned drawing it three weeks before the photo was taken."

"Probably." Brett shrugged again apologetically. "But regardless, why draw instead of paint?"

Paige stood silently for a moment. Announcing that she'd drawn it in her sleep —that she'd been drawing pictures in her sleep for the past two years— was not going to help with the investigation. Thus far Brett had avoided looking at her as if she was off her rocker, even given her unlikely claim of when the picture was drawn.

Paige knew if she told him the truth about everything then how he looked at her would change.

He'd given her the benefit of the doubt up until now, maybe because of high school, maybe because he was still just a great guy, but once he knew it would be different. Paige couldn't stand to have those brown eyes begin to look at her with mistrust, or even worse, pity.

"I don't know, really." Paige turned back to the refrigerator, taking the truth with her. "Trauma, I guess."

Pretty little Paige Jeffries from art class was lying about why she had drawn rather than painted the picture. But why would she lie? If she was willing to be open with a claim that she drew a picture three weeks before she could've logically drawn it, how much worse was the something she was keeping secret?

Or maybe she was just tired of how the Portland PD had treated her. She couldn't be blamed for not spilling secrets if everyone insinuated she was untruthful or fanatical at every turn.

Brett had very carefully avoided the question that was on his mind: how was it possible for her to have drawn something she had no idea would happen?

Because he'd been wrong. Paige Jeffries certainly didn't come across as some sort of attention-starved individual as he'd first suspected. No posse following her around catering to her ego, no fits of artistic rage or wild parties.

As a matter of fact, nothing about Paige was what Brett expected. Finding her here in her beautiful but empty house, in her socked feet with no shoes, jeans and faded University of Oregon sweatshirt, and the fact that she had stuck her head back in that damn refrigerator to keep from looking at him... Nothing was what he'd expected.

Maybe that picture had just been some freaky fluke thing that she really had drawn before the attack. Heaven knew, Brett had seen enough coincidences over the years in his police work that he no longer wrote off stuff like that.

If Paige Jeffries said she drew the picture three weeks before the attack, Brett would take her at her word. He'd just call it the old friend benefit of the doubt. It wouldn't make any difference in their hunt for the attacker, although in a case this cold you could hardly call it a hunt. And would probably make Paige a lot more at ease with the department. After all, she was the victim.

But the question of why she had drawn the picture instead of painting it? Something was definitely not truthful in her answer there. But again, it wasn't particularly relevant to the investigation. So Brett wouldn't push it right now.

Paige finally turned from out of the refrigerator with a loaf of bread in her hands. "Toast? I'm pretty hungry for some toast."

Brett looked down at his watch. It was one thirty in the afternoon. "No, I'm good. But you go ahead."

He watched as she took what seemed to be homemade bread over to the counter. She sliced two pieces thinly then walked over and placed them in the toaster. There was a fluidity to how she moved; a natural grace. Her movements were unhurried, although Brett highly suspected she was making the toast just to have something to do with her hands. Her light brown hair with strands of gold throughout tumbled over her shoulders and part way down her back.

But her eyes, despite rings of exhaustion under them, constantly darted around. Always hyper-aware and watchful; taking in everything around her. Maybe she'd been like that in high school too, or maybe it was because of the attack, but her crystal blue eyes seemed to notice everything.

Lord, she was beautiful.

Get a grip, Wagner. Here on official business.

"So are you going to ask me when I really drew those pictures?" Paige asked without turning from the toaster.

"No. I already have that information in my file."

She spun around to stare at him. "And you don't find that timeline odd in any way? The fact that I drew them before my attack?"

"Not the craziest thing I've heard in my lifetime."

She turned back and took the toast out of the toaster. "Well, I think you're the first person in your department to feel that way."

Brett shrugged. "I don't really know them well enough to say, but I'm sorry if that's true. I can tell you this: any person in the department would do anything they could to bring your attacker to justice."

Paige didn't have any response to that.

Brett watched as she buttered her toast silently. "Is there anything you've thought of or remembered that would help in the case? You know that even the smallest detail could be important."

She turned and took a tiny bite of the bread and shook her head. Tension tightened her shoulders again. "No, nothing. There's never been anything. You can go back and tell Chief Pickett you gave it your best effort so he can pass that up along the food chain. I'll be able to tell Melissa the same."

"I'd like to ask you some more questions, though." He really didn't have any more but found that he didn't want to leave.

Paige placed her toast back down on the plate and shook her head. "No offense, Detective, but I'm really not interested in answering any more questions. Nothing has changed. I'm well aware of that fact. Believe me, I live with it every day."

Brett wanted to push it, but decided not to. Like she said, she was the one who lived with her attack every day. If she had nothing more to offer, didn't want to talk about it anymore, he needed to honor that. And right now, he had no insight into the case, no reason to think any question he had would do anything but dredge up bad memories for her.

Brett stood up and tucked his chair under the island. "Okay. But seriously, please don't hesitate to contact me if you think of anything. Or need to talk."

Or wanted to go to dinner or a movie or a walk through town. He tamped down those words.

"And know that even if there's no pressure coming from higher up, I'm still going to be doing my damnedest to bring your attacker to justice." He reached out his hand to shake hers, although he was tempted to pull a card from his high school playbook and just grab her in a hug.

Paige stared down at his outstretched hand for a long time before finally reaching out and grasping it in a handshake. Brett felt a slight tremor go through her arm, but she didn't pull away. She continued to stare down at their joined hands without releasing him.

"Hmm," Paige finally whispered as she finally released his hand from her grip, the tiniest hints of a sad smile floating over her lips.

"Something interesting?" Brett couldn't help but ask.

"That's the first time in two years that shaking someone's hand didn't send me into a panic attack." That ghost of a smile again. "Thanks for coming, QB."

CHAPTER 5

SHE COULDN'T STOP THINKING ABOUT Brett Wagner long after he was gone, so Paige did what she had always done when she was stressed. Or scared. Or angry. Or happy.

She painted.

She wanted to capture his colors while they were fresh in her memory. Not that they'd be leaving her consciousness any time soon, or that they'd really changed much since high school. Deep, gorgeous teals and aquas were what surrounded Brett. A center that was so deeply blue it was nearly purple.

Colors as bold, strong, and sharp as the man himself.

Once she got started, Paige was immediately immersed in the painting. Colors mixed, chosen, without hesitation. She may be painfully shy around others, a nervous wreck around a group of people, and terrified in most social and even personal situations, but this —*this*— she could do. She painted with a boldness that was the exact opposite of her personal life.

She didn't doubt herself. Each stroke was purposeful and distinct. Each color fitting the way she envisioned it in her mind.

Paige had always felt like an outcast, a misfit. Except for when she was painting.

Painting had always been part of her life, even before her mother, the only parent Paige ever had to speak of, had died when she was six. Paige had been separated from her two sisters just after her mother's death. Because there had been no immediate family to claim them, the three were sent into the foster care system.

And then, despite the social worker's extended efforts, no foster family could be found to take all three troubled young girls together. Paige, and her sisters Adrienne and Chloe, were not only traumatized by the loss of their mother, but each seemed to have some sort of special need, or special *something*, that was obviously going to require a lot of attention.

Their mother had called it their special gifts. Adrienne and Chloe could hear things other people couldn't. Paige could see things. Colors.

It wasn't like they had superpowers or were psychic or anything. Paige and her sisters' minds just seemed to be more sensitive and receptive to different things.

Of course, when you were talking about triplet six-year-olds with that sensitivity, who'd just lost their mother, it came across as plain old trauma. And a lot of extra work. No foster family had been willing to take that on, so Paige and her sisters had been separated.

Once Paige had lost her mother and sisters it had been painting where she'd found solace. And she'd been finding solace there ever since.

Paige knew she painted colors and scenes no one else could see. That fact no longer gave her a moment's pause. She wasn't sure why she could see the colors that surrounded people, but she'd always been able to. Painting them had come naturally.

Growing up she'd tried to tell one of her foster mothers about the colors. But her child's limited vocabulary, coupled with her foster mother's busyness, had left Paige unable to explain. Over the years she had learned that she saw things other people didn't and to leave it at that.

Most of the time people's colors were beautiful to her, and always so very unique. Especially the children she'd been concentrating on lately. The hues were a joy, a comfort. Paige loved painting their auras for the same reason she loved the giant windows that made up most of her living room. Because she couldn't help but appreciate the beauty of it all.

Adults' colors were more complicated. Generally more muddied. And although Paige preferred the clarity of children's auras, she occasional liked the complexity of adults. Give Paige a strong woman —balancing work, family, love, and play— and Paige could almost guarantee a final painting that may not be beautiful, but would compel you to look. Then look some more.

But some people were surrounded by dark auras. Paige didn't paint those, didn't even try. The dark was too painful to paint. Most of the time it was too painful to even look at.

By the time Paige finished the painting of Brett, the sun was going down. She stepped back to look at it in the dwindling light, pleased with what she saw. It was beautiful. Breath-taking really. She knew her agent would want her to include it in next week's show.

Paige had no plans to do that. She didn't know what it was about this painting, but it compelled her. The same way the man himself compelled her.

She was attracted to Brett Wagner. Not in a freshman's high-school-crush way, but in a full-grown-woman-attraction way.

The thought both befuddled and delighted her. She was uncomfortable around him, but not in the same way she was uncomfortable around most everyone else. Her discomfiture with Brett had nothing to do with fears for her physical safety and everything to do with those butterflies in her stomach that she thought she would never feel again.

So no, she wasn't going to let her agent have this painting. Putting it on display at the show would be like displaying her own attraction to Brett.

It was something she just wanted to keep to herself. To let anyone else know, even Brett —*especially* Brett— would just make her too unbearably vulnerable.

The phone ringing from over at the door drew her attention from the easel in front of her. She answered it on the third ring.

"Ms. Jeffries. It's Jacob at the front gate. Just wanted to let you know that I'm leaving for the day. Tom is here and is taking over. I'll see you tomorrow."

"Thanks, Jacob. See you then."

Paige often thought it was ridiculous that people paid so much for her paintings. Honestly, she was going to paint whether they sold or not, so she would've given them away. But the great thing about her paintings fetching such a hefty price tag was that it enabled her to provide for her needs in an ample way.

One of her biggest needs in the last two years had been to feel safe in her own house. Paying for full-time security to guard the gate and monitor the grounds so she had that need fulfilled had been well worth the salary of the guards. She was often terrified when she stepped foot out of her house, but rarely within it. No one was getting through the gate without her being notified.

Paige hadn't set foot out of her house without security or some sort of entourage for the two years since her attack. It was too hard, too stressful, watching over her shoulder every second. Always afraid. She returned much more exhausted than when she'd left.

So mostly she stayed home. She had friends, a few important close ones that came to visit. And her sister Adrienne, who lived in California with her FBI agent husband, also came by a couple times a year. Her other sister Chloe too, although not as often. Paige was glad to have reconnected with her sisters as adults.

Between her small group of friends and her sisters, Paige's personal life was as active as she wanted it to be. The thought of dating had never even crossed her mind.

Until Brett Wagner walked in her front door earlier today, his large form causing wariness in her, but not fear. And the touch of his hand for the first time making Paige want to step closer rather than immediately rush away. And those soft brown eyes that hadn't looked at her like she was crazy despite what he had to suspect.

Maybe Paige was finally starting to move past her attack.

Now if she could just stop drawing dead women in her sleep.

She knew the Portland PD was frustrated by her inability to remember anything helpful. She'd seen her attacker's face, she knew she had. But she couldn't remember it. She'd worked with a police sketch artist, a therapist, hell, even a hypnotist to try to gather the details out of her mind. But all Paige could remember were the colors that had surrounded the man. Blacks and grays swirling like a steaming vat of evil.

Paige wrapped her arms around herself as she began to shudder. She could remember the colors surrounding the man to the smallest detail. To this day could paint them if someone asked. But somehow "steaming vat of evil" hadn't provided sketchable results for law enforcement.

Not to mention the man had hit her in the face so many times that seeing out of either eye had been nearly impossible.

Paige pushed that thought from her mind quickly. Nothing good came from dwelling on the physical violence she had endured. She knew that as fact.

It was probably time to stop thinking about the attack altogether. For good. It was time to let Portland PD off the hook. It had been two years. There was no reason to think they were ever going to find any new leads about her attack.

Paige wanted her attacker behind bars. Wanted to know there was zero chance she would run into him if she stepped foot out of her house.

But the man was probably never going to be caught. He probably wasn't anywhere near this area any longer. Her attack had been an isolated incident.

Without a description, they'd never catch him.

Every time the Portland PD had to send a good detective like Brett up to her house to talk to her, there was another case —a more active case that had the possibility of being solved— going ignored.

Paige would call Melissa MacKinven and tell her not to put any more undue pressure on the department. It was time. Past time.

And maybe she could talk to Brett Wagner again, but not about anything concerning her case, or weird drawings in her sleep, or violence. They would talk about... whatever normal people talked about.

It had been so long since she had been on a date she couldn't even remember what that was any more.

Plus she wasn't sure that someone as handsome and confident as QB Wagner would even want to go out with her. He was witty and engaging and brave. Paige, on the other hand, was not.

Not any of those things.

She was quiet by nature, introverted. She often was so caught up in painting that she forgot basic things like brushing her hair or eating full meals, for days at a time. She wasn't witty and fun like her sister Chloe or beautiful and tough like her sister Adrienne.

Paige was just mousy. In all the literal and figurative senses of the word: plain, afraid, in a constant state of mental scurrying, darting around looking over her shoulder.

Paige doubted someone like Brett Wagner would be interested in her for very long.

She rinsed her brushes in the sink in her studio and returned them to their rightful places, examining the canvas she'd just finished. It truly was beautiful —his colors were beautiful— but she wouldn't think about Brett any longer. She'd just be thankful she had the painting. It would have to be enough.

Exhaustion pulled at her. Hopefully she'd sleep more tonight than she had last night. And not draw.

Out of habit Paige checked the locks on the doors, then headed upstairs towards her bedroom. Exhaustion nearly overwhelmed her. She knew she should eat something — the few bites of toast she had with Brett hadn't provided much nourishment— but couldn't be bothered. She would get something to eat tomorrow. Sleep was the priority now, especially given how little she had gotten the night before.

The thought made her pause as she changed into the over-sized shirt she always wore to bed.

Would she wake up tomorrow having drawn another face? Another unknown woman covered in painful bruises? Or even worse, someone looking back from the canvas with the blank stare of death?

Paige crawled into bed. Sleep suddenly never seemed further away.

CHAPTER 6

HIS JOB WAS TEDIOUS, INCONSEQUENTIAL, *compared to his principal work. But it allowed him to pay the bills.*
And to pay her.

Rage rose like a savage black wave at the thought, but he forced it back. There was nothing he could do to her, all the things he desired would lead too quickly back to him. All he could do was save other men from the same fate.

As he had again a few hours ago. He thought of the woman's screams, how she'd begged him to stop. But he knew he couldn't trust her pathetic cries.

Betray. Abandon. Steal.

She would never do it to another man. As he'd strangled her with the rope he'd bought weeks ago in a different city far from here, he'd known he was doing some future man a great service. When he'd arranged her dead body on that dingy hotel bed, he'd stared down at her, memorizing that moment. Her dark hair, battered face.

A mental snapshot.

He longed to take a real snapshot with his camera, but couldn't. It was too risky. The photos of his prey while they were alive that he kept would be suspicious enough, if found, but at least partially explainable due to his job.

A job that allowed him to travel where he needed without anyone's notice. To select and track his prey where he was sure there would be nothing connecting them. Nothing leading back to him. But otherwise the job was just a means to an end. An annoyance.

Yet he would gladly continue, despite its tedium, until his pattern was complete.

The following week Brett had finally made some headway in familiarizing himself with the cold cases he'd been dealt, along with making progress in current ones. Captain Ameling still wasn't a fan but at least he wasn't actively trying to make Brett's life a living hell.

But right now Brett was standing over a dead woman and what Captain Ameling thought of him didn't matter. Brett and Alex Olivier, a ten-year homicide detective who'd joined just after Brett had left the area, stood in a motel room in a rather quiet, suburban area of Portland. Healy Heights had never been a particularly dangerous area unless something had changed while Brett had been gone.

"You get a lot of homicides in this section of town?" Brett asked Alex as they began looking around. The scene, which had been called in by the hotel manager after a member of housekeeping found the body, had already been processed by the crime lab techs.

The techs hadn't been very hopeful of getting much information based on what they'd found. The scene had been pretty clean; the body had obviously just been dumped here. The killing had taken place somewhere else.

"No, not at all," Alex responded as he knelt down next to the woman's body laid out on the bed. "You might get a couple of B&E's, maybe some domestic disputes, but that's about it. People here are not going to like a dead body coming so close to their suburban lifestyles."

Brett crouched down next to Alex. The medical examiner would give them an official cause of death, but Brett was willing to go out on a limb and say the woman died from strangulation with the heavy rope still wrapped around her neck. Just as disturbing was the state of her face. Both eyes swollen shut, extensive bruising all over her face.

It reminded him of what had happened to Paige.

He shouldn't be surprised that he was thinking of her again. After all, he hadn't been able to stop thinking about her all weekend. Or any of the days since.

He had enough work to do, and Randal and Terri constantly trying to set him up with someone, that Paige shouldn't be forefront in his thoughts. But the quiet artist had wedged her way, good and solid, into his head.

This was a murder case and Paige's was just assault and battery. *Just.* What had happened to Paige couldn't be described as "just" anything, but at least she was still alive, thank God. Unlike the woman here.

"Beating her that way then strangling her seems a bit over-dramatic, doesn't it?" Alex stood back up.

Brett looked down at the woman's face again. Nose was decidedly broken, maybe her jaw. It really did remind him of Paige's wounds. "Yeah. Damn brutal, that's for sure. And the killer had definite anger issues going on. This is up close and personal violence."

"We had another case a little similar a few months ago. Still unsolved."

"Beaten, then strangled?"

"Beaten, yes. But then stabbed. White female, roughly the same age and description: mid-20s, slender, auburn hair instead of black."

That pretty much ruled out the possibility of a serial killer. Serial killers, almost without fail, followed a pattern. Stabbing one victim, then strangling another? Would be very uncommon for one killer.

"That one was on my payday too, like today," Alex continued. "I remember because I knew my bank account was full when I went to the bar with the guys that night. Drank a pretty large hole in it. My girlfriend was pissed."

"We always get paid on the last day of the month, Alex?" Today was March 31st. Brett hadn't been in Portland long enough to know the paycheck dates yet.

"Yep. The fifteenth and the last day of every month. I know for sure because my girlfriend keeps threatening to call

Winston's Bar and have my tab privileges revoked. A few of us are headed there tonight. You interested in coming?"

"Definitely interested. But not sure about tonight."

"You got a wife? Girlfriend? Ah, you're the famous QB, you probably have both. Bring them along if you like to live dangerously."

Brett chuckled. "My mama didn't raise a fool. And I don't have a wife, at least not anymore. She didn't like a cop's hours."

Alex nodded again. Brett didn't need to say anything more. The life of a cop was hell on marriages. Brett's wasn't the first to fall apart because of all the time he'd had to leave his wife alone. The meals and occasions he'd missed. At first Heather had thought his life to be exciting, even with the abrupt departures he'd sometimes needed to make. But after two years she'd grown tired of it. Tired of *them*.

Brett hadn't fought for her. By the time he'd realized how bad things had gotten, it had been too late anyway. Their divorce eighteen months ago had been about as uneventful as their two-year marriage. He'd dated on and off since, but no one had really caught his attention and interest.

Until he'd met a tiny golden brown-haired beauty last week with haunted blue eyes. Brett wasn't sure anyone had ever caught his attention like Paige.

"Girlfriend then? Sounds like Randal's wife is trying to get you set up."

Brett barely held back a grimace. "Yeah, she's trying to reintroduce me to some of the gals I knew in high school."

Alex grinned. "Not interested in strolls down memory lane?"

Not with the people Terri had in mind.

Brett and Alex continued examining the room. If the body was anything to go by they weren't going to find much evidence anywhere else in this standard hotel room. But they would still look.

"You were with Miami PD before here, right?" Alex asked him as they both looked over the bed for anything that might have been missed by the crime scene technicians.

"Yeah, nine years. First four as uniformed, last five as detective."

"Sounds like you've got the experience needed for this job. I know the Captain is giving you a hard time, but he'll come around."

Brett used a pen-sized flashlight to look around the bedspread. "Let's hope so. The evil-eye every time I come in the precinct is getting a little old."

Alex smirked at that. "He's a good guy. Give him a little time."

Brett planned to leave no doubts in Ameling's mind that Chief Pickett had made the right call in hiring him. "I will."

"Offer still stands if you want to grab a beer."

"Raincheck. I'm actually going to an art show tonight."

Alex laughed. "Wouldn't have figured you as part of the art crowd. Maybe I should've asked if you had a boyfriend. Not that that's a problem."

"Yeah, it's not my normal thing. But thought I would check it out."

The two men finished their search of the room in relative silence. Both hoped the lab technicians would have more to report because they sure as hell didn't have anything.

Brett looked over at the dead woman one more time as the medical examiner began to prepare the body to take away. He was struck again at how much the bruises on her reminded him of what Paige looked like after her attack.

He was still thinking about battered faces later that afternoon back at the Precinct. A beating like that with the dead woman from this morning, the other dead woman Alex had mentioned, and Paige? It was at least worth looking into.

He grabbed Paige's file first since it was still on his desk. Looking at her bruised face was more difficult each time. But her face wasn't what he needed to see. He needed the date of her attack.

April 30th, two years ago.

Brett sat back in his chair. Paige made the third woman who'd had her face horribly beaten on the last day of the month. That was a weird coincidence.

Coincidences did happen in Brett's line of work. But he had learned over the years to never call something a coincidence until you were sure there were no deliberate links.

Brett began to look up state-wide crimes against women that happened on the last day of any month going back for the past five years. Anywhere the woman's face had been battered.

Within a couple of hours Brett had another dozen electronic files to go through. The first seven didn't have the same craniofacial trauma he was looking for, but then he found one that did. A murder victim from eighteen months ago. Brutally assaulted before being burned to death. Then he found another woman, also beaten before she was stabbed. A third from only six months ago. Strangled.

It was getting late now and he knew he should leave it until Monday, especially if he wanted to catch Paige's art show, but Brett couldn't force himself to stop. The more he looked into these cases, the more he began to recognize something evil.

Three women beaten and killed in the last three years in Oregon. Each on the last day of a month. But they'd all been killed in different ways and found in different locations across the state. At first glance there didn't seem to be anything that tied the women to each other, but Brett would be looking further the first chance he got.

Brett printed the electronic case files with the pictures and laid them out on his desk, standing so he could see the pictures more clearly. There was definitely a body-type similarity in the other three women and the body he and Alex had been processing earlier. As soon as they found out who she was, Brett would have even more to examine, especially once he knew what she looked like when her face wasn't covered in bruises.

"Wagner, what the hell are you doing?"

Damn it. Captain Ameling, and all his animosity, was not what Brett wanted to deal with right now. The man was obviously on his way out the door — rain jacket in one hand, briefcase in the other.

"Looking at what I think might be a pattern in some old cases, Captain."

"Ones I assigned you?"

"No, sir. Something else I found."

Ah, the evil-eye again. "Case load too small, Wagner? So bored you have to start searching for patterns in cases that have nothing to do with you? Don't you think one of the other detectives would've found it if there was a pattern?"

Brett shrugged. He didn't want to get into an argument with his new boss, but Brett was sure he was on to something. The older man turned away and Brett thought it was the end of the discussion. But Captain Ameling just put his jacket and briefcase down on another desk and turned back to Brett.

"Tell me."

Brett pointed down at the files. "Four women in the last three years. All with heavy facial trauma before being killed. And all were killed in Oregon on the last day of the month."

That got the man's attention. "Same month?"

Brett shook his head. "No, different month for each."

Captain Ameling bent to look more closely at the files. "Almost all of them were killed in different ways."

"Yes, two were strangled, one burned and one stabbed, including the woman we found today whose identity has not been confirmed yet."

The Captain cursed under his breath. Brett didn't blame him, this was like a smorgasbord of murder methods.

The Captain pointed to one of the files after looking through it. "This burn victim wasn't even labeled a homicide."

"I know. But she had the same battered face and died on the last day of July, so I pulled her."

"And what is that file under your arm?"

"Paige Jeffries. Beaten, but, of course, not killed."

Captain Ameling sighed. "Date?"

"April 30th. Two years ago."

"So, five women. Four with maxillofacial trauma, killed on the last day of any given month. Plus one who is still alive."

"Yes."

"But they were killed in different ways, found in different locations, with varying amounts of time between their deaths. And one of your dead ones was ruled an accident by whoever worked the case before. Not to mention the differences in the victim's appearances — you've got blondes here. Brunettes. Auburn. There's no reason to think this is the work of one person."

It sounded a little far-fetched when Ameling put it like that. But far-fetched didn't necessarily mean wrong.

"I know," Brett responded. Just like he knew the Captain was going to shut him down.

"It's not enough, Wagner. And I don't want the word *serial killer* even breathed unless we know something for sure. Especially not to Chief Pickett." Captain Ameling left Brett's desk and walked over to his coat and briefcase.

Brett didn't blame him. Nothing threw a city into a panic like announcing there was some sick killer on the loose.

"Yes, sir," Brett muttered.

Ameling turned and looked back at Brett and the files on his desk. "But it's a damn weird coincidence, so keep digging. That's what you were brought here for, right? To see things we might have missed?"

That wasn't what Brett had been expecting.

The Captain waved his arm out towards the files on Brett's desk. "So work your magic." The Captain turned and left without another word.

Brett looked at the files for a long time after Ameling left. Could they all be tied together? Ameling was right. There were lots of holes in the theory that these women had been killed by the same man.

But he looked at the pictures again. The women's appearances were different in terms of hair color and skin tones, but they were all similar in build... thin, petite, with long hair. Almost fragile in appearance.

Just like Paige.

If all these cases were tied together then that might mean that Paige wasn't just attacked.

She should've been murdered.

God, how it hurt him to see her battered face. He'd taken his fair share of punches to the jaw —scuffling with friends while growing up, not to mention a couple lucky hits from perps when he was a uniformed cop— but Brett had the build and stature to take it. Still each one had still hurt like a bitch.

Paige was so damn tiny. The thought of someone's fists being used on her in that way made him physically sick to his stomach.

He leaned back in his chair and took a deep breath. She had survived; was alive. That was what was important. But the more he thought about it, the more he was sure whoever had attacked Paige hadn't intended for her to live.

Captain Ameling didn't want Brett mentioning a serial killer. And Brett wouldn't, not until he had more proof. But in his gut he knew these cases were tied together.

And Paige was one of them.

Brett stood, sliding his chair back. He had to see Paige right now. Even though he knew she was fine, he had to look at her with his own eyes.

He would get back to these files tomorrow. They couldn't wait until Monday. Brett had a feeling that once he started digging, he would find even more connections.

More dead women linked in some way.

But right now he just wanted to see the woman who probably should've been dead, but somehow was alive.

Brett didn't know why Paige was alive when the others weren't. He just knew he was thankful.

CHAPTER 7

BRETT WASN'T SURE WHAT HE had been expecting at Paige's art show. He'd had a moment's hesitation when he'd arrived and immediately seen that getting into this shindig was definitely invitation-only. There was a line outside —longer than ones he'd seen for nightclubs in Miami— just for access. And none of those people, all obvious fans of Paige's, were getting into the show. As Brett walked up and gave his name to the man with a headset at the front door, he wondered if Paige had remembered to leave a pass for him.

He felt more relieved than he should when he found out she had. Although he told himself it was just because he didn't want to flash his badge to get inside.

Once in, he'd been expecting people milling around, looking closely at the artwork and quietly murmuring about the interpretive statement, or use of light, or rhythmic composition or any other number of phrases Brett wouldn't really understand. He'd planned to do a lot of smiling and nodding, if anybody deemed talk to him at all.

But instead it was more like a fun, over-sized dinner party. People were walking around, chatting, laughing. Part of it may have been because of the wine and champagne served by the waiters circling around in an unobtrusive fashion. Part of it may have been the three-piece band playing in the corner. An upbeat tune from *West Side Story*, if Brett recalled correctly.

When you're a Jet, you're a Jet all the way...

But mostly it was Paige's paintings that created the atmosphere. They were amazing. Compelling. Brett could barely drag himself away from one to look at the next. The *colors*.

And just one look made him realize he had two small Paige Jeffries originals sitting at his townhouse. He'd never known who'd left the paintings on his doorstep that had reminded him so much of the sisters he'd lost. If he'd had any time to research Paige's art he would've recognized the style immediately.

Given the popularity of her art, they would probably commandeer a pretty price. Not that Brett would part with them for any amount of money.

He looked around at some more of her work. They were all just as vibrant. Captivating. Sometimes even difficult to look at.

And in the center of it all was some sort of 3D rendering of one of her paintings. It burst from the ground into the air, over ten feet tall, reds and oranges and pinks flowing like waves at the top. Breathtaking.

Each canvas encouraged conversation, not just about the painting, but about emotion, life, joy and pain. About what it was to be alive.

Brett never knew he was able to wax so poetic about art. But honestly, Paige's work seemed to be beyond mere paintings to him.

The thought that Paige could've been killed in her attack two years ago ate at him. The world would've lost a truly great artist.

Brett would've lost the woman he hadn't been able to get out of his mind since the moment he'd met her.

"I wasn't sure if you would make it," Paige's soft voice was right beside him.

Brett couldn't stop himself, he pulled Paige into his arms. He just wanted to reassure his psyche that she was okay, unharmed, not in the clutches of some madman. Paige stiffened for just a second, then relaxed into his arms.

"Excuse me, Sir," a security guard tapped Brett on the shoulder. "I need you to release Ms. Jeffries immediately."

Paige looked at the other man. "It's okay, I'm fine, Jacob."

Brett let go of Paige. He hadn't meant to make her nervous in any way, hadn't thought about how his touch might cause her fear. He'd just needed to touch her.

She kept a hand on his arm. "Really, I'm okay." She looked up at Brett first when she said it, then turned to her security guard. "Thank you for checking, Jacob. I appreciate it."

The man faded back into the crowd.

"I wasn't thinking," Brett told her, trying, and failing, to force himself to ease back from her. "I'm sorry if I made you uncomfortable."

She smiled up at him. "Well, I wasn't exactly expecting a bear hug, but it didn't make me uncomfortable."

"It made Jacob pretty uncomfortable." Brett tilted his head towards the security guard who was still eyeing them.

"Jacob knows I don't like to be touched. Sometimes enthusiasts of my art can be a little fervent in their demonstrations of affection. It can be... overwhelming for me."

And then he had to grab her in a hug as soon as he saw her. Way to go, jackass. "I'm sorry, Paige. I didn't even think."

"Please, don't apologize." Her hand still rested on his arm and she gave it the slightest squeeze. "It was nice to be able to call Jacob off for once. Is that normally how you greet people you were questioning a few days ago?"

Brett gave a short bark of laughter. "No, I can assure you it's not how I traditionally greet suspects, victims, or witnesses."

"Good, then I feel special. Can I show you around a little bit?"

Paige was a little shaken by her brief embrace with Brett but not for the reasons she would've thought. She knew what it was like to break out in a cold sweat every time she shook someone's hand, to suffer full-on panic attacks when someone touched her shoulder from behind.

A full embrace? Paige could admit she hadn't let a man anywhere near close enough for a hug in two years. It would have sent her running screaming for the hills.

And yet, here she was, walking with her hand linked in the crook of Brett Wagner's arm. No running. No screaming. No hills.

Go figure.

She could still feel the imprint of his body —just the slightest bit— from when he'd been pressed up against her. Could still smell the manly scent of him. No cologne, just the vague residual scent of whatever soap he'd used. What it was had made Paige want to snuggle closer just for a second.

So different from her normal behavior, she knew it would catch other people's attention. She saw Melissa's surprised glance from across the gallery and knew she would have questions from the governor's wife before the night was over.

"So what do you think about the show?" she asked him, turning away from Melissa's gaze. She would deal with her friend's inquisition later.

"It definitely wasn't what I was expecting."

"In a bad way or a good way?"

His smile made something flutter in her center. "Definitely good. Although I have to admit, I don't have much basis for comparison."

Paige wasn't surprised. "Not a normal art-show attender?"

"No, not really. I always figured they would be more…" Brett seem to struggle to find the right word.

"Boring? Pretentious?" Paige arched her eyebrow at him.

Brett laughed. "Well, actually I was going to say too intellectual for me. But yeah, I guess either of those others would work too."

"Some art shows are everything you'd fear."

"But not yours?" Brett leaned just the slightest bit closer and she was amazed again when she didn't feel her normal need to draw back.

"My art is an extension of me. It's just what I do. I think it's crazy that people spend so much money for my paintings."

"It occurs to me that I didn't realize it, but I've had two Paige Jeffries originals for about fifteen years now."

She blushed, she couldn't help it. "I had painted those with your sisters the year before. Always reminded me of them, so I wanted you to have them. Of course, it never occurred to me that you wouldn't know that and you might just toss them."

"I didn't. They always made me smile. Even though I didn't know who they were from or what they meant, I couldn't get rid of them."

She squeezed his arm. "I'm glad. I was so shy back then, talking to you would've been nearly impossible."

"We talked in our class a couple of times."

She grinned. "I don't think, 'there are quizzes in an art class?!?' counts as much of a conversation."

"I'm still scarred about that. You painted long before high school, right?"

"Yes. I painted for as long as I can remember. What do you think of them?"

It wasn't a question she asked very often. Normally she didn't put much stock in other people's opinions, but she found herself studying Brett's expression closely.

She knew she shouldn't care if he liked her work, but she very much did.

She watched as he looked around the room almost 360 degrees before turning back to her. Her hand was still tucked in the crook of his arm as his brown eyes locked with hers. She took a step closer before she could help herself. Everything around them blurred into a background hum.

"I'm not great with words about stuff like this," Brett said in barely above a whisper. "But your work is compelling. I never knew that art could make me want to keep looking at it."

Paige felt a warmth spread inside her. Brett couldn't have said it more perfectly if he had a degree in art.

"Thank you." She squeezed his arm. "That's exactly how I hope people feel about it."

"And that centerpiece is amazing."

Paige studied it. "It's one of my pieces scanned then printed with a 3D printer. I never knew anything like that was even possible."

"Me either." They began walking around so he could see more. "How often do you have shows like these?"

"At least once a year. More if my agent can talk me into it."

"Will all these paintings sell? There's got to be, what, fifty or sixty in here?"

Paige shrugged. "Actually, most of them were already sold before tonight, I think."

"Wow."

Paige didn't like talking about the business of her art. She had no idea why people bought her paintings, although she was glad they did. "I just paint. I realize I'm one of the fortunate few who is able to make a living from doing what I love to do. I wouldn't know how *not* to paint. Even if I just had to stuff the finished pieces in a closet somewhere, I'd still paint."

Brett tucked her hand a little closer into the crook of his arm. "These paintings stuffed in a closet somewhere would be an absolute crime. And you've got a room full of people here who think so."

"Yeah, success is still a little surreal for me, even though it's been over five years since my paintings started selling."

They walked up some stairs of the converted warehouse that had been turned into the art gallery, further from the jazz band. Paige liked the big, open space of it all, and was glad for its largeness now. It gave her a chance to talk with Brett in relative privacy. She knew it wouldn't take long until her agent, Hunter Barnes, was looking for her wanting her to converse with some of her more important collectors.

Paige would much rather be here chatting with Brett.

"I'm a little surprised you showed up, actually," she told him as they took the last few stairs to the loft. From here, they could look down on the rest of the show. They weren't the only people up there, but at least it was less crowded.

"Well, I was surprised you remembered to leave me a ticket." He chuckled. "That line outside would put Miami nightclubs to shame. I never would've gotten in otherwise."

Paige let go of his arm and turned so she was leaning back against the loft's railing, her back to the show. She didn't want to be able to see when Hunter tried to get her attention. Brett put his hands on the railing, facing the show. Paige would swear she could feel heat where his pinky touched her waist against the railing. Their faces were close.

"I really am glad you made it tonight," she whispered, reveling in the intimacy, in the surprising desire *not* to pull away.

"I needed to see you." His voice was just as low as hers as he leaned closer.

She could tell there was more that he wanted to declare; shadows in his eyes that said his words held darkness and were more than just a statement of the attraction between them.

But he said nothing further, and the shadows melted away — whatever he might have said gone too. Only the attraction was left. She felt his hand slide to the side of her waist, his arm crossing her torso as he took a step closer, still to her side.

"You know what I've been thinking ever since last week?" he asked, voice deep.

"What?"

"How stupid I was not to ask you out in high school."

Paige couldn't help her blush again. "I couldn't have handled *the QB*. I was too shy. Too introverted."

He stepped closer, his cheek against hers as he looked out at her show and she faced the other way. She couldn't see his eyes anymore, but the feel of his cheek against hers —the stubble rough and masculine— stole her breath.

To anyone looking at them from below, it would just seem like a conversation between two people struggling to hear each other over the noise of the room. But Paige could feel every place where their bodies touched one another, and all she wanted to do was get closer. She leaned into him just the slightest bit.

"I hope you'll be willing to give him a chance now. Brett, not QB. He doesn't exist anymore."

She just nodded, caught in the soft brown of his eyes.

"I know this isn't the place, isn't the time," he continued. "You're needed elsewhere, I'm sure. This is your business. But I wanted to see you. To touch you with my own hands."

Slowly he stepped back from her. Paige forced herself not to move towards him, to keep their bodies in contact as she desperately wanted to do.

"It looks like your agent is looking for you," Brett continued. He reached into the breast pocket of his jacket and pulled out a card and held it out to her. "Here's my number at my office, with my cell phone number on the back."

Paige took it, holding it in her hand. Out of the corner of her eye, she caught her agent Hunter making his way up the stairs, his arm linked with Melissa MacKinven. Brett was right, their stolen moment was almost over.

She was surprised how disappointed that made her. Paige was usually thrilled to end a conversation with anyone. Especially a much larger and stronger man.

Brett placed his thumb under her chin and tipped her face back towards his. "I will call you soon so we can finish this," she felt his thumb caress her throat, "but I wanted you to have my number in case you need me."

His lips touched the corner of hers for just the slightest second before he stepped away. Their gaze held as Hunter crossed to them.

"Paige, sweetness, there you are!"

Paige managed to drag her eyes away from Brett to look at the older man who had been her agent, and close friend, for years. Long before Paige had become famous.

"Sorry, Hunter. I needed a little space. Hunter, Melissa, this is Detective Wagner, from the Portland Police Department."

Instantly Hunter's hackles went up. "Surely you're not questioning Paige now, are you?" Both Hunter and Melissa put themselves between Brett and Paige.

Paige realized she'd been letting other people, mostly Hunter and Melissa, run interference for her for too long. She had needed the buffer. But she didn't now, definitely not with Brett.

She stepped out from behind them, closer to Brett. Saw her friends try to hide their surprise as she did so.

"No, Brett is here as my guest. I invited him." She touched Brett on the arm and saw Melissa's eyes widen even more.

"Yes, I appreciate Paige's invite," Brett said, his smile for the other two people warm and genuine. "This is my first art show, and it has been nothing short of fantastic. But I've monopolized her long enough; I know she probably has other duties she's needed for."

Hunter's over-protective zeal melted away. "There are people who want to talk to her. Some have traveled quite a distance to be here."

"I don't doubt it at all." Brett smiled at her then leaned down and gave her a quick kiss on her cheek. "I'll call you soon. I'm going to wander around for a little while longer, but I won't keep you from business you need to conduct. Goodnight, everyone."

Paige murmured goodnight, but Hunter and Melissa seemed too shocked to say anything at all. All three turned and watched him walk down the stairs and across the gallery from their vantage point in the loft.

"Oh my gosh, Paige has a suitor," Hunter said as Brett disappeared from view around a corner.

"A suitor?" Paige laughed at the word.

"That's the perfect word for it," Melissa agreed.

"He's just a friend. We knew each other in high school. I'm not sure he's even interested." It had been a long time since Paige had read signals from a man. Maybe Brett's actions tonight were more casual than she'd interpreted.

The thought made everything around her feel colder and grayer. Paige turned away from the balcony rail and wrapped her arms around herself. She felt Brett's card still in her hand. Should she even keep it?

But then she heard both Hunter and Melissa chuckling. They turned around also and linked arms with Paige on either side.

"Oh honey," Melissa said. "I'll never be able to see and paint colors the way you do, but I know what a man looks like when he wants a woman. And believe me, Brett Wagner wants you."

CHAPTER 8

THE NEXT DAY MELISSA'S WORDS still rang through Paige's thoughts.

Brett Wagner wants you.

Paige had always been mostly a loner. Quiet and shy by nature, she found engaging men —the flirtation that her younger sister Chloe thrived on— exhausting. Paige had had a couple of intimate relationships with men years ago, but nothing that had become too serious.

She'd yet to find a man who didn't mind if she ignored him by painting for hours at a time, falling exhausted into bed only to get up the next day and do the same thing. A man who didn't mind if Paige forgot to brush her hair for days on end.

And then since the attack, she'd stopped looking for men all together. The thought of being touched by anyone was enough to make her physically ill.

Until Brett.

She had no idea how he would react to her forgetting to brush her hair. But for the first time in a long time she was willing to find out.

Something about Brett made her feel safe. No, not safe, that wasn't the right word. Safe was too close to boring. Safe suggested comfort, which she definitely didn't have. What she felt for Brett was too gripping, too exciting, to be called safe.

But she knew there was an element of shelter with him. That she never needed to worry about her physical well-being with him near. He had the heart of a protector — she could see it in the rich colors that surrounded him. He had chosen his occupation well.

She knew he would protect her. Never hurt her, at least not physically.

So no, he didn't make her feel safe, but he helped make her feel… brave.

Paige was just so tired of being scared all the time. A little bit of bravery was so very welcome.

She had felt it walking around the show last night after Brett had kissed her in the loft. Chats with people that would normally have been so torturous, while they weren't fun, at least weren't so exhausting. Because she knew he was nearby. Could sense him. Knew he was watching her.

She didn't need him for physical safety. She had her well-paid security team for that. But having him nearby sparked something inside of her she thought was gone forever.

And bravery was part of that.

Last night, long after all the guests were gone, while leaving the show from a back entrance, Paige had almost been to the car when she remembered a scarf she'd left inside. A member of her security team had offered to go back and get it, but Paige knew right where it was, so she'd gone back in.

Inside the darkened hallway leading to the studio, she'd gotten a chill. She could've sworn she felt eyes on her from outside in the distance. She looked but couldn't see anything but a deep, sticky blackness. She'd grabbed her scarf and immediately headed back to the car. Feeling the business card Brett had given her in her hand had helped. Like it was some sort of talisman.

The event had shaken her, she could admit it. But not as much as it once would have. Once she wouldn't have left her house for weeks after feeling like someone was watching her.

Now she could admit that she sometimes let her imagination get the better of her. That the ugly blacks she thought she saw in the night sometimes were just the dark, not malicious black colors surrounding someone with evil intents.

So… bravery.

Or maybe not bravery but just not allowing paranoia to rule her life.

Allowing herself to feel excitement and anticipation again. Who was she kidding? *Reveling* in the excitement and anticipation that being around Brett Wagner had caused.

Paige smiled as she stepped back from the living room windows, a cup of coffee warming her hands. It was a gorgeous spring day here in Portland. Sunny. They didn't get many of those.

She wanted to go out. By herself. With no guards or entourage.

Not a life-changing thought for most people. But totally new and unexpected for Paige.

She wanted to walk in downtown Portland by the Willamette River. Go to the Saturday Market — full of quilts and ceramics and jewelry and soaps. The people who sold there were artists like Paige, many quirky and strange, but always interesting. Paige had sold her paintings there years ago before they had become collectors' pieces.

Paige had let her attacker steal one of her favorite activities: walking around the market by herself just enjoying the unorthodox vibe of it all.

Not anymore.

She picked up the phone on her desk that automatically connected her with the guard office.

"Everything okay, Miss Jeffries?" She was glad it was Jacob, one of her two head security guards. He'd been with her longest. Understood her situation best. Never judged her.

"Jacob, I need your honest opinion."

"About a painting?"

Paige was pretty sure she had never asked Jacob, or any of the other guards, for his opinion about much of anything outside her work. She didn't tend to be chatty even with the guards that were around all the time.

"No, about my safety."

"Are you worried about something, Miss Jeffries?" She now obviously had his undivided attention.

"You and the team have been with me for two years. Since the incident. But nothing has really taken place since then. Do you feel my life is in jeopardy?"

"Hopefully, with me and the other men around, your life will never be in jeopardy. Are you thinking about paring down your security?"

"No, nothing like that."

"You're a celebrity. It will probably be good for you to have security for the foreseeable future, regardless of whether there are any direct threats or not."

"Yeah, I agree. Here's the thing: I'd like to go into town for the Saturday Market this morning."

"I'd be glad to take you there. It's no problem at all."

"Actually, I think I'd like to venture out a little by myself."

There was a long pause. "You pay me, pay all of us to stay with you. Why don't I just come with you?"

"Because I want to do it myself, Jacob. I want to stop being holed up in fear all the time."

Another pause. This one with a sigh at the end. "Miss Jeffries—"

"Just let me ask you one question. In your professional opinion, do you think I'm in any danger? Just to go downtown for a few hours?"

"Well, like I was saying earlier, you're a well-known artist—"

"I'm not talking about a fan who might possibly recognize me and want to post my picture with them on Instagram. I'm talking about being in *danger*. From the man who attacked me." Paige could feel herself getting agitated, just saying the words. "Do you think he will try again?"

"My professional opinion? No, I don't think you are in danger from that person. Based on what happened in your attack and because you've never heard anything from him since, no stalking incidents or weird gifts, I think you were randomly selected by him two years ago and aren't in any danger from him now."

Paige knew that should make her feel better, but now she wondered if this was a good idea at all.

"You know what? Let's forget it. I'll just stay here."

"Paige." It was the first time she ever remembered the security guard calling her by her first name. "You should go. We'll compromise. I'll drive you down there and drop you and will be nearby. You can walk around as long as you want and then come home."

Paige gripped the phone tighter. Could she do this?

Bravery.

"You're right. He's taken enough. Damn it, he's not allowed to have one single more of my sunny days to fill with shadows. I'll be ready in fifteen minutes."

An hour later, walking through the familiar grounds of the market, Paige knew she had made the right decision. Jacob had dropped her off, and although she had felt a bit like a teenager being dropped off at the mall by her dad, she was glad she was doing this.

Colors, noises, smells —some familiar, some not— surrounded her. And even though they weren't all entirely pleasant, they were fabulous, because they were her choice.

It was a brisk, sunny spring day. Paige walked from vendor to vendor, keeping her face low in her scarf, partially for warmth, partially so she wouldn't be recognized. Although the way people carried on around her, in constant movement and bustle, Paige didn't think anyone was really looking at anyone else, and even if they did get a good look at her she wondered if they would be able to place her.

Any general unrest she felt melted away as she walked and shopped and even chatted. The colors surrounding the artists here were bright and loud and jarring, for the most part. Difficult to look at sometimes, but obviously involving no malice.

After a couple hours of wandering, as much as she enjoyed it, Paige was ready to get away from the cacophony of colors surrounding her. But she wasn't ready to call Jacob to go home just yet. She decided to walk a little along the river. More nature, less people. Maybe she'd get a sandwich from one of the street vendors. Old town had them everywhere.

A grilled cheese from the Little T American Baker truck. She could almost taste it —had been one of her favorites years ago and was just up the block. The sandwich would be the perfect end to her outing.

The food trucks were through a little alley formed by a pedestrian pathway under the main road. People used it all the time to save themselves from having to go the long way around the busy street, but as Paige made her way towards it from the park, she stopped at the entrance.

There was no one in the alley that she could see in the dim light, but she could swear she felt eyes on her again. Like last night at the show.

Like her attack two years ago.

Her heart began to hammer against her ribs, her breathing hitched. She reached in her purse to pull out the phone to call Jacob. She didn't want the sandwich anymore.

The phone flew out of her hands and fell to the ground as strong arms came around her from behind.

"Hey, baby, there you are!"

The voice boomed in her ear. Paige jerked back, but the arms didn't release her. She was trapped.

Panic swamped her and Paige couldn't seem to force any of her muscles to move for a long moment. But when the arms tightened around her she exploded into movement. She flung her head back and could feel her skull hit her captor's face. She twisted and began flailing her legs.

But he still didn't let go.

From somewhere to her side Paige could hear laughter, but her panicked brain couldn't process who it was or why anything was funny. She opened her mouth to scream but a hand came up, covering her mouth over her scarf, which was now over most of her face.

"Damn it, Maggie, what the hell's wrong with you? I think you broke my nose!" The voice attached to the arms that held her said. Paige could barely register the words.

Maggie?

Another set of arms wrapped around her legs and stopped her flailing.

"Maggie, c'mon. Chill." This was the voice from her legs. "Eric, let her go, man. She's really freaking out."

Using every ounce of willpower she could find, Paige forced herself to stop struggling. The people holding her weren't hurting her; weren't taking her anywhere. The arms around her torso let go and Paige fell to the ground, crying out as her elbow cracked against the ground.

She pulled her scarf down from where it had covered most of her face as she scurried backward on the ground ready to run. She stared out at the three men now leaning over her.

"Oh crap. That's not Maggie," one of them murmured.

Not three men. Three oversized teenagers. Yellows and reds zig-zagging around them in jarring patterns. Hormones obviously ruled their every thought and action. But there wasn't any blackness. None of them intended her harm.

One had some questionable grays mixed in with his colors, but that could mean a number of things —from cheating on his girlfriend to plans to stuff some kid in a locker at school— and have nothing to do with Paige.

"Oh my gosh, ma'am, we're really sorry." This was the one who had grabbed her from behind and was bleeding from his nose. "We thought you were our friend Maggie."

The bleeding guy smacked the one with gray in his colors. "Dude, you told us that was Maggie."

That guy didn't make eye contact with Paige. "My bad. Sorry about that. She has the same scarf as you."

"Are you okay?" The third one reached down to help Paige, but she scooted away. She didn't want anyone to touch her right now.

"I'm fine," she said in the strongest voice she could manage. "You guys should just go."

The boys didn't seem to want to stick around, probably afraid they would get in trouble. They glanced at each other and left, quickly.

Somewhere in her subconscious, Paige knew she was safe. Those boys hadn't meant her harm. It had just been a misunderstanding.

But she couldn't get her body to stop shaking; couldn't get the muscles of her legs to work so she could stand upright. She needed to call Jacob to come get her, but her phone had fallen when the boys had first grabbed her and lay on the ground.

She scooted herself over to the phone almost in tears when she saw the screen cracked and no life in it whatsoever. Jacob's number was programmed into the phone, and right now she couldn't get her brain to function enough to recall any numbers from memory.

Even with the boys gone she still felt eyes on her. Wasn't sure if that was just residual panic or true danger. She needed to get out of this alley and back down near the market. Her breathing became labored again as she saw the inky blackness seeming to tendril out the alley behind her.

Paige forced herself up from the ground, wincing at the pain in her elbow. Everything seemed to be spinning as she took unsteady steps away from the mouth of the alley. She didn't know what was wrong. She hadn't been hurt by the boys, just scared. She hadn't felt this disoriented since...

Since the attack two years ago. The last thing she remembered from that day was feeling just like this before she blacked out and then woken up in the clutches of a madman, thrust further in darkness.

Her vision was dimming again as Paige took more steps. She wasn't sure which direction she was even heading, she just knew she needed to get away from here. From the blackness.

She put her broken phone in her jacket pocket, trying to steady herself. And she felt it. A business card.

Brett's card from last night.

"Ma'am, are you okay?"

Paige spun jerkily around at the words, and through her hazy vision could see a woman pushing a stroller. This person wasn't the blackness, but the blackness was still nearby.

"Could you please call the policeman on this business card? Tell him Paige needs him to come get her." She could barely get the words out.

The concerned mom helped Paige sit down on a nearby bench. The world kept spinning around her and ice seemed to have permeated her veins. With chattering teeth she watched as the woman looked at the card and dialed the number.

Then Paige just focused on keeping the darkness away.

CHAPTER 9

B RETT DIDN'T TEND TO PLAY games with women. When he said he would call, he called. And calling Paige today had definitely been part of his plan. He hadn't intended on making either of them wait and wonder.

But receiving a call on his personal cell phone from a stranger who told him Paige was sitting on a bench downtown in some sort of shock? *That* he hadn't been expecting.

"Can I please talk to her?" he'd asked the woman.

"Br-Brett?"

"Paige? What happened, honey? Are you okay?"

"Somebody grabbed me. I was walking. Somebody grabbed me." Her breathing was so labored it had been hard to make out her words.

"Where's your security team, sweetie?"

"Not here." Her teeth seemed to be chattering. "I— not here."

"I'm coming, okay? Just stay right there. I'll be there in just a minute."

He'd talked again to the woman who'd initially called him, making sure he didn't need to send an ambulance — was Paige bleeding, have broken bones? The thought that she'd been hurt again made him sick to his stomach.

But the woman had assured him that physically Paige seemed fine, although maybe in shock. He'd already been running out the main door of the station before disconnecting the call. Fortunately he wasn't far from downtown.

Thank God Paige had his card in her pocket. Why had she been alone? Where was her security team? From everything he'd heard, everything she'd told him, she rarely left the house alone, if ever.

Breaking quite a few traffic laws, Brett made it to Paige's location in record time. From where he parked he could see her huddled on a bench. The lady with the stroller was still with her.

"Paige?" Brett crouched down directly in front of her and placed his hands gently on her cheeks, brushing back the hair that had fallen over her face. She instantly began pulling away from him. "It's Brett, sweetheart."

"Brett?" Her voice was tiny, but at least she stopped pulling away.

"It's okay, alright?" He stroked her cheek again. "Nothing around here to hurt you."

The toddler in the stroller began crying and Brett looked over at the other woman.

"I've got to get him home," she said. "Is she going to be okay?"

He nodded. "I think so. I won't leave her alone. Did you see anything? Know what happened?"

"No, not really. I saw some teenagers running away, then saw her walking, unsteady and shaking. Her phone was broken but she had your card."

"Yes, I'm with the Portland Police Department. I really appreciate you helping her."

"It's no problem. I would hope someone would do the same thing for me if the roles were reversed." The toddler's wail got louder. "I hope she's okay. You don't need me for anything else, right?"

"No. Thanks again for your help."

Brett sat on the bench as the woman left. Paige was shaking. He took off his jacket and put it around her, even though it meant his belt holster was exposed. He pulled her close to him and just hugged her.

Anyone walking by would've thought they were lovers enjoying a rare beautiful day in Portland. Eventually Paige's tremors eased and she relaxed against him.

Brett just held her. He had questions, but wanted to give her time to regroup.

And certainly sitting here with her in his arms was no great hardship.

"It was such a beautiful day, I decided to come down to the Saturday Market," she finally whispered. "It's the first time I'd done that since…"

Brett nodded. She didn't need to say the words.

"After walking around a while, I decided to get a sandwich." Her quiet laugh was humorless. "A grilled cheese from a food truck I knew was on the other side of the highway."

"Little T American Baker?"

She nodded.

"Oh hell yeah. I used to have dreams about those when I moved to South Florida. Embarrassing dreams, inappropriate to mention in polite company."

That got him a ghost of a smile. Totally worth getting her off topic for. He could feel her pulling herself together, finding her strength.

"I got a little spooked at the thought of cutting through the alley."

"Not wanting to walk through an isolated tunnel isn't a paranoia."

"For most people, probably. For me?" She shrugged. "Before I even got to it somebody grabbed me from behind, in a bear hug."

Brett muttered a foul word under his breath, but let her continue.

"My scarf got caught up around my face when I started to struggle. I couldn't see." All the tension was back in her small frame. "I could only think that it was… It was…"

Happening again. Her panicked mind had thought that the attack was happening again. Brett didn't finish the sentence for her, but he easily could have. He let her trail off.

"It was some dumb teenagers, Brett," she told him after long minutes. "They thought I was their friend and were just messing with her. I think I broke one of the kid's nose when I was trying to get away."

"Good." Brett was damn sure not going to let her feel bad about popping some dumbass kid in the nose. "Do you want me to try to go after them? A broken nose could probably give me a pretty good lead."

"No." A ghost of a smile touched her lips again. "They didn't mean any harm, I could tell once I saw them. It was my own stupid reaction that allowed things to get out of hand."

He turned so they were more fully facing each other. "No, not stupid. Completely understandable."

Embarrassment tinged her cheeks. "I was so proud of myself for going out alone. And now look at me."

"Look at you what? You're sitting on a bench, enjoying a beautiful day, taking a breather after an event that would've shaken up anyone."

"I was sobbing on the ground, shivering, with a broken phone, unable to remember any phone numbers. If that lady hadn't come by, I probably never would've been heard from again."

He was relieved to hear a little spunk back in her voice.

"I was so scared, Brett." And just like that the spunk was gone.

He hooked a finger under her chin so she had no choice but to look into his eyes. "You had every right to be scared. This happening to you the first time you went out alone is the most crappy coincidence in the history of the world."

Brett would love to get his hands on those teenagers for about ten minutes. They'd never terrify someone in an alley again.

But right now his focus was Paige. He wanted the soft friction of anticipation filling her, like it had been last night when they talked at her show. Not the nervousness of residual terror.

Brett thought about the case files sitting on his desk. Dead women he'd been studying before he had to rush out. Paige wasn't one of those, and that was the most important thing. Tension he could handle.

But he liked it a whole lot better when her soft body wasn't tense. He needed to do something about that.

"I was planning to call, you know." He nudged her with his shoulder. "No need to create massive amounts of drama just to get me here quicker."

Her laugh might just be the most beautiful thing he'd ever heard. "Yeah, you know me. Attention seeker."

"How about, since we're both here, and I probably was only going to give you another six hours before I called and started begging you to go out with me, if we just go ahead and get that Little T grilled cheese?"

"I don't know... Sounds like you and that sandwich have a past history I'm not sure I can compete with."

He gave her a grave look. "I'll admit, leaving Little T's behind broke my heart. The only way for me to truly get over it is for you to take me there. Watching you eat a Little T sandwich? Now that is a fantasy and a half."

Her laugh chased the rest of the tension away.

"Okay, but if you start orgasmically moaning in the middle of eating it, I'm leaving you. But I'm willing to give you a chance, to help you get past your lost love."

Brett felt certain parts of his body sit up at attention at her words, but he kept a light smile. "Good. I was at the station when you called, but I don't have anything there that needs my immediate attention."

"On a Saturday?"

"Yeah, a few cases I'm following up on. But it will wait until Monday." He didn't want to mention the possible serial killer to Paige. She didn't remember anything about her attacker. And knowing she could've died —*should've* died— would only bring all her tension rushing back.

"I need to get in touch with Jacob from my security team. He drove me here. But my phone broke."

"I'm sure I have your security firm's number at my desk. It's in your file. We'll let them know you're with me and that I'll take you home later."

Her smile was the most beautiful thing he could remember seeing. "Yeah, that sounds great."

She stood and handed him his jacket. "Thanks, I'm feeling warmer now." She took off her scarf and stuffed it under her arm. "I think I'll just leave this off so no other teenagers try to accidentally strangle me with it and throw me into a full-blown panic attack."

Brett could see her irritation with herself again, but didn't address it. She wasn't running for her house, demanding to be alone. She wasn't crying, and even had some color in her face now. She'd had a scare, but she was working her way back from it. Refusing to let it control her.

Courage didn't always roar.

He kept his face averted as he slid the fifty dollar bill to the teenager.

"Dude, I had no idea she would wig out like that."

The boy paused, obviously wanting more information, but then thought better of it and just left. Which was good; he was tired of the boy already. The boy had played his role, tricked his friends into grabbing the woman, and now that role was over. He waved the boy away and he ran. Good. He didn't want to have to kill the boy, but he would.

But he would much rather kill someone who deserved it. He was reminded every single month of how a woman could continue to hurt a man, even after a relationship was long over.

Betray. Abandon. Steal.

Strangle. Stab. Burn. The perfect pattern for the perfect punishment.

Until her.

She had escaped.

Ruined the pattern.

It had taken him months to refocus, to find the pattern again. He'd almost lost control and gotten caught. But now he was back in control again, and she would not escape.

She didn't leave her house very often, he knew from the cameras he'd placed. He knew she would be out last night and he had seen her, had even watched her from afar at her art exhibit. And had been so close to her last night afterwards when she had walked back to the building.

It would have been hardly any effort at all to grab her, take her, and finish what had been started correctly two years ago.

But then she'd turned and left.

When she'd gone out today he'd quickly followed. Paid the boy to trick his friends into frightening her. Into getting her to walk down the alley alone where he was waiting.

And it had almost worked, until she had called that police officer. Ruining his plans again.

And although he could feel the anger singeing inside his veins that she was still alive, he knew it was for the best.

Her time was coming. She would suffer so much more. He would see to it.

And then his pattern would be perfect once again.

CHAPTER 10

B RETT TOOK PAIGE BACK TO the station so he could get the file that had her security firm's phone number. He spoke to Jacob, explaining the situation. But Jacob wanted to talk to Paige, to hear from her that she was alright. This assured Brett that her security team was doing their job correctly, even though he would've preferred if the man had been discreetly tailing Paige rather than letting her go completely alone.

"Jacob, it was just some kids. An unfortunate occurrence. If they had done it to anyone else but me, it probably would've been funny all around. I blew it out of proportion." Brett overheard her assure the other man. "Like you said, I'm not in real danger."

Brett stacked the files on his desk —no need for her to see the gruesome pictures some of them held— while she finished her conversation.

"No, I don't need to say it." She actually rolled her eyes. "I'm sure. Detective Wagner is going to give me a ride home later, so I'll see you tomorrow or whenever you're back on shift. Yes, I'm positive." Eyes rolled again. "Bye."

"Everything okay?" he asked her.

"This is all kind of new for me, so for the security team too."

"What, calling from a police station?"

"That, but everything else too. Me being out on my own. Me getting a ride with someone else. Me telling them I'll be late." She shrugged a delicate shoulder.

"You guys have an emergency word or phrase, right? That's what Jacob was double checking on?"

She looked surprised. "How did you know?"

He put the files in a neat pile near his keyboard. "I checked out the firm you use. They're one of the best around here. In a situation like yours, having an emergency phrase to communicate that you're in trouble but can't say it out loud is good practice."

"I brought an apple with me for lunch."

"That's your phrase?"

"Yeah. It's easy for me to remember. Not that I've ever had cause to use it. But the security guys and I agreed that if I ever start talking about apples with them, they should know I'm in trouble."

It was as good as any, since she probably didn't have cause to talk to her security team about fruit very often.

He hated that she needed a security team at all.

"You ready to face Little T's?"

Her eyes all but lit up. "Bring it. I can't believe how long it has been since I've had one."

He could see her process her own words. Her eyes lost their sparkle and she looked down.

"Hey," He hooked a finger under her chin to lift her face back up. "You're getting one today. That's what counts. You can get one tomorrow too, if you want. And any day after that if you choose."

"But I might be too scared to come out of my house tomorrow."

He brought his face closer to hers and shrugged, smiling. "Then you see if they do carryout and I'll come get it for you."

"I just feel stupid."

"You don't have to do all the hard things at once. You took a step today. You can take another tomorrow or next week or whenever you want to. Your timetable. No one else's."

She took a deep breath and nodded. "Okay. Well right now my timetable says grilled cheese."

He helped her into her jacket. "Lead the way."

Brett was pretty close to those orgasmic moans she'd threatened to leave him for an hour later at Little T's main restaurant that they'd decided to go to rather than the food truck. They were sitting next to each other in a small rounded booth in the back corner.

"This is just as good as I remember," he said. "I used to meet dad at the food trucks for lunch sometimes. He always wanted to try new ones, but whenever I could, I talked him into Little T's."

"He worked for the police too, right? Is that why you went into law enforcement?"

"He was the captain here. And honestly, I had no plans to follow in his footsteps, but found myself majoring in criminal justice, then joined the Dade County PD after college."

"Did you like it in Florida?"

"Yeah, it's so very different from here. The way you appreciate sunshine, you'd probably love it.

Paige smiled. "Of course Portlanders appreciate sun because of its often conspicuous absence. Were you happy to come back here?"

"I was. Florida was just my escape after my parents and sisters died. I liked it, but it was never home."

They talked for a long time. About his life in Florida, and even his divorce. She'd told him a little about her life as an artist, her relatively positive upbringing in the foster system and her sisters. Brett paid for their meal and since neither of them was ready to end their conversation or time together they decided to walk.

"Triplets, huh?"

"Yeah, Adrienne's my older sister, by seven minutes. She lives in San Francisco with her husband Conner, and they're expecting a baby. They're both kind of in law enforcement too."

"State or federal?"

"Conner is FBI. Adrienne has worked with the Bureau, kind of as a consultant for a long time now, ten years off and on."

"Wow, that would've made her a little young when she started."

"Yeah, not quite eighteen."

It wasn't unheard of, but still unusual for the FBI to use a teenager as a consultant. "What does she do for them? It must be a pretty unique skill set." Maybe she had creative skills like Paige. A forensic artist.

"She's sort of a... profiler, I guess is the best word for it. She's *really* good at it."

"What about your other sister? Where is she?"

"Chloe?" Paige rolled her eyes and chuckled at the same time, equal measures of love and exasperation clear in her tone. "She's currently living in North Carolina. She's a writer and the creative director for *Day's End* — a television show that's filming out there."

That wasn't just a television show. That was a *hugely popular* television show about zombies, vampires and all sorts of other apocalyptic stuff.

"Wow, that's a pretty big deal."

She smiled again. "Yeah, Chloe is super creative."

"And she's the youngest?"

"Yep, by seven minutes again. She's the wildest of the three of us. Fun, lots of spunk."

"Do you get to see her very often?"

"Not as much as I would like. When she lived in California I saw her more, but North Carolina is a little further out of my stomping grounds."

"So you're pretty much out here on your own."

She shrugged. "No more than anybody else. But they were there when I needed them to be."

"You mean after the attack?"

He could see her stiffen but she didn't withdraw into herself.

"Yeah, they came immediately. Stayed with me for weeks. I felt kind of bad because Adrienne and Conner were newlyweds at the time."

She seemed to be wandering, a little lost, so he directed them over to an empty bench. "Did it help having them here?"

"As much as anything could. I was completely out of it for the first couple of weeks, on so much pain medication and the swelling in my face made me almost unrecognizable. I don't know what I would've done without them after that."

"Did you ever try to talk to them? Go over details?" He didn't want to bring this back up, but now that he feared they were dealing with a serial killer, her remembering his face could mean the difference between life and death.

"Believe me, I tried with everyone. Adrienne and Conner were so patient. Worked with me every time I asked them to. I should've been able to see my attacker's face. There is no way he could've hit me the way he did without me seeing him."

"That's not necessarily true."

"I could've been knocked unconscious with the first blow? And the rest done while I was out? Yes, but I know I wasn't unconscious." He could feel her small frame tighten. Her voice was hoarse as she continued. "Not at first. Not for a while. I felt every blow."

The thought made Brett sick, but he held firm to his resolve to keep her talking. "Do you think, or the doctors, that it was head trauma that cause you not to be able to picture him clearly?"

"'Head trauma is a delicate thing' - that's a direct quote from the neuro-specialist. She said that I may never fully remember, or even partially remember, what happened that day."

"It sounds like there's a *but* in there somewhere."

She looked over one shoulder at him. "*But* she also said that I didn't necessarily have wounds that should affect my memory."

He shrugged. "It happens. The brain protects itself."

She seemed to switch topics. "You saw all my paintings last night at the exhibit. Saw all the colors. My paintings are based on colors of people I choose to paint. Their *auras*. Different shades and hues based on their thoughts and emotions and intents towards others."

"So when you're painting people you see colors."

"Actually, I see the colors around people all the time, whether I'm painting them or not. It's one of the reasons I don't necessarily like to be around people a lot of the time. It can be pretty overwhelming."

Brett wiped a hand along his face. He had no idea what to do with this information. He guessed it was possible. Paige was an artist, in tune with colors and stuff. Maybe that part of her senses —if you could call seeing *auras* around people *senses* for God's sake— was just more developed. Not unlike his skills in detective work. He had certain senses that were more well-developed than the average person. Even had a sixth sense about criminals a lot of the time. Could he really explain that? No.

But *auras*?

Her features were tight as she sat next to him. She had slid her leg back down on the bench and was now holding her midsection. Almost as if to protect herself from a blow, at least the emotional one she figured was about to come from him.

"Most of the paintings you saw last night were of children. I love their colors most of all. Usually so bright and clear. Adults' colors are more muddled; more complicated."

He studied her for a long time. "Has painting always been this way for you? The auras."

She nodded. "For as long as I can remember."

"Those paintings you left for me at my house in high school. The ones of my sisters. Were they…?"

Paige nodded giving him a sad smile. "Yes. Lydia and Audrey were my friends, only a year younger than me. They were always so animated and affectionate. They talked to me at school all the time even though I was painfully shy. Their auras were so vibrant. I wanted to make sure they wouldn't be forgotten."

Brett grabbed her hand. "Thank you. For painting them. I never knew why those paintings reminded of my sisters, I just knew they did."

"I'm glad. When Mr. Ragno saw the paintings in class before I gave them to you, he encouraged me to keep working with that style. So those paintings are what started my career."

Brett sat back trying to take it all in. Auras. People having colors. He could accept it. But he wanted to get back to where this conversation had started.

"Okay," he said. "It's a little strange for me, but okay. But what does that have to do with you not being able to remember your attacker?"

Her arms wrapped more tightly around her middle and insecurity washed off of her in waves. "I can't remember him because I don't think I ever saw him. His aura was so black it blocked out all his features to me. All I could see was darkness."

CHAPTER 11

BRETT THOUGHT SHE WAS WEIRD. He might not have said the words outright, but he had to be thinking it. She knew better than to talk about the colors and auras she saw around people. It was odd to her and she lived inside her own head every day. How could anyone else understand it at all?

But he hadn't run. Hadn't made a polite excuse and driven her home as soon as possible when she'd told him about them. And that they were sometimes so overwhelming —like in her attacker's case— that she couldn't see anything else but them.

"Things happen in law enforcement that I can't always explain or even begin to understand. Once saw evidence that an 80-year-old woman had lifted a two hundred pound refrigerator to save her grandson trapped underneath." He'd shrugged. "The body and mind work in ways we don't always understand."

After that they'd moved on to other subjects. More neutral subjects not about her seeing auras or hinting about her sisters' abilities. First date stuff about his life in Florida and what made her laugh. Places where they'd like to travel and favorite movies of all time.

She could almost forgive him when his was *The Matrix* rather than *Star Wars*. Nobody was perfect. Han Solo could take Neo any day. Everyone knew that.

Paige had to admit she was fully charmed by the adult QB by the time the afternoon was over. Sitting next to him in his car as he drove up the isolated road leading to her house, Paige stole a glance at him.

The evening setting sun threw a stunning light on him, one she could appreciate without being an artist. His dark hair and hard cheekbones should've given him a dangerous look, but his half smile as he told a crazy story about some shenanigans in college, softened the hard look. The late afternoon stubble on his cheeks made her want to reach out and touch him. To see if he felt the way she imagined he did.

But then they pulled up to the gate at her house and the moment was lost. They were back at her house, her fortress, the place where she hid from the world. Paige entered the code. She'd had a good time today with Brett, but would she be willing to go out again on her own after what had happened with those teenagers? And would Brett even want to hang around her after what she had told him?

Now instead of feeling like a coward, she felt like a nutcase *and* a coward.

He pulled around the circular drive until the car was in front of her door, then shut off the engine. Almost immediately, Tom, the other main member of her security team was at the car.

"Ms. Jeffries, Jacob reported what happened downtown today. Are you okay? Is there anything you need?"

Paige stole a glance over at Brett who was walking his way around the car. "I'm fine, Tom. Seriously, it was nothing. Just some kids being rowdy and I totally overreacted."

The thought of how scared she'd been, how stupid she'd been, caused her stomach to tighten. She was just so tired of it all.

"Definitely not an overreaction based on her history," Brett told Tom while shaking the man's hand. "Teenagers can be morons and rarely think about how their actions may affect someone else."

"Jacob was upset and felt that he had made the wrong call allowing you to walk alone."

Paige sighed and shrugged. "You guys can't protect me from all the bad, scary teenagers in the world."

The man looked like he might argue the point, but Paige wouldn't let him.

"Jacob didn't make a mistake. I wanted to get out alone. I probably pushed it too far for it being my first attempt."

She rolled her eyes at herself. "If my phone hadn't broken, I would've called Jacob right away to come get me. Nobody's fault; just bad luck."

But then Paige thought about the black she saw down the alley after the teenagers had left. The same blackness she had seen and felt last night after the show. Just like the day she'd been attacked.

Had it been bad luck? A shudder ran through her. The most frustrating part of this entire situation was her inability to trust her own judgment. She had no idea when she was safe or when she was just allowing her imagination to run away with her.

"But maybe a discreet distance tail might be in order in the future," Brett was telling Tom.

Yes, please. Somebody follow her around because evidently she was unable to determine the difference between safety and danger. She had no idea if the shadows she saw were real or only in her head.

Paige murmured her thanks to Tom and headed inside. Brett was still talking with him, but she didn't want to listen any longer. She just walked inside to the kitchen, taking off her jacket and putting it on the kitchen table. She got the pieces of her broken phone and laid that out too.

"Hey, you doing okay?" She felt Brett's gentle touch on her shoulder.

"Sometimes I don't think I'll ever recover from what happened to me." She turned and walked over to the sink, facing out the window. "That I'm broken."

She could see his vague reflection in the window as he came to stand behind her, but he didn't touch her again.

"If you're talking about what happened today, I think you're being too hard on yourself."

She turned to face him. "I'm talking about how I've lived inside this house for nearly two years, afraid that something that was probably a random occurrence will happen again. I'm afraid that I've let some silly teenagers goofing off force me back into this house for two more years. I'm afraid that I told you about seeing auras and now you're looking at me like I'm a few Bradys short of a bunch."

He smirked. "I was going to say a few marshmallows short of a bowl of Lucky Charms."

She smacked him on the arm as he laughed. "That's not funny."

"A couple tires short of an eighteen wheeler?"

She groaned, wiping her hand across her face. He was joking she knew, but he didn't even know the full extent of everything. "I don't blame you if you want to leave. If you think I'm crazy. If I was you I'd get as far as possible—"

She forgot what she was going to say as he stepped closer and took the hand she was using to rub her forehead. He gently brought her fingers up to his lips and kissed them before lowering them down to her side.

She couldn't stop looking into his soft brown eyes — was almost mesmerized by the flecks of gold in them— as he reached down, grabbed her by the waist and hoisted her up onto the counter by the sink. Then he reached down and gripped her hips and slid her all the way to the edge until she was flat up against his hard body.

All without any hurry.

"You're not crazy. And there's no one else I'd rather be with."

Perched up on the counter put them much closer to being eye to eye. Brett's hands slid up her back to either side of her neck, threading into her hair.

And then he kissed her.

It wasn't brief like last night at the show. It was thorough. Hot. Wet. Every single thought about anything flew out of her mind and all Paige could do was feel.

She saw in colors all the time, but never before had she *felt* in colors. Even with her eyes closed colors seemed to bombard her.

It went on and on. She pressed her body closer to his, hooking her leg around his thigh, her fingers finding his hair and raking their way through its thickness.

She couldn't remember ever feeling like this. Not even before the attack.

Paige shuddered and couldn't hold back a soft moan as his lips left hers and trailed their way down her jaw and began taking soft nips at the side of her neck. She slid herself closer, but winced from the pain in her elbow before she could stop herself.

"Wow," he murmured against her mouth. "That got out of control a little faster than I thought possible." He backed up from her. "Is your arm okay?"

"Yeah, it's fine. I just moved it the wrong way and it caught me off guard."

A throat cleared from the entrance of the kitchen.

"Ms. Jeffries?" It was Tom. "I just wanted to let you know that I've done my security sweep through the building. I'm retiring to the guard house for the evening."

Color flooded Paige's face. Had Tom come through earlier and she and Brett hadn't even realized it? Brett turned so he was standing in front of her, blocking her from view of the older man. Not that Tom was trying to look. He seemed to be looking everywhere but directly at her.

"Thanks, Tom. I'll talk to you tomorrow," she said from behind Brett's back. That was the normal security procedure. Whoever was working checked the big house then went out to the smaller guard house for the night. They still had both audio and visual communication channels open if needed, and they always kept close watch over the grounds and gate, but Paige preferred to be alone in the house.

The thought of which right now both thrilled and terrified her.

With Tom's exit she was left alone in the kitchen with Brett. Again, leaving her both thrilled and terrified.

He stepped away, leaning back against the side counter so he could see her, grinning.

"If Tom had gotten here a few minutes later, he might have gotten quite an eyeful."

Paige couldn't help it, she laughed. "Yeah, the guys aren't used to me having gentlemen callers/detectives around. Especially in the evening."

"Especially making out with them in your kitchen."

Paige laughed again. "Yeah, that's only happened three or four times in the last week."

The smile he gave her caused heat to pool in her belly. "Well, I hope I at least rank in the top half of your suitors."

"You're not too bad. Maybe even the top third." Oh my gosh. Was she actually flirting with the QB? Her sister Chloe would be proud. Hell, Paige was proud of herself.

She walked over to him. "Want me to show you around the rest of the house? I do have other rooms besides the kitchen."

Paige just prayed she'd have enough nerve to show him the room she really wanted him in: her bedroom.

Paige was nervous. Not that Brett blamed her. It had been a long, stressful day for her.

She showed him the living room again —the view was even more tremendous with twilight falling on Portland as it had been last week in full sun— and then moved on to show him her studio.

She was most comfortable in the studio. Obviously spent a great deal of time here, her movements were almost muscle memory. She knew where everything was and everything was obviously placed to her liking.

The room was the epitome of artistic chaos. Canvases of all different sizes, multiple easels, hundreds of paint containers. The paints were all lined up in a methodical fashion on the wall. Obviously when Paige wanted a color she didn't want to have to search for it.

Although her supplies were neat and organized, nothing else was. Paints that had either missed the canvas entirely or had been forcefully removed lay splattered all over the walls and floors. Clothes lay strewn everywhere. Obviously as Paige had gotten hotter or colder when she worked she had used the different items of clothing, mostly sweatshirts and sweaters, but then had forgotten about them. There were at least a dozen lying about, on chairs, on the floor, over the sink.

He could see the exact moment she looked at the room through his eyes rather than her own.

"Wow, it's a mess in here." Color was high on her cheeks.

He grabbed her wrist gently as she moved to begin straightening. "It's perfect. It's exactly what you need it to be. Leave it."

"But—"

Brett gave the hand that encircled her small wrist a light jerk, pulling her up against him. "It's perfect," he murmured again before kissing her.

Brett knew he shouldn't kiss her. Not again. He was just torturing himself when he knew he couldn't stay tonight.

Shouldn't stay tonight. Paige's day had been traumatic and she was emotional. He didn't want her to feel pressured into anything. He could wait.

But damned if he didn't want to keep kissing her almost as much as he wanted his next breath.

And the way she was wrapping her arms around his neck to pull him down closer to her was not helping. It made him want to forget all good intentions and just lay her down right here —amongst all the colors and canvases— and add some more clothes to the haphazard piles around them.

And he would. Soon.

When Brett eased back from her, they were both out of breath. Paige touched her swollen lips, staring at him with her crystal blue eyes.

"I don't mind this mess. You're obviously comfortable here."

She looked away, glancing back around the room. "It's amazing I have any clothes left."

If she only knew.

"The room works for you with your painting, that's what counts."

"Yeah, it does." She shrugged. "And it gets good light from the windows."

They walked back out of the studio and down the hallway. There was a closed door she didn't mention at all before moving on to the next one. "This is my guest bedroom. Or really, I should say my sisters' room, since they're the only ones I have stay overnight here."

"Okay. What's that?" He pointed his thumb at the closed door she'd ignored. "Bathroom? Linen closet?"

Her features became shuttered. "Nothing. Just a room. Stuff."

She immediately moved on down the hall.

Brett looked at the door. It didn't take any particular detective skills to know that she didn't want him to see whatever was in there. Maybe it was just more of a mess than her studio and she didn't want to be embarrassed.

But maybe it was something different.

He wasn't going to push, although it went against his nature not to do so. He caught up to Paige where she'd made her way down the hall. She was leaning against a door frame.

"This is my bedroom. Where the tour ends."

CHAPTER 12

P AIGE DIDN'T WANT TO TALK about the room with the drawings she did in her sleep. Didn't even want to open the door to it. She didn't know who those girls that she drew were or when they would tragically die. She didn't even know if they were real people. Maybe they were figments of her traumatized mind.

But most of all she didn't want to try to explain it to Brett. He'd done the best he could just getting past the "I see auras and black scares me" conversation. She didn't want to talk to him about dead girls.

She wanted to make love with him.

Paige would've thought she'd be afraid. Nervous. Something. But she wasn't. Looking at Brett as he walked towards her down the hall —a deliberate lack of suspicion about the unopened door in his eye— all she could feel was the heat pooling in her.

"Paige." Chivalry floated off the word. He stopped his forward progress.

He was concerned about her. Going to try to stop this before it even got started.

She felt a deep, feminine bravery come over her. Whatever battle with himself Brett was envisioning? He'd already lost it.

She took a step closer to him and hooked the crook of her finger into his shirt between the second and third button. She pulled him closer.

"Brett." She mimicked his same tone, but smiled instead of frowned.

"You've had a pretty traumatic day today."

"Yes, scary teenagers everywhere."

"You hurt your elbow."

She stretched out her other arm to show its functionality and pulled him closer with her finger. "I think I'm going to make it."

"This," he sighed and referenced between them and her bedroom with his hand, "Is a big deal. For me, but for you especially. I think we should take it slow. That you should make sure this is what you really want."

She let go of his shirt. She wasn't prone to anger, but felt it coursing through her now. Not at him, at life in general. She was tired of being fragile, of being the one everyone always worried about. She'd been that way her whole life, even before the attack.

The quiet one. The one that needed protection. The scared one.

But damn it, not tonight.

She pushed Brett back against the door frame with a little more force than either of them were expecting. She poked her finger into his chest.

"I'm not scared. And I'm not making some knee-jerk decision based on what happened today. I want you and unless I've misread everything and you don't want me too, then just shut up and kiss me."

She grabbed both sides of the collar of his shirt and pulled him down to her. And although he kissed her back, it wasn't like before in the kitchen. Didn't have the same passion.

Something inside her died a little.

Oh God, maybe she *had* misread him. Maybe he'd just been friendly, not truly interested in her romantically. The bravery coursing through her veins a moment ago fled.

"I'm sorry," she murmured pulling back from his mouth, stepping away. "I shouldn't have done that. You don't want this. I'm sorry." She couldn't bear to look at him.

Then the world seemed to spin around her as Brett propelled her through the door. Paige found herself lifted and pinned up against the wall, his hands on her hips.

His hard body met hers in all the places she'd been mentally screaming for his touch.

"Don't want you?" There was something desperate in his lips as they raked over her throat. Paige heard herself moan, but couldn't seem to stop it. "There are a lot of things going on in my head, but not wanting you is not even in the realm of possibility."

His lips met hers and this time the kiss was what she had been wanting. It wasn't a gentle, searching kiss. It was hot. Demanding.

The colors were back where their bodies touched. Paige struggled to get closer, clutching Brett's shoulders. He pushed her harder against the wall, hitching her legs over his hips. Paige gasped into his mouth, colors blurring all around her.

They had too many clothes on, but Brett made quick work of those, stopping their kisses only to pull her sweater over her head. He released her legs to unfasten her jeans and she shimmied them down her hips as he removed the rest of his clothes and put on protection.

Immediately he was back against her body at the wall. She gasped at the cold hardness against her back, so opposite to the hot hardness against her front.

Brett looked at her more carefully. "Elbow?"

"No," she shook her head, drawing his lips back to hers. "Cold wall."

Brett laughed. "Should we take this to the bed?"

"No," she cupped his face with both hands. "I want you right here. Hard and hot."

This time when he grasped her legs and hooked them over his hips there was nothing between them.

"I'd be more than happy to oblige."

Then Paige just held on as Brett pushed forward and the world exploded in colors around her.

Brett threw an arm over his head against the headboard and looked down at the small woman lying curled, sleeping against his side. He hadn't had any real forethought of what their lovemaking might be like, but if he had, the words raw, hot and demanding wouldn't have been the ones he would have used.

But that was exactly what their lovemaking had been.

And Paige had given every bit as much as she'd gotten. He grinned and his breath whistled through his teeth as he thought of it. She had categorically refused to be treated as breakable. As fragile. Good for her.

And hell, definitely good for him.

He was glad she was sleeping now. After they'd showered, together, which had led to even more lovemaking, he'd helped her slip on some extra-large t-shirt —the Oregon Ducks again— and she'd promptly fallen into an exhausted sleep.

Despite what she'd said, it had been a stressful day for her. Even good stresses like the two of them being together, were still stresses. Took a toll on the body and mind. She needed rest.

Tomorrow he needed to get back to the station and finish the work he wasn't able to complete today because of the time he spent with Paige, even though it would be a Sunday. If there really was a serial killer on the loose then Brett wanted to prove it as soon as possible. So they could catch the bastard. But for right now a little bit of sleep.

Brett woke up to Paige sliding away from him in the bed. It was still dark outside. He looked over at the clock and saw it wasn't quite four o'clock. He pulled her back to tuck in next to him, but a few moments later she was scooting away again.

"You okay?" he murmured. Maybe she had to go to the bathroom or something.

Paige didn't respond and he figured she had gone back to sleep when all of a sudden she sat up completely straight and draped her legs over the side of the bed.

"You all right, sweetheart?"

No response. Brett rubbed his eyes with his fingers, he could make her out through the moonlight coming through the window, but just barely.

"Paige?"

She abruptly stood straight up and began walking towards the door.

Did she hear something? Was she freaking out because he was in her bed? A number of things could be going on in her head. Should he give her privacy?

But something in how she was moving seemed strange, stiff. As she went completely out the door, Brett grabbed his pants from the chair by the bed and pulled them on. He followed her out into the hallway.

"Paige, just let me know you're okay. If you want to be alone that's fine, but just talk to me for a second."

She didn't even slow down.

But when she got to the door of the room she wouldn't show him earlier, she stopped. Then opened the door and went inside.

Now Brett really wondered what the hell was going on.

He quickly walked down the hallway and followed her through the door, determined to get some answers. But what he saw made him stop in his tracks.

This wasn't some messy storage room or closet like he'd thought it might be. This room was perhaps the cleanest in the whole house. It had a sofa and coffee table in one corner and an easel with art supplies in the other, with an artist's portfolio resting against the wall next to it.

Why wouldn't she have wanted him to come in here?

Brett watched as Paige walked over and stood in front of the easel, grabbing a colored pencil from a package on a nearby table. Once there, she didn't move for a long time, so Brett circled around her so he could see her face. Her eyes were wide open, but unfocused, obviously not seeing him.

She was sleepwalking.

He felt better. Sleepwalking happened a lot. One of the twins had walked so much in her sleep as a kid that their parents had put an extra lock at the top of the front door to make sure she didn't go outside to play on the swing.

They'd found Lydia on the swing, sound asleep, multiple times before putting in the lock. She'd never hurt herself, but it had freaked them all out a little bit to see her ready to play, in her pajamas, eyes open, but unseeing.

Just like Paige was now.

On one hand he was glad she wasn't upset or trying to run away somewhere where she could freak out privately, overwhelmed by what had happened today. Or tonight.

On the other hand, what was he supposed to do with her? Let her stand here at her easel until she came back to bed? She wasn't doing anything. But surely this couldn't be restful for her body.

"Paige? You want to wake up, sweetheart? We could go back to bed," Brett said it softly, not wanting to jar or scare her. You weren't supposed to wake sleepwalkers up, right?

Brett gently wrapped an arm around her shoulders and began easing her back from the easel. She took two steps without any fight before jerking free from him and stepping back up to the easel.

He was surprised by the violence in her movement, but was about to try again when the hand holding the pencil moved up and began drawing.

It was spooky to watch, he had to admit. Her hand moved with grace and precision, not stopping at all once the drawing began, except to change colors. But her face never actually looked at what she drew. Whatever it was, however it was happening, it was not because Paige was carefully watching and controlling every stroke.

As a matter of fact it was almost like she was just a puppet and someone else was using her hand to draw.

Brett didn't want to stop her. He wasn't sure he could anyway. Soon it was obvious that she was drawing a woman's face on the large paper attached to the easel. The detail was remarkable, almost like it was a photograph.

He grimaced. Exactly the same style as the one she'd drawn of herself from the hospital. Was this how she'd drawn herself — while she was sleeping? She hadn't mentioned that.

Of course, nobody would've believed her. Hell, he was standing right here watching her draw in her sleep and couldn't really believe it.

Brett's relief was palpable when it became obvious that the woman Paige was drawing didn't have any bruises on her face. It was a testament to Paige's talent —if you could call drawing without even being awake a *talent*— that she captured the woman's expression so precisely.

The woman was smiling. But as Paige added more detail, Brett realized the smile didn't reach her eyes. She was slightly apprehensive, as if something was causing her concern, but not enough to cause real worry to cross her face.

Paige continued to add more detail with different colored pencils, never hesitating or unsure, reaching for the next pencil without even looking at them.

She drew for at least an hour. Every time Brett thought she must be done she would go back and add another layer of detail, her arm in constant motion. After she was finished with the face, she began to draw in some of the background. It didn't have nearly as much detail, but he could tell the woman was in a parking lot of some sort.

Paige kept drawing.

If she was awake, she would have to be exhausted. There was no way she could keep her arm moving like that for so long without stopping to stretch it or rest it or something. And it was obviously having further effect on her physically, the pallor in her face grew and at some point her nose began bleeding.

He needed to stop this. Whatever was happening was hurting her. No drawing could be worth the physical price she was paying.

But before he could figure out the best way to wake her, she stopped herself as abruptly as she'd started. Her arm dropped to her side and the pencil fell from her fingers. Brett came closer, waiting for her to do something else, but she didn't do anything. Just stood there facing the easel.

Brett once again wasn't certain what he should do. Would she eventually wake up? Go back to bed? Fall in a heap on the floor? She looked like she was about to collapse.

"Paige, are you done drawing, baby? Why don't you come back to bed?" He realized she was cold, her legs were covered in goose bumps, the arm she hadn't been using chilly to the touch. He wrapped an arm around her. "Let's go back to bed."

She didn't resist as he turned her from the picture and began walking towards the door. The same visionless gaze still filled her eyes.

Brett walked slowly down the hall with her, in case she stumbled or woke up, but she never faltered. He helped her back into bed and as her head touched the pillow her eyes finally closed. He grabbed some tissue from the bathroom to wipe her nose then wrapped the big comforter around her. He stepped back and watched as she curled up on her side, hugging a pillow, trying to get comfortable. Her body was stiff, obviously in pain. The hand she used to draw rested curled unnaturally against her chest.

Brett realized her fingers were cramping from holding the pencils for so long. He could see her fingers spasm every few seconds. He crouched down so he could take her fingers in his hand, gently rubbing and stretching them, helping to ease the overworked muscles.

Paige relaxed into the bed under his ministrations and was soon obviously deep asleep. Brett released her hand and laid it gently against the pillow she was clutching.

It was after five o'clock now, the sun would be coming up soon. He knew there was no way he'd get back to sleep. He sat down in the overstuffed chair by the bed and looked at the woman lying there. In peace, finally.

He had no idea what he'd just witnessed in that room. All he knew was the more he knew about Paige the weirder things got.

CHAPTER 13

PAIGE WOKE UP A LITTLE groggy. She seemed to have aches all over her body. In her elbow where she fell yesterday, but also… other places.

She had to admit those aches didn't bother her one bit.

But she was totally exhausted even after sleeping all night. She peeked out from under the covers to see what time it was on her bedside clock. After nine. She needed to get up.

She rolled over to see if Brett was still in bed, maybe she could take advantage of him again, despite her soreness.

He was there, but wide awake, sitting up against her headboard. A cup of coffee in his hand, one leg stretched out in front of him, one leg hanging over the side of the bed.

"I made you a cup too," he gestured with this head towards her nightstand. "But I think it has probably gotten cold by now."

"Oh, okay. Thanks. I'll just go warm it up in the microwave."

"No, it's fine. I'll go get you a fresh cup. Cream? Sugar?" He was already getting out of bed. His jeans were on, as well as the light blue button-down shirt he'd had on last night, although it wasn't buttoned.

"Neither, thanks."

He grabbed her mug and was out the door without saying another word.

Was she crazy or was Brett acting a little weird? She didn't know exactly what she'd been expecting, but he just seemed distant.

Or maybe that was just how things were the morning after. It had been years since she'd had one.

Then she saw it. A little bit of blood and traces of colored pencil on her pillowcase where her hand had rested. Her eyes flew to her hand. Yes, even more evidence on it.

She had drawn again while she was sleeping.

Paige flew out of bed, throwing on a pair of yoga pants from a nearby drawer, and ran down the hall.

The door was open. Paige knew for a fact it had been shut last night as she brought Brett through. But it was open now. She slowed as she reached it.

She immediately looked at the easel, feeling relief pour through her when she saw a *live* woman's face. Maybe if Brett had seen it she could just tell a few fibs —she'd woken up in the middle of the night with the need to draw and this is what happened— not mention drawing in her sleep.

She was trying to back out of the room and close the door when he showed up.

"Here's your coffee."

"Thanks."

Brett walked right into the room. "So, that's a pretty amazing drawing. Is she a friend of yours?"

So he had seen it. Did he know the truth about *how* she had drawn it? "Um, no. Just someone I saw in my head and drew."

He walked over to study the picture more closely. She forced herself to take a sip of her coffee and not fidget.

"You just saw her in your head? This wasn't from a photograph?"

"Yep. Just from my head. No picture." Her voice sounded a little high and unnatural even to her own ears.

"That's pretty amazing detail." He glanced over his shoulder at her where she stood in the doorway. "And this is drawing, right? Not painting like you normally do."

"Yeah. Colored pencils." She always used them when she created a picture in her sleep. Definitely not her normal medium.

"Do you know what this reminds me of?"

Paige knew what he was going to say before he said it.

"The picture you drew of yourself from the attack," he continued. "The style, I mean. I'm no art critic, but it is the same style, right?"

He'd obviously been thinking about this for a while. His words were too carefully chosen for it to be otherwise. But maybe he'd just seen the drawing when he went down to make coffee this morning.

"Yes. Both from pencils. Both same general composition and size."

"But no bruises on this lady."

Not this time, thank God. "Nope. I guess I'm not always morbid when I draw."

"Yeah, about that. I thought you said last week that you really only paint, don't really ever draw."

Paige gripped her coffee mug more tightly. How was she going to explain to him that she *couldn't* draw like this normally? Pictures of dead women aside, that was the hardest part to accept about her ability to draw in her sleep: she didn't have the same skill when she was awake. If he asked her to grab the pencils right now and draw him, she wouldn't be able to do it.

Exhaustion poured over her. She was tired of having to hide this. Tired of it happening. Tired of the toll it took on her body every time she did one.

"Painting is definitely my primary medium," she verbally side-stepped.

"It's a good thing you're already a world-renowned painter or I would say you need to switch to drawing. You definitely have a talent there."

She just shrugged. Yep. She had a talent for drawing dead women in her sleep. That wasn't bat-shit crazy or anything.

"So she's not a real person? That's a shame. I would think someone would really appreciate having a drawing of this caliber —a Paige Jeffries original no less— of herself."

Paige would be thrilled if the woman wasn't real. If she was just a figment of Paige's imagination. If that was true then the next time she drew a dead face staring out at her she could say that woman was a figment also.

Not someone who had died a horrible death that Paige somehow saw in her sleep.

"Nope, not anybody I know. I probably saw her somewhere yesterday and my subconscious remembered her or something."

"Have you done this a lot? Drawn people you don't know?"

Paige walked over to study the drawing more closely.

"I do it every once in a while. Like I said, painting is definitely my primary medium. I don't really... enjoy drawing like this." That much she could say with utter truthfulness.

"What do you do with the drawings? I'm sure you could sell them."

She didn't want to tell him the truth. That she had tried destroying the drawings at first, particularly the ones with the dead women. But she had just drawn the same scene again each time she'd destroyed them. So now they were all stuffed in a portfolio file. At least that way she didn't have to look at them.

"No, I don't want to sell them." She looked at the woman in the drawing. Young. Beautiful.

Was she dead? Paige had no idea. She closed her eyes, trying to take in enough air to tamp down her panic. She didn't want to have a breakdown in front of Brett.

When she opened her eyes she found he had circled around to the other side of the painting so he could see her, rather than the woman on the easel.

He knew. Something about the look he gave her told her. His questions were all neutral and without judgment, but they were attempting to lead her down a path where she confessed to drawing in her sleep. He was a detective, after all.

"You saw me, didn't you?" she whispered.

Even after the dozens and dozens of times she had done it, Paige wasn't totally sure what happened when she drew in her sleep. Usually she woke up in some awkward pile on the floor, bloody and stiff from how she'd slept, her right arm sore from overuse. She never knew how she'd gotten there or how long she'd been there or how long the drawing had taken her.

"I woke up when you got out of bed," he said. "I wasn't sure what was happening. I thought maybe you were upset or overwhelmed by yesterday or... us."

It was the first time since she had woken this morning that his eyes had softened and his voice wasn't so distant. He wasn't mad, she realized. Confused, but not mad.

"I really just wanted to make sure you were okay," he continued. "Although I'll admit my curiosity was a little piqued last night when you didn't show me this room, so when you went in here, I didn't hesitate to follow."

Paige both wanted and didn't want to hear the rest. But she knew she didn't have any choice.

"I finally realized you were sleepwalking. Not uncommon. Lydia did it all the time when she was young. I tried to get you to come back to bed, but you wouldn't leave the front of the easel. Standing almost exactly where you are now."

She knew this spot. She had woken up here on the floor many times.

"And then I watched as for the next hour and a half you drew that picture right there." He gestured to it with his hand from where he stood at the side. "Without waking up even once, or even looking at the easel."

Paige wrapped her arms around her middle, certain she might fly apart any second. How was she supposed to explain this? It seemed like every day she had something more outlandish to tell Brett. She glanced over at the portfolio folder leaning against the wall. He didn't even know the worst of it.

A folder full of drawings of women. Some fine, some beaten, some dead. Because she was sick. Because her brain had some sort of morbid fascination with brutality towards women.

He seemed to have handled the auras conversation yesterday without too much pause. And to his credit, he hadn't left in the middle of the night when he found her drawing in her sleep. But to show him those pictures in the folder would mean the end of whatever this budding relationship was. Those pictures were abnormal.

She was abnormal. She gripped her stomach tighter and tucked her head down and away from Brett. Maybe even more than what had happened to her physically in the attack, this was the reason she had shied away from any sort of intimacy. No man in his right mind would want to deal with all this.

"Hey," he whispered and she felt his hand stroke her arms where they hugged her body. "It's okay, you know."

She stepped back. "It's not okay. It's weird!" She could feel tears welling in her eyes but didn't know how to stop them.

He stepped forward again, his palms cupping her shoulders for just a minute before he pulled her hard up against his chest. Paige knew she should step away but she couldn't seem to force herself to do it.

His arms felt strong enough to protect her from the terrifying images she drew. From the evil black colors she sometimes saw swirling around people. Maybe he could protect her from her own mind.

"Lydia used to play outside on the swing in her sleep. That's much more freaky than drawing," he said into her hair.

Paige couldn't quite laugh, but his statement at least stopped the tears that were threatening. When she didn't pull away, he tucked her even closer into his hard body.

"I know I draw in my sleep. But I don't know why and I don't know how to make it stop" she murmured into his chest.

"Maybe you shouldn't try to make it stop. Maybe it's your brain's way of trying to release something."

She knew she should show him the other drawings; the more gruesome ones. They would make him understand why she wanted it to stop. Nobody wanted to wake up in the morning to those scenes.

He was a detective, so the images probably wouldn't phase him. But it would change what he thought about her, wouldn't it? It would have to.

She would show him the drawings eventually. But not today. Not this soon.

She just wanted to stay with him like this, for him to keep holding her, as long as possible.

"It's just exhausting. Usually I wake up on the floor after I've drawn in my sleep."

"Yeah, you might have done that last night, but I led you back to bed."

"Thanks. That's a lot more comfortable than in a heap on the ground."

Brett pulled her back so he could look her in the eye. "Are you okay? It has to take a lot out of you to do that. Your poor arm was working non-stop for nearly two hours. I was exhausted just watching you. *Your nose was bleeding*."

"Yeah, it's not easy on my body." And it had been getting worse over time. "I'm usually wiped out for the day after it happens. That's why I wish it would stop."

"Does it happen often?"

Paige shrugged. "Five or six times a month."

He led her over to the couch. "And you always draw people?"

She tucked her legs up under her as he sat next to her and pulled her close. She was grateful for his warmth. Even talking about this made her feel cold.

"Yeah, always women." But not usually alive and relatively happy like the woman on the easel. If that was the case, Paige would just chalk it up to more weirdness. But the death, the violence that she drew. Over and over. Always the same, just different women.

"I don't really want to talk about it anymore, Detective."

Because she knew where all these questions would lead: showing him the drawings.

Not today. Not this soon.

She moved from his side onto his lap so her legs were straddling his hips. She wrapped her arms loosely around the back of his neck, linking her fingers in with his hair.

"Isn't there anything else we can talk about? Or maybe not talk at all?" she lowered her head and kissed him, nipping his bottom lip.

He was aware of her diversion technique, she could tell when she looked him in the eyes. But he was willing to let it go. "Anything else peculiar I should know about?"

Oh God.

She kissed him again. "Well, I do dance around naked during the full moon."

Brett flipped her around so she was flat on the couch and he was lying on top of her.

"I might need a preview of that immediately to make sure it's acceptable."

Paige hooked her arms and legs around him and pulled him close. "Whatever you say, Detective."

CHAPTER 14

B
Y MID-AFTERNOON ON MONDAY BRETT wasn't any closer to proving his serial killer theory even after focusing most of his attention on it the whole day. He didn't want to admit it, but it was looking more like Captain Ameling was right: there wasn't enough of a pattern tying the deaths of these women together to blindly attribute it to one killer.

He hadn't been able to find any more deaths on "payday" dates in Oregon. He'd expanded his search to include the entire state, but had only found one more murder. That one had been six years ago, and although it did fit the right dates and a matching killing method as one of the other women, someone had already been arrested and found guilty of the murder.

Brett leaned back in his chair, closing his eyes. Was he pushing? Looking too hard for a pattern that wasn't really there?

His gut told him no. That there was something more. Something he was missing.

But his gut wasn't going to get him anywhere with Captain Ameling. Brett needed something solid.

Maybe it would help if they could get more information about the woman from Friday's crime scene. Brett walked over to Alex Olivier's desk. Alex held the phone handset on one of his shoulders, but motioned to Brett to have a seat in the chair in front of his desk.

"What's up?" Alex left the phone hanging on his shoulder. "I'm on hold waiting for some details about a homicide from a couple weeks ago."

"Do we have any info from Friday's scene? Confirmed cause of death? ID on the victim?"

Alex was the primary investigator on the case so all the info would go through him. Brett watched as the other man searched through some emails, phone still hanging off his shoulder.

"Let's see. Here's a tech report: in preliminary tests, nothing of any use found so far at the scene." He scanned through more reports. "Victim ID? Nothing yet. Evidently there was some issue with the downtown coroner's office and morgue this weekend. Water valve broke. Everything — including bodies and files— had to be relocated to secondary locations. It's holding everything up."

"Damn it."

"Yeah, I want to find out who that lady is so we can notify her next of kin. Somebody's got to be looking for her."

"Thanks man, keep me posted."

"I'll do better. I'll put your email on the list so you get any updates from the ME's office or anything the crime techs find."

Whoever Alex had been holding for picked up and Alex started talking. Brett waved and headed back to his desk. There was nothing he could do on this case until he knew a little more about the victim. Then he could see if she had anything in common with the other women besides gender and general age.

But Brett suspected that even when he could put a name to the victim he wouldn't be able to tie her to any of the other women. The killer was too smart for that.

If there even was just one killer.

Paige walked into the downtown police station, the picture of the woman she'd drawn on Saturday night tucked in a file under her arm. It struck her as interesting that in the eight years she'd lived in Portland she'd only been here twice and both times were within forty-eight hours of each other.

When she'd been interviewed about her attack, the police officers had come to her, first in the hospital and then to her home. She'd been here on Saturday with Brett so they could call her security firm's number. Although there had been people around then, it had been a weekend so anyone who wasn't required to work hadn't been around.

Now it was Monday and there were *a lot* of people here.

Her security team had given her a ride to the station and since they knew she was, ahem, *friendly* with Brett, they hadn't given her grief when she told them she needed to go to the precinct.

But she wasn't here to see Brett. As a matter of fact she was hoping she could get in and out of here without seeing him at all. She wasn't visiting her boyfriend.

Because honestly, she wasn't even sure if he could be called her boyfriend. They'd had a great night together Saturday night, and an even better morning yesterday morning —she could feel her core temperature rising just thinking about yesterday morning on the couch— but that didn't mean she would call him her boyfriend.

But it didn't matter because boyfriend or not she wasn't here to see him. She had an appointment with a missing person detective named Schliesman because of what she had seen in the newspaper this morning.

A picture of a young woman. Not just any young woman, the exact one Paige had drawn Saturday night.

Her name was Teresa Cavasos.

There had been a missing person's ad in the newspaper from the woman's family. Evidently she had been missing since Thursday and the family and police were looking for any information.

Paige wasn't stupid. She didn't plan to tell the police that she had drawn the picture in her sleep. She already had a reputation as an attention-hungry kook around here. She would tell them she drew a lot and that she had drawn this picture of the woman in the last couple of days, and when she saw the woman's picture in the paper thought it might help.

It wasn't a perfect plan, but it was better than admitting the truth.

It wasn't the woman herself that Paige hoped the police would find helpful in the drawing. It was the details around the woman. She was obviously in a parking lot and there were buildings that were unique in their shape and size. Paige didn't know where they were located, but she hoped someone working the case might.

For the first time Paige could put one of the faces she had drawn to an actual name, which both excited and terrified her. If somehow she could help the police find this missing woman, then Paige had to try. Maybe it would make all the nights she'd lost drawing those painful pictures worth it. Just helping one woman would do that.

The precinct was busy and pretty overwhelming, but at least she felt safe here. Of course, her sister Adrienne had once been kidnapped in the middle of an FBI building by a psychotic killer, so maybe Paige shouldn't feel too safe. But she wouldn't hang around. She'd just do what she needed to do and get out.

Unless maybe she happened to run into Brett. Her not-boyfriend.

She stepped up to an overworked uniformed officer who was attempting to single-handedly direct people who came through the door and also answer the phones. "Excuse me, I have an appointment with Detective Schliesman who is working Teresa Cavasos' missing person case."

The man handed her a visitor's pass. "Take a seat right there." He pointed to some hard plastic chairs by the door. "I'll call for your escort."

The colors surrounding all the people were varied and dramatic, to be expected in a place full of both the best and the worst society had to offer. Although Paige did notice that sometimes it wasn't always just the criminals with the dark, muddy colors. People's intent wasn't always obvious by the clothes they wore — uniform or not.

"Ms. Jeffries? I'm Detective Schliesman. You said on the phone that you have something pertinent about Teresa Cavasos' possible disappearance?" She began leading Paige down a hall where it was a little more quiet.

"Yes, um, I'm an artist," she told the older woman.

"I've heard of you." The woman didn't smile or give any sort of encouragement. The clear reds surrounding her assured Paige that Detective Schliesman was honest and a good person overall, but the woman was angry. Exhausted.

"I won't waste any of your time, Detective. I just have this picture." She got the drawing out of the file that held it. "It's Teresa Cavasos, I'm sure."

The detective didn't take the picture like Paige expected. But the red surrounding the woman flared momentarily.

Although she hid it well, whatever Paige had just said caused a flash of irritation or anger to course through the other woman. That wasn't good.

"Can you just hold that until we get to my desk, Ms. Jeffries?"

Paige didn't understand, but nodded. "Sure."

When they got to the woman's desk, she surprised Paige again by pulling out a pair of latex gloves to grab the drawing. Without touching it anywhere with her own skin, Detective Schliesman placed the paper in a clear evidence bag.

So much for Paige's concern that they wouldn't take the drawing seriously or pay it any attention. Schliesman was definitely paying attention to it now.

"Please, sit down." She gestured to the chair crammed into the small space between her desk and the one next to it. "You drew this, Ms. Jeffries?"

"Yes."

"When was that?"

Paige wanted to keep as close to the truth as she could. "Saturday night."

The woman looked at her through narrowed eyes. "Are you friends with Teresa Cavasos? Know her from somewhere?"

Paige had known these questions would be tricky. "No. I don't know her."

"But you drew what could only be called an amazing resemblance to her. With remarkable detail. Were you watching her? Studying her, in order to get this much detail?"

This was where Paige knew deviating from the truth was going to be necessary. "No. It's an artist exercise. After a day of being around people, I try to pick one and recreate the person and scene from memory. I've gotten pretty good at it over the years."

"And you happened to pick out Teresa Cavasos to draw on Saturday?"

And the red surrounding Detective Schliesman kept flaring. The woman was keeping her temper at bay, but just barely. She was frustrated and what Paige was telling her was not helping.

"Yes. Normally with this type of exercise I draw strangers and never know who they are and never think any more about it." A partial truth — Paige never knew who she drew, but she definitely thought more about them. "But when I saw the ad in the paper Teresa's family had taken out, I thought I would bring the picture down here."

"Are you hoping to claim the reward?"

Paige shook her head. "No. No, I don't need or want any money. I'm just trying to help."

That was the absolute truth. But she was beginning to think this whole thing was a bad idea.

"Look." Paige turned a little more towards Detective Schliesman ignoring all the chatter, ringing phones, and general chaos going on at desks all around them. "I don't have any agenda here. I just wanted to bring this drawing because it has so much detail about the location around Teresa."

"But you weren't watching Teresa at that location?"

"No. I don't recall seeing her at all. But an artist's mind works differently somehow." That was putting it mildly in her case. "I just drew what I pictured in my mind and here it is. It might be nothing."

Another officer walked by and Detective Schliesman grabbed him, showing him the drawing. "Randal, you recognize this? The area in the background?"

The man stopped to look. "Whoa. Hey, isn't that Teresa Cavasos?"

"Yep."

"Isn't she—"

"The background, Randal. Do you recognize that area in the back of the drawing? I just need confirmation of what I'm thinking."

The man looked at the detective, then over at Paige then finally stared down at the picture.

"Yeah, sure Janet. It's that fancy boutique strip mall over in Healy Heights, right? I can tell by the way the flowers are laid out over here and the angle of this building." He pointed to the edge of the drawing.

"Thanks. That's what I thought too."

Relief coursed through Paige. The officers knew the area. So maybe this would help them, in some way, find the missing woman.

Randal handed the drawing back to Detective Schliesman. "Isn't that strip mall just a couple blocks away from the hotel where—"

"Yep." The woman definitely cut him off.

"And I thought this had turned over to hom—"

"Thanks for your help, Randal. We'll talk later."

The man was wise enough to know he wasn't going to get a full sentence out around Detective Schliesman, so gave Paige one more look and left.

There was something going on here that Paige didn't understand. But she had done what she had set out to do. She would let the police take it all from here. She stood up.

"That's really all I had to offer, Detective. I hope it is helpful in some way."

"Ms. Jeffries, do you mind waiting just a few more minutes? This drawing is very interesting and I'd like to show it to a few other people who might have some questions for you."

The detective's tone was as friendly as the smile on her face, but Paige could see the pulsing red that still dominated her entire person.

Detective Schliesman was angry. What Paige didn't know was whether it was directed at her or the case or what.

"Well…"

"Let me take you somewhere where it's not so chaotic to wait." She gestured around her with her arm. "It can be overwhelming in here, I know."

The woman took her and led her down the hallway, opening the door to a small room with a table and chairs. Paige had to admit, the quiet was a relief.

"If you could just wait here," the other woman told her. "And this is a non-cell phone use room, if you don't mind. I'll be back in just a few minutes."

Detective Schliesman didn't wait for a response and the door closed behind her with a resounding click.

Paige looked around the room —gray walls with no decor whatsoever. There were cameras in two corners and a large mirror taking up the entire far wall. The only furniture was a sparse table with four medal chairs surrounding it.

Paige had seen enough TV to know where she was. She walked over to the door and tried to open it.

Locked. She went back and dropped down into one of the uncomfortable chairs.

She was in an interrogation room and was evidently now a suspect in Teresa Cavasos' disappearance.

CHAPTER 15

Y O, BRETT," ALEX SHOUTED FROM his desk, that
damn phone receiver still glued to his shoulder even
two hours later. The man was the king of multitasking.
"Report of our Jane Doe from Friday. Got a positive ID.
Sending it your way."

Brett threw his arm up in acknowledgment —no need
to add to the late afternoon chaos around all the desks by
yelling— and sent the electronic file directly to print.

Call him old school, but he preferred a hard copy of
information in his hand. The tactile nature of it helped him
think. He walked to the office's common printer thankful it
was fast. It was time to see their Jane Doe without any bruises,
and hopefully be one step closer to proving, or disproving, his
serial killer theory.

The name and general info sheet came up first: Teresa
Cavasos. Single, Caucasian female, twenty-eight years old.
5'5, 120 pounds. No criminal record, so she hadn't been
in the system for easy identification. Between that and
whatever had happened in the coroner's office requiring
bodies to be sent out to county morgues, it had caused a
much slower identification of the body. Brett noticed the
report had also been sent to an officer in missing persons
a few hours ago. The missing person wasn't missing
anymore. She was dead.

The picture of the woman covered in bruises came next. Brett didn't need to study that one, he remembered the bruising clearly enough from the crime scene. But the picture he grabbed from the printer after that had his stomach dropping; the picture of Teresa Cavasos with no bruising.

This was the woman Paige had drawn in her sleep.

Brett forced himself to loosen his grip on the papers so he wouldn't crush them as he walked back to his desk. What the hell was going on?

He had totally believed Paige when she'd said she had no idea who the woman she'd drawn was. That it was just someone Paige had made up in her mind. But obviously she had to have known Teresa Cavasos. The image couldn't have been anyone but her.

Brett grabbed his cell phone to punch out a text message to Paige, since he knew her security team had gotten her a replacement one this morning.

I need to talk to you ASAP. Call me.

It wasn't very romantic, or even gentle, but Brett didn't care. He needed to know how the hell Paige was connected to Ms. Cavasos.

He stared at his phone for five minutes, willing Paige to reply. Nothing. He was still staring at it when Alex came over and picked up the picture.

"Teresa Cavasos." Alex whistled through his teeth. "That's a shame. Her family has been looking for her. They took out multiple ads in the paper, went on television, everything."

"Really? I totally missed it. I've been caught up in so many other cases, I hadn't even seen anything about her."

"Yeah. They've got money. She was their only daughter, I think. I was hoping they'd get a ransom note or something. But at least now they know."

Brett nodded. "I guess that's better than never knowing."

"Always."

Alex left, leaving Brett staring at the picture of Teresa Cavasos. Damn it, he wanted to believe the best about Paige. The absolute best case scenario he could think of was that maybe Paige saw one of the ads Alex just mentioned and didn't remember. Then had drawn Teresa from her subconscious.

The medium case scenario was that she had seen the ad, and drawing Teresa was a way of getting attention. Like what the other members of the police department had accused her of with the drawing of her own attack.

The worst case scenario was that she knew Teresa and didn't tell him. That she had lied outright.

Actually, the really worst case scenario was that Paige had something to do with Teresa's murder.

But no, Brett categorically refused to believe that. Actually, he had a difficult time believing any of the scenarios except the first. Paige wouldn't purposely deceive him.

Right?

Her subconscious might have deceived them both. But she wouldn't have lied to him outright.

Although Brett had been doing this job long enough to know that everyone was capable of deceit. And everyone was capable of letting their emotions cloud their better judgment where attraction was concerned.

And damn it, why had she not texted him back?

Brett called and left a message —similar to what he had said in his text— when the call went straight to voice mail. Then he sent another text.

If this all turned out to be nothing, she was going to think he was crazy. But Brett needed this cleared up for him. Right. Now. He willed her to call.

"Hey QB."

Brett looked up to see Randal Younker standing by his desk. This was not the time that Brett wanted to turn down another dinner party invitation.

"Hey Randal. What's going on? I'm pretty busy."

"Janet Schliesman from down in Missing Persons sent me up to get you."

"Okay. For what?" Brett asked.

"She heard you and Olivier are taking over the Cavasos case now that it's officially a homicide."

Randal motioned for Alex to join them.

"They've got a present for you downstairs in Interrogation Room A having to do with the Cavasos case. A suspect."

"Already? It just became a homicide case," Alex said. "Based on what? Ransom? Family member?"

"No. Much better," Randal shook his head in disbelief. "Woman came in with a drawing of Teresa in a strip mall parking lot in Healy Heights."

Brett felt his stomach drop out. They had Paige in their interrogation room. It couldn't possibly be anyone else but her. He stood up.

"Healy Heights?" Alex looked over at Brett. "The strip mall is just a couple blocks from where she was found in that hotel."

Brett looked over at Randal. He didn't want to give away that he knew the person they were holding was Paige. "A picture of Cavasos? Weird, but what makes the person a suspect?"

"The woman said she drew the picture, which is fine, Teresa's picture has been all over the paper and news. Anybody could've drawn her."

"Okay…" Alex said. "So?"

"So," Randal continued, drawing it out in his usual dramatic fashion. "In this drawing, Teresa is wearing the outfit she went missing in. The one she showed up dead in. Which is not the same one her parents put in the paper or on TV. Only someone connected with Teresa's death would've known what she was wearing."

"And she just walked in and volunteered her drawing?" Brett asked. "That doesn't seem very smart if you're involved with a murder."

Randal shrugged. "Actually, I think she came in under the pretense of helping with the missing person's case. She thought the scene in the background might be helpful."

"Still not particularly smart if you're guilty and trying not to get caught," Alex said.

"She said it was some sort of artist exercise where she just picked someone at random to draw. Replicates a scene from memory and then draws it."

"And she just happened to choose Teresa Cavasos." Brett said it and could see how the detectives downstairs would've found it pretty suspicious.

"Said she didn't know Cavasos was missing at the time, and when she saw it in the paper today she came down to the station to see if she could help."

Why the hell hadn't Paige come to him?

Of course, Brett had no idea what he would've done if she had.

Alex stood up. "Sounds like someone needs to go question our artist friend downstairs."

CHAPTER 16

PAIGE WASN'T SURE WHAT TO do. Was she under arrest? Could they just leave her locked in here?

She knew she wasn't supposed to use the phone, but maybe she should before Detective Schliesman returned.

But who would she call?

Brett? He was probably at his desk. But what position would that put him in? Plus, she didn't want him to have to tell the entire police department that she drew in her sleep. Not to mention he would have to tell how he knew that for a fact.

Should she call her sister Adrienne? Her husband was FBI and maybe could help. But they lived a couple hours away.

If she was being arrested she should probably call a lawyer. But she didn't even know one. Her manager did. Or Melissa, the governor's wife, surely did.

But Paige didn't want to drag Brett or her sister or even a lawyer into this. All she wanted to do was help them find Teresa Cavasos. And to be honest, if her picture couldn't help them do that, then Paige really wasn't of any more use to them. She didn't know anything beyond what she'd drawn on that paper.

Her phone buzzed in her bag, and Paige grabbed it. A message, actually a voice message and two texts, from Brett to call him. She'd missed his call a few minutes ago.

Should she call him back? If they were just going to leave her locked in here, maybe she shouldn't worry about breaking the rules. What were they going to do, arrest her?

Seems like they may have already done that.

But Detective Schliesman walked in —the reds around her still spiking— so Paige dropped the phone back in her bag. Maybe they'd be releasing her in just a minute.

"Ms. Jeffries, you have the right to remain silent. Anything you say may be used against you in a court of law."

Paige listened as the detective read her the rest of her rights. Evidently they wouldn't be releasing her in just a minute.

"Do you understand these rights as I've presented them to you?" Schliesman finished.

"I don't understand, am I under arrest?"

"Do you understand your rights, Ms. Jeffries?" the detective repeated.

"Yes, I understand my rights. What I don't understand is if I'm under arrest?" Paige was trying to remain calm, but it was becoming difficult.

"No, you are not under arrest," the other woman replied. "Reading rights is normal procedure before doing any questioning."

"Do I need a lawyer?"

Detective Schliesman looked at her steadily. "Have you done anything to need a lawyer?"

"All I'm trying to do is help find a missing woman."

"Then let's go over the details of the picture again."

Brett and Alex watched from the other side of the mirrored glass as Schliesman questioned Paige. The two women had been at it for over an hour. Question after question about the drawing and Paige's relationship with Teresa Cavasos. Schliesman never let Paige know Teresa was dead.

Brett knew why. The detective was hoping Paige would trip up and say something that would give away that she knew Teresa was dead. That would catch her in a lie, and because the news of Teresa's death hadn't been released, would link Paige to the murder. Brett had interrogated suspects before and had to admit that Schliesman was doing a good job.

But it might possibly be the most painful thing Brett had ever had to watch.

Everything about the interrogation room was designed to make the person being questioned feel uncomfortable. The chairs, table, color of the walls, lighting, everything. They were hard, cold, sterile. A suspect's subconscious noticed, even if their conscious mind didn't.

Given Paige's artistic mind and senses? He'd bet she was well aware of the damage the room was meant to ensue on the psyche. He watched Paige shift again on the uncomfortable chair, her expression pinched as she attempted to answer Schliesman's questions.

He couldn't watch this any longer.

"I'm going in there."

Alex held his hand out. "This woman have anything to do with the art show you attended Friday night?"

Brett glanced over at him before looking back through the mirror. "Maybe."

"You go in there right now and this situation gets a whole lot more complicated, whether she's innocent or not. Think about that."

Brett ran a hand across his face. Alex was right.

"Right now this is my case," Alex continued. "There's nothing to report involving you and her. You walk in there as anything other than a homicide detective and that changes."

"I don't think she had anything to do with Cavasos' murder, Alex. She was a victim of violence herself a couple of years ago."

"Yeah, I remember."

"She didn't do this," Brett said again, leaning closer to the mirror.

"That may be true," Alex responded. "I hope it's true. But you need to let someone else establish that as fact. Not just barge in there as her boyfriend. In the long run that won't help you or her."

Damn it.

Brett watched as Schliesman questioned Paige again about the clothes the victim was wearing in the drawing. That was key, the fact that Paige had drawn Teresa in the clothes she had been taken in. Had died in. That was what was so suspicious about Paige's drawing.

"These clothes. Why did you draw her in this particular shirt?" Schliesman asked.

"I don't know." Paige's exasperation was clear. "I just drew her in what I saw in my mind."

"From seeing her in the parking lot, on McDonell Street but not really paying any attention to her."

"Yes, like I said. It was an artist's exercise. Trying to recreate something from memory; focus on details."

That definitely sounded a lot better than saying she had drawn Teresa Cavasos in her sleep. And she had been sleeping when she drew the picture, Brett had no doubt about that.

"But you can agree it's a little suspicious that out of everyone in that strip mall parking lot you chose to draw the one person that went missing that day," Schliesman said.

And Brett knew the other half of what the detective wasn't saying: that Paige conveniently brought in the picture of Cavasos just as she was discovered dead. Too late to be of any help finding her as a missing person.

Paige looked down at her hands. "Yeah, it was unfortunate."

"Are you sure this isn't a situation where you're trying to get attention in your own case?"

Schliesman reached down and pulled a file out of a bag she had brought into the room. Paige's file. She didn't open it, but set it on the table.

"Your attack from two years ago is unsolved. Maybe you feel like the police should be working harder on your case. That bringing in a picture of a missing lady might get you back into the limelight."

"No," Paige responded. "I have pretty much made peace with the fact that my case won't ever be solved."

The sympathetic look Schliesman gave her was almost believable. Probably was believable to Paige who by now must be desperate for any sort of friendly relief.

"That's a shame. To have to live with that? Knowing the police no longer care enough to keep looking for the man who did *this* to you?" She took the picture of Paige's battered face out of the file and slid it across the table to her.

Paige barely glanced at it. "I'm well aware of what happened to me, Detective. I don't need to see it. And no, I do not hold any ill will against the Portland Police Department. I believe they tried their best with the information they had."

"But you have to admit, this will put you —and your case— back on their radar."

"Detective Schliesman, I'm just here to do whatever I can to help find a missing woman."

Brett turned away from the questioning as the door to the observation room opened. Captain Ameling walked in, making an already bad situation worse.

"I heard she was back." He pointed at Paige through the glass. "Is this another weird issue like the supposed drawing of herself after the fact?"

"No, sir," Brett responded. "She says she saw Cavasos at a parking lot in Healy Heights and drew her as part of some sort of artist exercise where she draws someone from memory."

"And the person she happened to draw showed up missing and now dead. Very convenient." The captain turned to Alex. "Do we have enough to arrest her?"

Brett knew he needed to stay out of this. The captain already didn't like him. Speaking up now would just make it worse for Paige.

"No, I don't think so," Alex said. "Plus, you know the chief will have a fit if we try."

"Yeah, well, the chief is in meetings off the premises all day. So if we have enough to book her, you do it. I'll handle the chief." He turned to Brett. "And you damn well better not call him about this or I'll make sure you're working traffic cases for the rest of your very miserable time here."

Brett's lips pursed. "I'm not going to call the chief. I want to find out who did this to Teresa Cavasos as much as anybody else."

They all watched Schliesman question Paige. Back to info about the clothing choice in the drawing again.

"Why hasn't she lawyered up?" Captain Ameling asked.

And then Brett knew. Any lingering doubt he'd had was wiped away. Paige hadn't asked for a lawyer because she wasn't guilty of anything. She was just trying to help.

She didn't know what almost everyone in this building was hoping to pin on her. She was in way over her head and had no idea she was even in the water.

Brett needed to do something. Calling the chief wasn't an option, and wasn't the route Brett would want to go even if he could get in touch with Adam. But he did have the number for

Paige's security team. He got out his phone to send a text as discreetly as possible.

Paige is being held for questioning at downtown precinct. She needs a lawyer here, stat. Get one here now.

Her security team was competent, and what's more, Brett believed they really cared about her. He hoped they would get someone here for her.

"You bored by what's going on?" Ameling asked, glancing at Brett's phone.

"No." Brett put it away. "But believe it or not I have other cases I'm also working on, that also require my attention."

They turned back to what was happening inside the room. Paige shifted uncomfortably in her chair and rubbed the bridge of her nose with her hand.

"Look, I've answered all your questions, multiple times. I'd like to talk to Detective Brett Wagner if that's okay."

"Why?"

Brett could feel Alex and the captain looking at him. If Paige mentioned their relationship now, it could be disastrous. But she didn't know that.

Alex looked over at Ameling. "Captain, I think we're going to need to let her—"

Captain Ameling held up his hand. "Wait, I want to hear the answer to this."

Brett appreciated Alex trying to run interference for him; to distract the captain. But the man was looking for dirt on Brett and he was afraid Paige was about to give it to him.

Paige stared at Schliesman for long moments.

"Detective Wagner was nice to me when we talked last week. He was respectful, didn't treat me like a freak the way the Portland PD has been known to do."

Brett let out a breath he didn't even realize he was holding. The captain was still wary, but the crisis had been averted.

"Well, you're going to get to see him very soon," Schliesman told Paige. "I'm actually turning this case over to him and Detective Alex Olivier."

Brett knew what was coming. Schliesman was about to let Paige know the case was now a homicide. The detective wanted to shake things up to see how Paige would respond when she found out Teresa Cavasos was dead.

And she'd do it in the most jarring way possible.

Brett couldn't even blame Schliesman for her methods. Under matching circumstances he'd do the same thing.

Schliesman pulled out another case file, Cavasos' he was sure. She took out some pictures.

Brett knew which ones. The ones from the hotel where they'd found her body. The ones that showed that Teresa was obviously beaten —very similarly to Paige— and stabbed. The ones that showed that the missing person Paige had been trying to help for the last few hours was very definitely beyond help now.

Schliesman put the pictures right in front of Paige.

Paige took one look at them, and flew out of her seat, vomiting in the trash can by the table.

CHAPTER 17

P AIGE FELT WEAK. DAZED. SHE glanced around the room. Everything in here was gray: the walls, the floors, the furniture, the two-way mirror thingy. It was difficult to get her bearings.

She'd been in here for hours, answering question after question. The *same* question after question.

And then the pictures.

Oh God, she was too late. Teresa Cavasos was already dead. The pictures. They were still sitting in front of her right now, but Paige had turned them over.

Detective Schliesman had put them right in front of Paige so casually. They were gruesome. Horrific. The woman had died from being stabbed, after being severely beaten.

Paige knew what a beating like that felt like. The debilitating pain that throws your entire body into a panic. Hearing your own bones break and knowing there was nothing you can do about it. Your own blood filling up your nose and mouth until you wonder if you might choke on it.

It was impossible for Paige to ever forget it. She didn't need a picture to remind her.

But more disturbing than the violence of it all, more disturbing than the fact that the detective had obviously wanted to catch Paige off guard —and had succeeded— was the content of one of the pictures Schliesman had shown her.

Like she was playing some sort of twisted game of solitaire, Paige flipped the middle picture over and studied it again.

Paige had drawn that very image a few weeks ago. It was sitting in the portfolio where she kept all the drawings from her sleep.

With all the bruising, Paige hadn't realized she had drawn Teresa Cavasos twice: once when she was alive and once when she was dead. Although her clothing had been a prominent part of the picture she'd drawn of Teresa in the parking lot, only the top part of her collar was in the other picture she'd drawn of the woman's death.

The same as the photograph she was looking at now.

But it was obviously the same shirt, now that Paige was studying it. No wonder Detective Schliesman had asked her so many questions about the clothing in the photo. It was what Teresa had been wearing when she died.

Paige needed to call a lawyer. Through the exhausted haze of her mind she knew that was true. Schliesman had known Teresa Cavasos was dead the entire time she'd been questioning Paige. She must have been hoping Paige would confess or say something incriminating against herself.

Paige vaguely wondered if saying 'hey, I drew a picture of this exact death scenario too' would be incriminating enough for the detective.

She didn't know how to get a lawyer. Who to call. Was she allowed to use her phone now? Could she leave the room? She knew the door was still locked.

God, she just wanted to see Brett.

Not as her lover or to fall into his arms. Just to see someone who didn't think she had killed some poor woman in a horrible way. Just to see someone whose colors weren't an angry, accusatory red.

Or the chilling gray of this entire room. Paige turned the picture back over and wrapped her arms around herself.

After showing her the pictures, Schliesman had started asking her more questions about where she'd been last Thursday, before a knock on the door had interrupted them and the detective had left.

Paige had been so distraught over the pictures, over finding out she was too late, over realizing she had also drawn

Teresa Cavasos dead, to even remember last Thursday or where she'd been on that day.

She'd asked to see Brett again. If he was here, he would help her. At least he would be a friendly energy off of which she could feed. Someone to help her focus.

Someone who could hopefully help ward off the panic attack Paige could feel stalking its way closer.

She wrapped her arms around herself tighter, but knew it wouldn't be the barrier she needed. She wanted to get out of this room.

A few minutes later the door opened. Instead of Schliesman, another detective with wavy blond hair and a much less angry aura walked in. Followed by Brett.

She wasn't sure what exactly she had expected from Brett, certainly not any romantic greeting, but he stayed far back against the wall as the other man walked closer and took a seat.

"I'm Detective Alex Olivier from the homicide department. And I think you already know Detective Wagner." He gestured to Brett.

"Yes," Paige nodded. "He and I met last week." And made love two nights ago.

And now he was standing on the other side of the room like he could not care less what was happening with her. Even his colors were colder.

She'd been through a lot today, but she was afraid this was what would tip her over the edge. So ridiculous to think coldness from someone she wanted warmth from would be what did it.

"Like Detective Schliesman said, we'll be taking over the case now that it is officially a homicide."

"Have you been listening to what I said to Detective Schliesman?" she asked the surfer looking detective.

"Yes. For almost all of it."

"Both of you?" She looked pointedly at Brett.

He looked away. Paige had her answer without Detective Olivier saying a word.

Brett had sat behind that mirror and listened to everything that had been asked of her, knowing what Schliesman suspected her of. Oh God, he had known it was a homicide the whole time, had known they were trying to set her up, and had done nothing.

Maybe he'd actually thought she had something to do with it. Paige wrapped her arms around herself, for warmth and because she was afraid she might shatter into a million pieces.

"Miss Jeffries," the detective moved closer. "I understand it's been a difficult day for you."

"I'm going to go get you some water." It was the first thing Brett had said to her. She didn't even look at him.

But the other detective nodded. "Good idea, Brett."

Brett knocked on the door and left when it opened electronically. Paige looked at the man sitting across from her.

"I'm sorry, I don't remember your name."

"Olivier. Alex Olivier. I'm a homicide detective."

Exhaustion washed over Paige. First, all the questions by Detective Schliesman, then finding out Teresa was dead, then seeing her dead *in the same method* Paige had drawn?

And then Brett.

Brett walked back into the room, two water bottles in his hand. He put one in front of Detective Olivier and crouched down next to Paige, opening the other one.

"I'm not thirsty," she said, staring at the collar of his shirt. She couldn't bear to look him in the eyes. And she totally ignored the deep blues surrounding him. He was troubled.

"You need to drink it anyway," he said, gently disengaging her fingers from where they were clasping her arms.

Paige shivered slightly. His touch. How could she still feel such heat at his touch? How could she still want to lean towards him —towards his strength— and rest against him after he'd amply shown how little she really meant to him?

She brought the water bottle up to her lips and sipped. He was right, she had needed the water. She drank down nearly the entire bottle.

He stood, his fingers running unobtrusively along her arm as he stepped back.

She slid away. He could not be gentle now. Not when her heart was lying in pieces around her. He needed to go back over to the wall and blend back into the gray. She had to focus on keeping herself together, not on him.

Detective Olivier slid the other water bottle over towards her, but Paige didn't open it. "The last question Detective Schliesman asked is probably the most important one for you to answer. Unfortunately, you were pretty upset when she asked it."

"Which question was that?"

"Where were you last Thursday?"

"Is that when Teresa Cavasos went missing?" she asked.

"I'm not at liberty to discuss any specifics. But if you could just think about where you were on Thursday."

Paige closed her eyes and worked her way backwards: the night with Brett, the art show, preparation.

For the first time since she'd found out Teresa was dead, Paige felt a slight release in the pressure built up in her body. If whatever happened to Teresa happened on Thursday, there was no way they'd be able to think Paige had something to do with it.

A knock on the door startled Paige. Both Detective Olivier and Brett looked over at it sharply. Brett opened it.

"Gentleman, I'm Christine Thomas, Ms. Jeffries' attorney."

Paige was surprised. She hadn't ordered an attorney, despite this one being delivered, like a pizza. But the woman's aura was pretty clear, even if constantly moving. She was a multi-tasker, but had good intentions. At least right now.

She walked to the table and shook Paige's hand, giving her a reassuring nod.

"We'd like all questions to desist immediately and for my client to be released unless she's being formally charged," Christine told the men. She didn't sit down.

Detective Olivier sighed. "Ms. Jeffries has not been charged. She's always been free to go at any time."

Paige looked at the detective then Brett then her new lawyer. She'd been free to go all this time? Why hadn't Brett told her that?

Maybe because he thought she'd been guilty of murder.

"I can see by my client's face that's news to her," Christine said.

Paige shook her head. "The door was locked."

The lawyer put a hand on Paige's shoulder. "Are you ready? They can't keep you here any longer."

Paige stood. "Yes, but there's one question I want to answer before I go."

"What was the question?" she asked.

"Where I was on Thursday."

"You don't have to answer that, Ms. Jeffries," Christine told her. "It's not an admission of any sort of guilt not to answer the question."

"But if she does answer, and has a good alibi, it goes a long way towards us eliminating her as a suspect," Detective Olivier put in. Brett had come to stand closer to the table, although Paige still didn't look him in the eye.

"It's okay," she told Christine. "I want to."

The lawyer nodded but looked ready to jump in at any time.

"Last Thursday, I spent the entire day surrounded by a dozen people at the Barnes Gallery preparing for my art show that happened Friday night. We were there at least twelve or fourteen hours, long past midnight. My agent Hunter Barnes, and any number of assistants, can verify this."

"I think that pretty much eliminates my client as a suspect," Christine told them. "We'll make sure you're given the contact info. But right now, I'm taking Ms. Jeffries home."

Paige stood and followed Christine out the door. She could feel Brett's eyes on her the whole way.

Back at his desk, Brett stared at the computer screen, but didn't actually see anything on it.

The look in Paige's eyes in the interrogation room was the only thing he could see right now.

The most Brett could do to help her had been to stay away. To let others —whose neutrality could not be called into question— determine that she was not responsible.

But that look in her eyes.

Anger he could've handled. She had the right to be pissed off at how Schliesman had blindsided her with the news of Teresa Cavasos' death. Had the right to be furious at how they'd accused her of wanting attention. Had a right to be angry when she found out the man she'd just spent the weekend doing incredibly intimate things with, had been listening to the entire conversation and doing nothing.

Even though there was nothing he could've done that wouldn't have made it worse.

But she hadn't been angry. She'd been hurt.

That look in her eyes.

Brett rubbed his hand over his face, exhausted. He should've done something earlier. Should've insisted he and Alex go in instead of letting Schliesman try to set Paige up. Should've pulled the damn fire alarm for heaven's sake. Anything to stop what was happening to her.

But Brett knew deep inside he hadn't done any of those things because he'd wanted to see how Paige would answer the questions, how she would react to the news of Teresa's death.

He wanted to know what the hell was going on with these pictures she drew.

If Brett hadn't been there to see it with his own eyes, he would've never in a thousand years believed she had drawn it in her sleep. And Paige was wise enough to know not to mention that detail to anyone else. She'd learned her lesson from drawing herself.

Then a thought hit Brett: had she drawn the picture of herself in her sleep also? She hadn't mentioned that. Of course, she wouldn't have mentioned the sleep drawing at all if he hadn't literally stumbled onto it.

He planned to ask her.

Alex walked over to Brett's desk. "Just got off the phone with Hunter Barnes. Jeffries' alibi checks out. She was with multiple people all day Thursday, actually most of the week."

"Okay."

Alex snickered. "Yeah, I'll bet you're pretty relieved to know your lady friend isn't involved in a homicide."

Brett never had any question about that. What he didn't understand was the drawing. Brett and Alex both studied it where it sat on his desk.

"It's strange, right?" Alex said. "How did she draw it if she didn't know Cavasos? Why would she draw it?"

Drawing a random person in her sleep was weird.

Drawing a specific person in her sleep who had been abducted and killed in the very outfit she'd been wearing at the time went straight into Bizarroville. Brett knew there was no way he could mention it. Ever.

"She's an artist." Brett shrugged, attempting to be as casual as possible. "World renowned. Maybe her brain works differently than other people's. Like she said, she saw Teresa in the parking lot and drew her later. Her subconscious picked her out to draw."

"Well, Paige's subconscious made a hell of a choice."

"That's for sure."

"As far as I'm concerned, we've eliminated her as a suspect unless something changes," Alex said.

"The captain will be less than thrilled."

Alex raised an eyebrow, nodding. "Yeah. He doesn't like her."

"He doesn't like that she gets special attention from higher ups."

"Yeah, well, he doesn't like that about you either. So watch your back." Alex gave a little wave before walking back to his desk.

Brett didn't care right now about the captain's lack of love for him. What he cared about right now was Paige.

That look still haunted him.

When she left today he hadn't been able to go after her like he wanted. Hadn't been able to drive her home, explain his actions, ease that look in her eyes.

He hadn't been able to go after her then, but he'd damn well be there as soon as he could.

CHAPTER 18

O N THE LONG DRIVE UP to her house Brett prepared
what he would say to Paige. How he would explain
his actions at the station and why he hadn't stepped
in to help.

That he'd wanted to, but it would've made the situation
worse. That he'd done what he could by getting word to her
security team so they could get a lawyer in to her.

But to be honest, Brett didn't even know if she was
going to allow him past the guards to see her. And although
he wouldn't blame her, he didn't know what the hell he was
going to do if she did that.

So when the guards allowed him through, his relief was
tangible. Perhaps she wasn't as upset as he had thought.

She opened the door after his brief knock, but didn't look
him in the eye. Just like she hadn't looked him in the eye since
she'd realized he'd been present during her questioning at the
station. She closed the door behind him and walked back to
her living room to stand in front of one of the huge windows
that looked out onto that magnificent view, resting her hand
against it. She didn't say anything.

Brett watched from the doorway. Paige wasn't pouting,
wasn't pissy. He knew her well enough to know that. She
wasn't planning to lord over him what happened today.

But she was withdrawing.

Brett knew it with every fiber of his being. She was closing herself off to him. And although she'd probably never be rude or even unfriendly, she never planned to let him close to her —body or emotions— again.

That was just totally unacceptable. A fire burned through Brett, something carnal, primitive. She would *not* shut him out. He wouldn't allow it.

Couldn't bear it.

All the words he'd so carefully planned were not going to help him now. They were just words. To Paige words would always be secondary.

He needed to bind her to him in the quickest, strongest, most basic way possible.

He had his jacket and tie off before he was a few steps into the room. He draped them over the couch.

Her back was to him so she didn't know what he was doing. Brett didn't care. He would take every advantage —fair or unfair— that he could get. He unbuttoned the top buttons of his shirt as he crossed the rest of the way towards her.

She had showered recently, he could tell. Her mass of golden brown hair was still damp, sticking slightly to her t-shirt. She had on soft gray pants, her feet were bare. She was still leaning against the window, looking out silently at the twilight in front of her.

Brett knew he had only one chance at this. If he gave her the opportunity to close him all the way out, she'd never let him back in.

He felt her stiffen when he took her hair and tucked it over one of her shoulders, leaving her neck exposed on the other side.

He didn't give her a chance to protest. He brought his lips down to her neck, softly biting then easing the spot with gentle kisses over and over. His hands came down and slipped under her shirt and the elastic of her pants. One grabbed her hip, the other splayed wide over the soft skin of her belly, pulling her back against him.

His lips continued to nip and lick along her throat. Not wanting to give her time to think —only feel— he slid one hand up to her breast and the other down further to the juncture of her thighs.

She stiffened, but he didn't stop. Felt her nipple pebble under his fingers before he slid to the other one. His other hand slid lower easing one finger inside her, immediately moving to touch the spot he knew would make her tremble. A sigh rushed out of her lips before turning to a soft moan.

He felt her arch her back into him as both his hands teased her, his touches too soft to give her the release she wanted. She tried to turn, but he wouldn't let her.

"Put your hands on the window," he whispered into her ear. "And leave them there. Just feel me. Feel *us*."

She did what he asked and he rewarded her by dipping his fingers further into her wet center. She moaned as he kissed her ear on his way down her neck again, his other hand moving between her now erect nipples, rolling them between his fingers.

He eased her hips back with his hand so he could thrust against her through his clothing. But right now he planned to make her come apart with just his fingers.

He slipped them deeper inside her, touching her where he knew she needed to be touched. She stiffened and her arms fell from the window. He immediately stopped.

"Window, baby. Keep your hands there."

She groaned and put them back up and he immediately restarted his movements. Applying more pressure; gently flicking that little bundle of nerves that tightened even as she became wetter. Soon her head fell against the window too and she was nearly panting.

"Brett, I can't…"

She couldn't get there. He knew. He was keeping her from her release on purpose and it was taking every ounce of his concentration because all he wanted was to ease the rest of their clothes off and take her right against this window.

And he would be inside her later, he promised himself. Taking her hard and fast until neither of them could tell where he ended and she began. But not yet. Not until he had bound her to him in every way he could figure how.

He kept her on the edge as long as possible, her face flushed, body trembling, soft keen falling from her lips between begs for more. Finally he slid his lips to the place where her neck met her shoulder and bit. Hard. Just as his fingers put pressure on that tiny nub of flesh that hurled her over the edge.

Her entire body jerked and she called out his name, grinding her hips back against him. He almost lost it right then, but held on to his sanity. Barely.

Paige sobbed as she came down from her release, her body slack, arms falling bonelessly from the window. Brett eased his fingers from her, sliding her pants all the way off as he did so.

As she turned and melted against him, he slid her shirt over her head. He carried her naked form over to the overstuffed chair and ottoman. He laid her gently on it and she finally started to regain some measure of focus and composure.

Brett unbuttoned his shirt the rest of the way and threw it to the side. Paige's eyes were still mostly shut as residual shudders flowed through her.

But they flew open as he reached down and grabbed her legs and slid her down further on the chair, spreading them on either side of the ottoman, leaving her wide open to him.

"Oh, we're not even close to done," he said as he bent and began kissing his way up her leg from her knee.

Not even close to done? Paige's whole body felt like jello. How could there be more?

She hadn't planned on there being anything at all. Had just planned to politely let Brett know that she understood he'd just been doing his job today, but that she didn't think it was going to work out between them personally.

She had thought he might be relieved at her words. Save him the trouble of saying them.

But now, good heavens, *now* he was currently kissing his way —with tiny little nips that were driving her crazy— up her thigh.

By the time he reached her center, Paige couldn't think of any words, much less the words of goodbye she had planned to say.

She had thought her body had shattered a few minutes ago against the window. That was nothing compared to the way she came apart with his lips moving on her.

He knew exactly what to do, how much pressure to apply and where, to ratchet up her hunger until she could hardly breathe.

And with her legs sprawled out over the side of the ottoman, all she could do was feel and see all the colors that flew around them like a meteor shower. They burst into tiny flames as she screamed out grabbing hold of the arms of the chair as if they were lifelines. His hand gripped her buttocks hard, keeping her in place for his masterful tongue when she would've slid away. All she could do was sob his name.

He eased back, kissing his way back down her trembling thighs. But before Paige could even catch her breath Brett had removed his pants and was easing himself inside her. She cried out as he hooked his arms under her knees, bringing her legs up to wrap around his waist.

His face was a look of sheer concentration, moisture dotting on his forehead, as he moved in and out of her. She realized he was waiting for her pleasure to build back up to that peak again. Realizing her needs were more important to him than his own was all the invitation her body needed. She could feel her body tightening, pleasure simmering back through her. She wrapped her arms around his neck.

"You come with me this time," she whispered.

He hooked one of her legs higher, changing their angle and Paige gasped. She hadn't been sure another release would even be possible for her. Now she had no doubt.

His eyes locked with hers as he moved within her, his hand cradling her head like she was the most precious person on earth.

Then gentleness was gone as need took over. Groaning, he reached down and nipped hard at that place on her neck where he'd kissed her before. It was all it took to throw them both over that final edge.

They called each other's names as they fell.

CHAPTER 19

I 'M A LITTLE SURPRISED YOU didn't have me turned away at the gate."

A couple hours later Paige sat on one of her kitchen barstools, wrapped snuggly in her robe. She had a cup of coffee in her hands and a piece of toast in front of her that he'd made. For himself he'd made a sandwich to go with his coffee.

She watched him with just a hint of wariness. Considering she had planned to just let Brett in, let him make his professional justification for his actions earlier today, and let him leave, she was pretty darn surprised by the shivers that were still racing through her every few minutes.

"I thought about it," Paige admitted. She knew now it would've been the much safer decision. "What you did at the station... I know it was because of your job, but it sucked, Wagner."

He winced. "I know. I'm sorry. It was the best of pretty poor options."

"And once you got here? What was that blitz attack?"

He came to stand right in front of her on the barstool, his hands gripping either side of her hips so that they were face to face. "You were going to keep me out. Emotionally. You'd already decided it. I wasn't going to let that happen. Wasn't going to let you go."

"Sex as an emotional weapon?"

His forehead touched her. "I'm finding when it comes to keeping you in my life I'll use just about any weapon I have available to me."

Silver simmered all around him. Determination. It was hard to stay aloof—not that she'd been doing a good job of that anyway— when confronted with a man determined that you would be his. When that was what you really wanted anyway.

"Thank you for contacting my security team so they sent a lawyer," she finally whispered. "Jacob let me know it was you who let them know what was going on."

He kissed her briefly then moved back to the table. "I'm glad they got one there so quickly."

Paige was too. Today had been pretty torturous.

"Why didn't you come to me with the picture?" he asked her.

"When I saw the ad in the paper this morning I recognized Teresa. I thought she was a missing person. I thought maybe I could help." Paige shrugged. "I didn't think the case had anything to do with you. Besides…"

After a few moments of silence Brett prompted her. "Besides, what?"

She took a sip of her coffee, which she recognized as a stalling tactic. But it couldn't be avoided. "I wasn't sure exactly what was between you and me. We'd only spent one night together and I wasn't even sure you wanted to see me again."

Brett cocked his head towards the living room. "Well, I hope that's been cleared up."

As much as she liked the thought, she still couldn't stop thinking about this afternoon at the station. "The way you looked at me today in that interrogation room. It's hard. Knowing you were watching the whole time. Could've stopped it." She huddled down into her robe. "I'm having a hard time with that."

He put his sandwich down and took a step towards her. "Paige—"

She held a hand out to stop him. "Did you think I had something to do with Teresa Cavasos' death? Is that why you didn't intervene?"

The thought that he could've sat there, *suspecting* her, made something hitch inside Paige, wanting to break apart.

This time her outstretched hand didn't stop him. He came around the island until he was standing right in front of her.

"No," he told her. "I never once thought you were a part of Teresa Cavasos' death. The entire time Schliesman was questioning you I knew you were innocent."

Paige felt she could breathe again at his words.

He cupped her cheek with his hand. "I couldn't go in there and stop it. And once I was in there, I couldn't give you any special treatment."

"You were doing your job, I understand."

But it still hurt.

"There were people watching you. Watching me. Going into that interrogation room as your lover would've been the worst thing I could do for both of us."

She shrugged but didn't look him in the eyes.

He took the coffee cup out of her hand and put it on the island then cupped her cheeks with both his, forcing her to look up at him.

"I was caught off guard. A new homicide comes across my desk and low and behold it's the same lady you'd just drawn in your sleep. I had no idea what that meant."

She nodded. It was freaky. And he didn't even know the half of it.

"Then they tell me they have a possible suspect they're questioning. I'm trying to get in touch with you when I walk into the room and find you sitting there. The suspect."

He drew his thumbs across his cheeks. "But I never thought you did it. I'll admit, I ran scenarios in my mind and one of them was that you were in some part of Teresa's murder. But I dismissed it almost immediately."

He hadn't suspected her. He'd just had to keep his distance. She could understand it even if it had hurt her at the time.

"I knew I needed to let someone else establish your innocence. Because if I had rushed in there forcing everyone to accept my word for your innocence, once our relationship became public, there could be all sorts of blow back and accusation of favoritism."

"Not to mention, your department probably frowns upon you sleeping with a suspected criminal."

He gave her a half smile. "True. Although you weren't a suspected criminal at the time we slept together. But that probably wouldn't have mattered much to my direct supervisor. He's looking for any reason to get me out."

"Brett, I swear I didn't know her until I saw her picture in Sunday's paper. And that was this morning. I didn't even look at the paper until then."

Brett nodded. "I know. I was out of the media loop all weekend too or I would've recognized Teresa Cavasos when you drew her."

"Am I a suspected criminal now? Are you going to get in any trouble if someone was to find out you're here?"

"No, your alibi checked out. Hard to be part of a murder plot when you're working fifteen hour days with a dozen other people. Not to mention the fact that you have 24/7 security who can vouch for your whereabouts."

"I just wanted to help them find that woman, Brett. I really thought the details in the background might be some sort of clue. I couldn't have lived with myself if there was something I could've done, but didn't just because I was too chicken to go to the police station."

Just once, out of all those pictures she'd drawn over the last three years —all those dead and bruised women— faces she didn't know, she wanted one good thing to come of it. All the exhaustion, the nose bleeds, the muscle spasms, if just this one time she'd been able to help, then maybe it would've been worth it.

But she hadn't.

"I know seeing that dead woman was jarring for you. I'm so sorry," Brett told her. "The reason they were so suspect of you is because the blouse Teresa was wearing in your drawing was the same one she was found dead in. She was actually found Friday, although her body wasn't identified until today."

"It was difficult to see her dead, especially since I was hoping otherwise. And I knew the shirt had something to do with it because Detective Schliesman kept coming back to that."

It was time to show him, Paige knew. Not all the pictures, because she wouldn't wish that on anyone. But it was time to show him the other picture of Teresa Cavasos she'd drawn. The one just like the police photo where she was dead.

"But the reason I had such an extreme reaction," she told him, touching him on his arm, "with the vomiting and everything, wasn't just because of the shock of seeing her dead."

"What was it?"

She took a deep breath and got down from the stool. This probably wasn't going to go well.

"I have to show you."

That wasn't what Brett had expected Paige to say. She wrapped her robe tighter around her and led him out of the kitchen and down the hall.

He was glad she had listened to him, had understood why he had acted the way he had today at the station. The crisis seemed to have passed, the aloofness he'd felt from her that had been so intolerable to him was now gone.

His relief was all but palpable. He had no idea why someone who'd been in his life such a short time meant so much to him, he only knew it was true. She wasn't shutting him out, physically or emotionally. Nothing else was as important as that.

But as they walked down the hall he realized that although she wasn't distant any more, wasn't holding herself apart from him, there was another type of tension. And it had to do with whatever she was about to show him.

When he realized which room she was taking him to, tension filled him too.

The room with the easel.

She stopped in front of the closed door and turned to him.

"I don't know exactly when I drew this. I don't date them. But it was months ago."

Brett didn't know what he was about to see, but he knew it wasn't going to be good. They both took a breath as she opened the door and turned on the lights.

On the easel was a drawing of one of the crime scene photos of Teresa Cavasos. The exact replica of one of the photos Schliesman had shown Paige today. The crime scene photo after Teresa's body was found.

Thoughts flew through Brett's head as he studied the picture.

"Did you draw it in your sleep?"

Paige nodded.

Brett just stared at the picture. Now he was officially at a decision point. Knew that whatever he said next, how he reacted to this picture, was going to choose the path for their relationship.

Because seriously. What. In. The. Hell. *Another one?* Another picture, the exact replica of a crime scene photo?

He could either choose logic: she'd drawn the picture this evening after Schliesman showed it to her this afternoon. Paige was an artist, she could remember details normal people wouldn't remember, even after only seeing the photo for a few minutes.

Logic dictated she was telling him she drew it months ago as an attempt to get attention. That there was something in her that needed people —maybe law enforcement personnel specifically— to provide her succor. To make her feel important, visible, not forgotten.

It wouldn't be unheard of, and would even be understandable, given her attack. Logic would argue that it was natural for her to want to keep law enforcement focused on her, to make her feel safe, since her attacker had never been apprehended.

It was even logical that she could've faked sleeping while drawing the other picture of Cavasos Saturday night, just to draw Brett closer. Or maybe her mind even *believed* she was sleeping.

Perhaps this was all a desperate cry for help. One Brett needed to take seriously.

Logic was one option.

Or he could completely ditch logic and believe the almost impossible: that Paige really had drawn this picture months ago, before Teresa Cavasos was dead or missing or even in danger.

Just like Paige had drawn the picture of herself before the attack.

Brett was in conflict. Because in order to believe that Paige was of sound mind and emotional stability he had believe that she was somehow psychically connected to hideous violence.

Which was, ironically, crazy.

Or in order to believe this picture had been drawn in any sort of reasonable way, of conscious mind and at a logical date and time, he had to believe that Paige —who was watching him so calmly from the side, not saying anything— was just a stop short of the loony bin.

Brett felt like the oxygen was being systematically extracted from the room. Breathing was becoming harder and harder. He had to get out of here. Clear his head, think things through. He couldn't do that with Paige's big blue eyes watching him so intently.

He turned to her. "I've got to go. Just for a while. I've got to figure out…" What? If he needed to find someone who could provide psychiatric help for her? If he could go against ten years of police detective methods and suspend everything he'd ever held true?

She nodded. "But Brett, there's really something else I should show—"

He held out a hand to stop her. Whatever she wanted to say or show him, it would have to wait. Right now he just had to figure out his own mind.

He grabbed her gently by both her upper arms and brought her close. He kissed her forehead breathing in her scent.

"Whatever it is you need to show me, it has to wait, okay? It's all I can do to process this."

He finally felt her nod against his lips.

"I just need some time to sort things out. I've got to go," he said again. He released her and took a step back. "No matter what, you do not show that picture to anyone, do you understand me?"

Brett had no doubt, alibi or not, Paige would be arrested if she showed up at the station with that picture claiming she'd drawn it months ago.

He could tell she was about to say something more but stopped and just nodded. Her features were pinched and she had her arms wrapped around herself as if she was expecting a blow.

To think he'd put that damned expression on her face twice in one day crushed him.

She was confused. Was hurt. But he couldn't do or say anything to help her right now.

Not until he figured out in his head what the hell was going on.

CHAPTER 20

BRETT DROVE AWAY FROM PAIGE'S house, not exactly sure where he was going to go. It was nearly midnight and there wasn't really anyone else he wanted to see.

The person he wanted to be with was back in the house probably wondering if he was driving away forever. Brett scrubbed a hand across his face. He had to admit he was also wondering if he was driving away forever.

He slammed his hand against the steering wheel. The dichotomy of his feelings were tearing him apart. And it all came down to the question, could he believe that Paige really drew that picture in her sleep.

He could call Chief Pickett and ask him his opinion. The chief was his friend, had known Brett all his life, but Brett didn't want to do that. For one, he didn't want to run to the chief every time he had a problem. And for another, Brett wasn't sure exactly how to explain all this.

It was crazy to him and he'd seen it actually happening. How could he explain it to someone else?

And once the chief was involved there was no going back. Friend or no friend, the chief would not be able to just turn a blind eye to this once he was aware of the full scope of Paige's involvement.

Brett turned on his hands-free phone system and called Alex. He cringed just slightly as the phone rang for the first time. He didn't really know much about his new partner. Alex might not be the type to want to discuss case related matters outside of office hours.

He may not want to talk to Brett at all.

"Wagner, you in trouble?" Alex answered the phone without any greeting.

"Nah, man." This was a bad idea, Brett shouldn't have called. "Never mind. I was just thinking about the Teresa Cavasos case."

"Important enough that it couldn't wait until tomorrow? Unless you're like everyone else and just can't stand to go a few hours without hearing my voice." Alex's chuckle broke the tension. "It's a real problem, believe me."

Brett at least smiled. "So I've heard. I just had some thoughts about the case that were a little unorthodox. They were sort of consuming me so I was gonna see if you wanted to grab a beer real quick and talk this out."

"Why didn't you just start with that? I'm always up for a beer." Alex gave him the name and address of the local sports bar that a lot of the guys from the station hung out at. "I'll meet you there in fifteen."

Brett hung up and drove the rest of the way. He would try to run some of this past Alex without giving him the full details. His new partner had already proved to be level-headed, maybe he would be able to help Brett see the truth.

Because God knew he couldn't see it on his own.

Alex already had a booth near the back and a beer for himself when Brett arrived. Brett grabbed a beer from the bar and made his way over.

But now that he was sitting here across from his partner the idea of explaining this seemed more complicated than ever. He decided to keep Paige's name out of it for as long as possible. He didn't want to do anything that might implicate her and didn't want to put Alex in a position where he felt like he had information about the case but that Brett didn't want him to use it.

Not to mention that the entire thing sounded so impossible that even the thought of explaining it was giving him a headache.

Alex nodded at him. "So this is about the Teresa Cavasos murder? Did something new happen that I haven't heard about? Or maybe it has something to do with the lovely Ms. Jeffries?"

So much for keeping Paige out of it.

"You ever believe in using unorthodox methods to solve cases?" Brett finally asked after taking a sip of his beer.

"Like what? Psychics and stuff?"

"Yeah. Like that. Techniques outside what would be considered customary."

Alex shrugged. "I basically believe in using any legal method available to solve cases. Particularly when it involves a violent crime and murder. Is this about the picture Paige Jeffries drew?"

"Nah." Brett leaned back in the booth as casually as he could. "I'm just talking hypotheticals. Nothing to do with Paige."

Alex raised an eyebrow and leaned forward on the table with his elbows. "I will say that I've been on the force long enough to know that cases are not necessarily always solved in a linear fashion. I don't necessarily think that all information needs to be shared with every single party at the moment we get it."

"Yeah, me too."

"Since something was obviously bugging you enough to get me out of bed in the middle of the night, but you haven't already shared it, then why don't we come to an agreement. As long as we are working towards the same goal, finding and arresting Teresa Cavasos' killer, then as far as I'm concerned anything said here tonight doesn't need to be official record."

Brett knew that didn't mean anything officially. Just meant that Alex wanted to be a good partner and give Brett the sounding board he needed.

But he had said the most important thing: that they were both trying to catch Teresa Cavasos' killer.

"It is about the picture Paige Jeffries drew."

Alex rolled his eyes. "Uh, *duh*."

Brett smirked a little. "Yeah, it's a little weird."

"Yeah, that amount of detail. I guess it's the fact that she's an artist or whatever but it was pretty amazing."

Brett shifted back against the booth. "And suspicious. That's what you mean, isn't it?"

Alex shrugged. "As far as airtight alibis go, hers is one of the tightest I've ever seen. She's not the killer." He looked a little harder at Brett. "Is that what you're worried about? That you were in bed with a killer?"

"No," Brett said immediately. At least he honestly knew he wasn't worried about that. Brett had no doubt that Paige was not involved with these crimes. "I don't think she has anything to do with it."

Alex nodded. "Good. That's the first step. We couldn't even go any further if you weren't sure about that."

"But the drawings are freaky. I know that. Hell, she knows that."

"Drawings plural? As in, more than one?"

"She had another drawing that she showed me a few minutes ago. One of Teresa Cavasos, but dead this time. An exact replica of one of the crime scene photos. The one Schliesman showed her."

Alex put his beer down mid sip. "The *exact* same? With all that detail and everything?"

Brett nodded. "Yes."

"She was able to draw it after only having seen it for a few seconds? The same photo that made her throw up in the trashcan?"

"It seems like the photo made her throw up in the trashcan because she had *already* drawn it. Before she ever came to the station. Like months ago."

Alex twirled his beer glass with his fingers. Brett appreciated that he didn't laugh or scoff outright.

"If memory serves, that's what she said she did with the photo from her own attack, correct?"

Brett grimaced. "Yeah. Of course, no one wants to believe her because that sort of stuff is as weird as shit isn't it? I mean, if someone could draw crime scenes before they happen?"

Alex stopped twirling his beer glass. "Yeah, definitely eerie."

"So that's where I stand," Brett said. "When I got to her place tonight she showed me this other picture of Teresa Cavasos. Logic says she's just an artist who's desperate for attention."

Alex took another sip of beer. "Yeah."

"Like Paige has found a way into the Portland PD computers, draws these pictures, says they happened much earlier, and is just trying to get someone to pay attention to her."

"I've seen the file for her case," Alex said. "That assault she underwent? If she camped out at the police station demanding everyone listen to her and pay attention to her case, nobody would blame her."

Brett rubbed his forehead. "Believe me, I've thought of that."

"And what does your gut tell you? Do you think that's what this is? Because legit. nobody could blame her for needing serious help. Psychiatric help. Doesn't make her crazy or anything. It would sort of make sense."

Brett took a long time to gather his thoughts. It came back to the internal argument he'd had with himself at Paige's house. Logic versus crazy.

He thought of Paige's pretty face, blue eyes, soft smile. Those hadn't changed since high school. She'd never wanted attention. Not then, not now.

"Honestly, man, I don't think this is about attention for her. As a matter fact, she goes out of her way not to be the center of anyone's focus. Hell, she almost never leaves her house at all. She's almost agoraphobic."

"But even someone who doesn't like to leave her house might still want someone to be paying attention to her case. To find the person who did that to her. It would certainly be understandable."

"I know. Trust me, I have thought those very things myself."

Alex leaned back in the booth. "But you don't think that's what's happening now. You think Paige is telling the truth, no matter how illogical it is."

Brett realized the other man was right. "Yeah. But hell, man, I wouldn't be the first person who's been snowed by a beautiful woman."

"You know her better than I do. I don't have a personal relationship with her so I can't say what type of person she is. But I do trust you. I trust your judgment. I trusted Chief Pickett when he chose to bring you in here for a reason. So if you say that's not what's going on, then I think we should work under that assumption until we're given any different information."

Brett scrubbed a hand across his face. "So to recap: believing that Paige had some sort of premonition and drew both her own attack and Teresa's murder long before either event happened." Mentioning the sleep part would just muddy the waters.

"Yep." Alex saluted him with his glass.

"You know that means going against everything I've learned in nearly ten years in law enforcement. I'm not into hocus pocus type stuff. It goes against logic."

"Hey, I'm not suggesting we take up casting spells or voodoo dolls. But maybe your gal has some sort of sixth sense or something."

Like her sister did with the FBI.

Brett didn't bring that up because this conversation was already one of the weirdest of his life. Brett needed to put in a call to the San Francisco FBI field office. Just to get an understanding of what Paige's sister could do.

"Yeah, sixth sense. I guess it's not unheard of."

Alex shrugged. "If you don't think she's crazy, and you don't think she's a killer, then your only option is to believe what she's saying. And use it. Because what if the next person she draws is still alive and we can use that to help save someone's life? If that's the case, then I don't care when or how she draws it, or if she does it with her toes."

Brett nodded. Alex was right. Who cared *how* it was happening, it was happening. Hell, he'd seen it himself. Seen her draw in her sleep. Seen the toll it had taken on her. She hadn't been making that up.

Brett raised his glass in a small salute to Alex. "To using whatever methods we can to catch a killer."

They clinked glasses. "Even the zany ones."

CHAPTER 21

I DON'T DATE THE PICTURES.

Paige's words about her drawings were echoing through Brett's mind when he woke up the next morning.

What she'd said to him when he'd asked her when she'd drawn the picture of Teresa Cavasos. That she wasn't sure because she didn't date *them*. Plural.

He hadn't really paid attention to her exact words at the time because he'd been reeling from the drawing she'd shown him. But now his brain was thinking about it full force.

How many more did she have?

He called her last night after his beer with Alex. He hadn't wanted her to worry that he deliberately wasn't contacting her.

But when the call had gone straight to voicemail he had to admit he was a little relieved. He left a message saying he would call her today, and he would. He hoped she wasn't at her house upset. Worried that she'd never hear from him again.

He couldn't leave her alone now if he wanted to. He had to know what other information she had about murders that were possibly tied together. Especially now that his subconscious was remembering that she had more than one drawing.

Truth was he couldn't leave her alone even if she had nothing to do with any case for the rest of his career.

But Brett knew he wouldn't truly be able to be with Paige until these cases were sorted out. Not the way he wanted to be with her. Which scared him a little bit.

It scared him more that it didn't scare him more. When he'd moved back to Portland, he'd known his football past would come into play, at least for some people —like Randal and Terri— who wanted to bask in the glory days their whole lives. Thought he might even date an ex-cheerleader or two once he got here.

He'd never expected Paige Jeffries. She wasn't a cheerleader. Wasn't part of the glory days.

She was so, so much more.

But right now, he needed to get back up to her house and see exactly what other pictures she hadn't shown him. Maybe they were just more of Teresa Cavasos, but maybe it was much more than that.

Brett got dressed and went into work. Before he could go back to Paige's house he needed to look into something else she'd alluded to. Paige's sister and the work she did for the FBI. Some sort of profiler, with a special gift. Brett didn't know exactly what he was hoping to gain from the information. Maybe just an affirmation that unorthodox law enforcement methods did exist.

Affirmation that Brett wasn't crazy for even considering this.

Alex and Brett nodded at one another from across the office, but didn't mention their conversation last night. Right now there wasn't anything more to mention about it. They were both waist deep in details from Teresa Cavasos' murder, studying the details as they were handed over from missing persons.

It was after lunch before Brett was able to make his call to the San Francisco field office of the FBI. All he knew was the person he should talk to was named Conner Perigo and that he was Paige's brother-in-law.

It took a minute for the call to be routed to the correct desk. Brett wasn't sure what he was going to say at all. He would keep this official. Businesslike. Maybe keep Paige's name out of it all together.

"Conner Perigo." The other man answered the phone without any other greeting.

"Special agent Perigo, this is Detective Brett Wagner, with the Portland PD."

"Detective Wagner, what can I do for you?"

"I'm working on a case of what I think may be connected murders. I haven't confirmed that they're all related, but I have reason to believe they are."

"Okay," Agent Perigo said. "Do they have to do with a case I'm working on or someone here in this office?"

"Not exactly." Brett wasn't sure exactly how to start this conversation.

"Then why don't I connect you to someone who has more familiarity with the Portland area. I don't think I'll be very much help to you if this isn't related to any of my cases."

Brett realized he wasn't going to be able to keep Paige's name out of it. In order to get Agent Perigo to focus on this, he was going to have to use the connection between the man's wife and Paige.

"No, this case isn't directly related to your caseload, as far as I know. But I believe that the killer I'm tracking has a victim that got away. Her name is Paige Jeffries."

Perigo didn't say anything, but Brett could tell by the way the noise shifted that the other man was moving into a quieter space.

"You're looking into the Paige Jeffries attack?"

"I am."

"I'm assuming you're contacting me because you know the connection between her and me."

"Yes, I know she is your sister-in-law."

Silence met him on the other end for just a moment. "Do you know this because you're good at detecting or because Paige told you?"

"Does it matter?"

"Yes, it does very much. If you're contacting me because you figured out on your own that I'm related to her by marriage and that the FBI might lend some resources to the case that you may not have, then that's one thing."

"And would that be a problem?"

"Absolutely not. I would use both my own personal resources and resources within the Bureau to help arrest the man who did that to Paige." Another length of silence. "But you're not hunting me down because of your detective skills, are you?"

"No," Brett said. "Paige told me that her sister's husband worked at the FBI."

"Well, I guess actually it doesn't matter because my offer is still the same. I'll do anything to help find Paige's attacker."

"Including using your wife's nontraditional profiling skills?"

"Well, now I know you're the one who's been talking to Paige. You didn't get that from any database search. Adrienne's work at the FBI is pretty classified."

"The one talking to Paige?"

"My wife and her sister are pretty close. Paige mentioned that she'd been spending time with a Portland detective. Someone she knew in high school."

"Yeah, I guess that would be me."

"Spending time with her about the case or more than that? I didn't pry."

"Both."

"I'll be honest with you, Detective Wagner--"

Brett interrupted him. "Under the circumstances I'd appreciate it if you'd call me Brett. I'm not calling you in any official capacity."

"Likewise, Conner. I looked into this case when it first happened. Did everything I could."

"Which I'm suspecting wasn't much given its unsolved status. I haven't found much to go on either. At least as an isolated case."

"We looked at it in conjunction with other attacks, but didn't find anything. And, I have to be honest, the Portland PD wasn't interested in much federal help on what was a local case. What have you found that made you think Paige's case is connected to some other attacks?"

"Not attacks. Murders. I think that Oregon might have a serial killer on the loose."

"Why?"

Brett explained the payday details as well as the similarity between the women: unmarried, in their twenties, attractive despite having different hair colors. He also explained the problems: different locations, different methods of murder.

"How do you think this ties in with Paige?"

"All the victims were severely beaten in the face and head like Paige. I think Paige was meant to be a murder victim, but got away."

"Damn," Conner muttered.

Brett nodded. "And, of course, that picture she drew of herself."

"The one of herself in the hospital that she drew a long time before the attack."

"You say that with pretty calm assurance. Most people around here found it difficult to believe that she could've drawn that with such eerie accuracy before the assault occurred."

"Well, let's just put it this way. Compared to what my wife can do, Paige's gift seems pretty tame."

"And exactly what can your wife do?"

Conner chuckled. "I could tell you, but you won't believe me. Or at least you won't believe quite as much as when you watch it yourself. I'll send you an electronic file with Adrienne at work. It's a sight to behold."

Brett could feel his eyebrow raise. "Can you at least give me a rundown?"

"Let's just say they used to call her the Bloodhound. Adrienne can sense and track people with evil intents. Get readings, so to speak, from items they've touched. The solving of dozens of cases, more, are directly attributed to her. And she doesn't even work full-time for the FBI."

Brett didn't push why Adrienne Perigo did not work full-time for the FBI, if she had such a gift. That wasn't his business.

"Paige has drawn more pictures. Not of herself, of another woman. A murder victim."

He heard Conner curse under his breath.

"And if I'm not mistaken," Brett continued. "Paige has more drawings that she hasn't shown me. What I'm pretty sure are other victims."

"She didn't have anything to do with the crimes, that much I can tell you. I made the same mistake of suspecting Adrienne as a criminal when I first learned what she could do. Thought she was in on it."

"Yeah, well, I've already rounded that corner. I don't believe Paige had anything to do with these crimes, but I don't believe many of my colleagues are going to support my theory if it comes down to it."

"So are you calling to see if my wife can come do her particular type of profiling for your case? I should warn you that Adrienne already tried everything related to Paige's case when it first occurred."

Brett rubbed his forehead. "No, I guess I was just looking for confirmation that everything I know about how law enforcement cases are solved might be incorrect."

Conner sighed. "Not incorrect. The Jeffries sisters will just force you to open your mind to other possibilities that might *also* be correct. But it does take some getting used to."

No doubt about that.

Conner continued. "I have to admit I don't know Paige very well. Adrienne and I had just gotten married when the attack occurred and Paige hasn't really been interested in a lot of outside company since then."

"She draws these pictures in her sleep." It was difficult to even say the words out loud. "I know that sounds crazy, but I've seen it myself."

"Trust me when I say I understand. When Adrienne is sensing an object she goes into a sort of trance. Damn scary."

"I'm not sure if that makes me feel better or worse."

Conner chuckled. "All I had to do was open my mind to the possibility that it *could* work. Adrienne's track record pretty much spoke for itself."

"I'll go talk to Paige right away. Figure out what other pictures she might have that she hasn't been willing to show."

Why would she? Every time she showed a picture to someone in law enforcement they either told her she was crazy or threatened to have her arrested.

"Good," Conner said. "Use them. If this guy is a serial killer like you think, forget about whether it makes sense as to when or how these pictures were drawn. If this helps you catch this guy that's all that matters in the long run."

"And look," Conner continued. "I don't know if Paige is anything like Adrienne, but if she is then using this gift costs her. Physically takes a toll on her body. I'm able to help offset the physical price Adrienne pays, but I don't know that Paige has ever had that."

Brett had seen the physical demand the drawing had taken on her. Paige very definitely pays the price for these drawings.

"I'll do what I can to help her."

"And you're going to have to protect her. I don't think you're going to have any more doubts after you watch what Adrienne can do, but not everybody is going to believe. You've got to protect her from the people in your department who are going to want to make a judgment call without all the facts."

"It's understandable. I've seen her actually draw one of the pictures and I still can't believe it."

"You're going to have to run interference for her. You can't just bring these drawings into the station and expect everybody to not want to know where they came from."

"Believe me, I know."

"And if you're right and her case is connected to a killer, then you're going to have to be even more careful. Paige has never been in much danger because it's well known that she could not remember the face of her assailant. If he finds out she's working with you and she knows more than has been let on…"

"Then a murderer might be back on her trail."

CHAPTER 22

P AIGE WAS PRETTY SURPRISED WHEN the security at the front gate announced that Brett was back. It was late afternoon and after how he looked when he left last night she wasn't sure she'd ever be seeing him again. His face. The way he'd been so torn. She knew that was only to be expected, after all he was a police officer and everything he did was based in logic. In fact.

Drawing murder victims in her sleep did not exactly lend itself towards the logic and fact side of things. She'd gotten his call last night. Had purposely let it go straight to voicemail because she couldn't bear to talk to him. He said that he'd call today, that he wasn't mad, that they would work this out.

But how could they? She felt like every time she saw him she dropped another bomb on him: I drew a picture of myself in a coma two months before it happened, I paint auras, I draw dead people in my sleep.

Her life wasn't just like an episode of the Twilight Zone, it was like a whole damn season.

And the worst part was she *still* hadn't told him the worst part. Hadn't shown him. Had another bomb to drop on him.

She needed to show him the portfolio. The one full of pictures of the women she'd drawn. If he had thought seeing the one picture of Teresa Cavasos was hard, seeing them all really wasn't going to sit well with him.

Paige rubbed at the ache in her chest. There wasn't any way her relationship with Brett was going to survive this. She wasn't even sure how *she* was going to survive it.

Now that she knew how isolated she'd really become, how was she going to just go back to that?

Especially when the only person she really wanted to be around her was Brett. Everywhere she looked around this house now all she could think of was him. Of them. Of their lovemaking.

When she heard his knock on her door she didn't falter in her steps to it. Better to just rip the band-aid off. She would show him the pictures, all of them, and he would hopefully be able to use them in some way. If Teresa Cavasos was a real person then maybe all the other drawings were real women also.

Paige rubbed her chest again. They were all dead. She knew that too. She might've always known that.

She braced her hand against the door frame, before opening it, taking a deep breath. She could survive this. She'd survived worse.

She opened the door to let him in. He looked at her so intensely she had to glance away, and couldn't stop the small flinch when his knuckles grazed her cheek gently.

"Are you okay?"

A loaded question. She couldn't look her best, not after not sleeping all of last night. She'd stayed up for hours trying to draw. Trying to draw the way she did while she was sleeping. Trying to force her mind to come up with the images of the women she knew were in her subconscious.

It's hadn't helped. Hadn't done anything but exhaust her physically the way she'd already been exhausted mentally.

She felt Brett's arms slowly slide around her. There was nothing more she wanted to do than lean into his strength. To steal these moments while she could, because she knew soon enough they would be gone.

But she couldn't. It was time, past time, for her to show him the pictures she'd been hiding. At least with Brett she knew she wouldn't be arrested.

She pulled back from him. "There's something I need to tell you. I know hearing those words from me have to send a chill up your spine, but it's important. And yes, strange."

"There's more pictures, aren't there? That you've drawn. Other women."

Paige's eyes flew up to his. "How did you know?"

"I figured it out sometime this morning. Something you said in passing last night."

"Yes, that's what I was trying to tell you."

He nodded. "I know. And I'm sorry that I didn't let you get it out, but honestly it was probably for the best. Sometimes I just have to process stuff in smaller doses."

"I feel like I drop a bomb on you every time I see you."

His arms wrapped around her again and this time she did lean into his strength.

"My bomb shelter is pretty strong. But I will admit I do hope that this is the last one for a while. You're not some sort of shape shifter or something, right?"

She appreciated his attempt to put her at ease, but she was afraid when he actually saw the pictures he wouldn't be able to find any humor in any situation.

"I hope you still feel that way once you see these. My only defense is, that until Teresa Cavasos, I didn't know that these were actual real people. Real women. I thought that maybe it was my subconscious playing out some issues from my attack."

She pulled back from his arms and led them into the living room where she brought the portfolio, wide horizontally and vertically but without much depth. It was meant to store different sized papers or canvases to be carried.

She didn't know why some of the paintings were larger and some were smaller any more than she knew why she drew these to begin with.

The portfolio was on the coffee table. She opened it and looked over at Brett.

"I'll admit I'm a coward and couldn't go through them. I haven't ever gone through them once I put them in here."

He just nodded.

"I'm going to go get some water and let you look through this on your own for a while."

She didn't want him to have to hide his reaction from her. Wanted to give him the opportunity to look through things objectively without her in the room.

Plus, she knew what was in there. She didn't want to see the pictures of these women again. They were burned into her mind forever.

He trailed his knuckles down her cheek again. She nodded. "I'm just going to stay out. Call me when you're ready for me to come back in."

She didn't wait for him to answer. She didn't go into the kitchen like she planned, knowing that was just going to drive her crazy, wondering what he was thinking in there.

Instead she headed to where she'd always gone when things were too much. Her art studio.

"Paige, stop."

It took her a second to focus, to figure out what was going on. She'd been so deep into her painting that she'd lost track of everything around her.

It wasn't the first time it happened but usually it was because she was lost in the joy of her art.

She looked at the easel in front of her. She'd painted what any neutral observer would've called a black hole. Umbra, penumbra, and antumbra --the different types of shadows-- filled the entire canvas.

She wasn't exactly sure when she had switched to this. She'd been trying to lose herself in painting, anything, but hadn't been able to do it. Even painting the auras of Chloe and Adrienne, which she knew from absolute memory, had been impossible.

And then the dark aura had taken over.

Paige knew what this was. This was her painting of the man who had attacked her. This is what she saw when she tried to remember him. The blackness. The shadows.

Brett was standing behind her with his hand gently grasped over hers. She felt the stiff muscles of her arm as he lowered her hand down to her side.

"Are you all right?" His deep voice was a whisper in her ear.

"I think so." She set the paint brush in a jar of cleaner on the table by her easel. "That's him. That's what I remember when I think of the day that I was attacked. Instead of seeing his face, I just see this."

She felt Brett's hands come up and begin rubbing her upper arms, his long fingers easing her tight muscles.

"You need to eat something. And definitely drink some water if you haven't had any this whole time."

She spun her head back slightly to look at him. "How long has it been?"

"Almost five hours."

No wonder she was so stiff and tired. She sometimes got caught up in painting like this but usually had a bottle of water and some fruit within easy reach of her easel. Her mind had learned to take care of her physical body –grabbing whatever hydration or nutrients she needed- so that she could continue long hours of painting.

But she hadn't planned on long hours of painting today.

She fully turned so she could face Brett. "The drawings. Did you see them all? Will it help you in any cases?"

"Let's eat a little and then we can go over it. But yes, your pictures are definitely going to be helpful."

In the kitchen they worked together to make some soup and sandwiches. Neither of them said much as they ate, both caught up in their own thoughts.

After cleaning the dishes Paige didn't resist when Brett led her back into the living room. She had to face those pictures. Knew he would have questions about them. It was time.

Most of them she hadn't seen since the day she drew them. She didn't know the order or the dates, but now wished desperately she did.

"I haven't studied these pictures. I just want you to know that. I don't know much about them and haven't looked at many of them since the mornings I found them and then just put them in the portfolio."

She was relieved when Brett nodded. "It's understandable. Some of them are pretty graphic in their violence."

Paige hardly recognized her living room as they walked through the entryway. Brett had moved the couch all the way back to get more space to lay out the pictures.

The drawings, there were well over one hundred of them, were laid out in very specific groupings all over her floor.

"Wow." She murmured.

"I found some sticky notes in your kitchen drawer and used them. I hope that's okay. Normally I wouldn't do something like that with artifacts involving potential cases, but I figured we were never going to log these into official evidence."

Paige walked closer to the pictures trying to figure out the patterns Brett had used. "That's fine."

"The first thing you should know, if you don't already, is that you drew every single picture more than once."

Paige's eyes flew to his. "I did? I knew I drew them again if I destroyed them, which is why I started to keep them. But I drew them *all* more than once?"

"Yes. Every single one. Most at least half a dozen times."

At least that meant she hadn't drawn a hundred dead women.

Brett took a step further in the room. "The yellow stickies have numbers on them. I didn't want to lose the order you had them in the portfolio, just in case that means something."

She looked around more carefully. "But you don't have them laid out in the order that I drew them, right?"

"No, they are laid out by victims. I tried to group together each woman that you've drawn as best as I could. Although some I'm not sure about."

The pattern was obvious now that he laid it all out on her living room floor. What Paige had assumed were dozens of women that she'd drawn were actually less than ten in total. If you eliminated the repeats she'd just drawn them in different stages of an attack. So she hadn't recognized that some of the drawings of the women with no bruising were the same women *with* the bruising. Alive and dead. The same women.

Brett had grouped the drawings according to victims.

"It looks like you drew two or three pictures of each victim. One before the trauma and one after the trauma for all of them. And then the third picture for some of them is obviously once they are dead."

Brett's voice was not cold, but he obviously had been trained to look at this from a professional point of view. Paige didn't have that same training. She struggled to hold on to the contents of her stomach.

In most of the later pictures the bruising was so severe Paige couldn't believe Brett had been able to recognize them as the same woman as before the attack.

Paige walked to the first grouping of pictures. "How can you tell that this is the same woman? In the before picture she's wearing what's obviously a lower cut dress and in the after picture" –after meaning the woman had been beaten to where she was unrecognizable– "she's wearing a collared shirt."

Paige didn't wait for Brett to answer. She studied the other groupings of pictures more closely. "It's like that with a lot of them. Is there some detail I'm missing? How are you able to group these pictures together?"

"Because four of them, including Teresa Cavasos, are all murder cases I've been looking into."

Paige shut her eyes. So that confirmed at least four of the women she'd drawn were dead. There was no reason to believe any of the other ones were still alive either.

"More than that," Brett continued, "I think all of these women were murdered by the same person. And that he meant to murder you too, but you got away."

CHAPTER 23

BRETT GAVE PAIGE A LITTLE bit of time to look over the pictures as he grabbed his phone to call Alex, even knowing he would've already gone home by now.

"I need you to meet me at the station in a few minutes."

"Wagner, you know we're not dating, right? This is two nights in a row you're dragging me out of my apartment."

Brett chuckled. "Just do it. Get a conference room where we can spread out and make sure Captain Ameling is gone. I'm going to be bringing Paige with me."

"This is sounding dirtier and dirtier. "

"In your dreams, Olivier. We've got a serial killer on our hands. I'm sure of it now."

Alex whistled through his teeth. "All right, I'll see you in a few."

Brett walked back to where Paige was still studying the pictures.

"I can only recognize some of them because of their files," he told her. "If I hadn't already seen pictures of them like this I would never be able to reconcile them with the earlier pictures either. There's no reason to think you should've been able to."

"I really had hoped I was just crazy. That my brain was broken after the attack or whatever. That I just had something dark inside me that needed to get out while I was sleeping and I was just drawing violence against pretend women."

He knew it had to be hard. "I wish they were just figments of your imagination too." Not only because of the loss of human life but because it would've made Paige feel so much better.

"Don't you think it's really freaky that I did this? Aren't you tempted to arrest me or question me further?"

Brett took her hand and led her out of the room.

"No. Not at all."

Her eyes narrowed as she looked at him. "How can you say that? There has to be some sort of doubt. That I had to be present at these crimes or something like that."

Brett sat her down at the table so that he could face her eye to eye.

"This is why I left last night. I had to work through what I saw to be my three options."

"That I was a criminal had to be one option."

Brett nodded. "Yes, that was an option. Actually, honestly, it was really less that I thought you were involved in the crimes and more that I thought you could've hacked into the Portland PD computer files or something."

Realization dawned in her eyes. "That I saw the pictures and then drew them. That I lied about being asleep when I did it."

Brett could see the possibility of it hurt her. But this conversation was necessary. He had to let her know that he had considered all the options, but when it was all said and done, he trusted her.

"Yes. That was actually the most logical choice. Nobody could blame you if you needed law enforcement attention focused back on you. "

He hated that tears welled in her eyes.

"You thought I was crazy."

Brett smiled at her gently. "Actually, wanting attention made you *not crazy*. Believing you drew murder victims in your sleep? That made both of us a little crazy. I needed something that was a possible logical explanation."

"I can't blame you for that. I know I'm telling the truth and it still sounds completely nuts to me."

"It was less about believing you and more about it going against everything I knew about law enforcement. If you could do this, Paige." Brett gripped her arms gently, wanting to make sure she knew how difficult this was for him. "If I accepted that you could draw murder victims in your sleep, then it had to change how I looked at law enforcement in general."

Paige nodded. "Adrienne's husband said the same thing when he first worked with her."

"Yeah, I talked to Conner Perigo today."

"To see if I was a nut case?"

Brett chuckled. "No. More to deal with what I was just saying. I needed someone to tell me that there were other ways of solving crimes than just the way I've always done it."

"So you believe me because Conner said I wasn't a murderer."

She wasn't understanding him at all. "No, the opposite. The reason I called him was because I knew I could trust you. That you were *not* a murderer, crazy, or someone just seeking attention."

"Really?"

"Yes. I knew I had to either be all in –completely believe in you– or just walk away altogether. Once I decided I trusted you? Then it was just a question about how to best use the information you could provide. While also protecting you."

Brett had no idea how much his faith in her had meant to her until that moment.

"Thank you," she whispered.

He reached over and grabbed her hands. "Thank you for trusting *me*. I can't believe you've carried this burden alone for so long. No more. We're going to use your gift to catch a killer."

"I hope so."

As planned, the homicide area of the Portland police department was almost empty by the time Brett arrived with Paige. Brett wasn't exactly sneaking her in, there wasn't anything illegal about what he was doing, but he knew Captain Ameling would throw an absolute fit if the other man knew Paige was here.

Which was nothing compared to the seizure he would have if he saw Paige's pictures.

Alex was waiting for them when Brett ushered Paige into the conference room.

"I feel like I'm doing something risqué," Alex chuckled. He turned to Paige, shaking her hand. "Glad to see again the lady who is going to get both of us fired."

Paige turned alarmed eyes to Brett. "I don't want anyone to get into trouble."

Brett slipped an arm around her shoulder, to reassure her, but also because Alex hadn't let go of her hand yet and was still smiling charmingly at her.

"Nobody's going to get fired. But Olivier may get a punch in the jaw if he doesn't let go of you."

Alex grinned and dropped her hand. "And trust me, we'll take the risk of getting in trouble if it means catching a killer. So what have you guys got?"

Brett took out the drawings and began placing them in groupings around the conference room table.

He had to give Alex credit, the man took the drawings pretty well.

While he studied them, Brett went to his desk to get the files he'd been working on last week. When he came back he was able to place a file on top of three different groupings of pictures.

"Victim A, Charlotte Winters. Victim B, Heather Brown. Victim C, Alexandra Dobbs. All three of these women have been murdered in the last two years."

Alex picked up the pictures Paige had drawn of victim A and compared it to the case file. He then did the same with victim B and victim C. There was no doubt that these pictures and cases belonged to the same women.

"No arrests for any of them. Different causes of death and no seeming connection between the victims," Alex said.

"That's basically what Ameling told me when I thought these might all be the work of the same killer."

Alex shrugged. "Honestly, outside of the fact that Paige drew them all I don't see much connection between them either."

"Let's try to identify the women in these other drawings and see what we're looking at once we've got all the information."

It took hours and it was why Brett had taken the chance at bringing Paige and the drawings into the station. Only here could they access the information and databases they needed to try to identify the other women based solely on a picture.

Because most of them had been declared missing before they were murdered, they were all in the facial recognition database. Four hours later they had identified the women in every picture Paige had drawn except for one.

"OK, we'll come back to her in a minute," Brett said. "Let's see what patterns we can find with the others."

They had a total of eight dead women. Alex and Brett had rearranged the piles on the table and arranged them in chronological order.

"I know you think this is all the same killer," Alex said, looking over the photos again. "But it's possible that Paige is just drawing women who die." He turned to Paige. "Which still sucks for you, so I'm sorry. I can't imagine that drawing these are any fun."

Paige had helped them in any way she could for the last few hours, but as they became more and more certain that all the women were dead she had withdrawn. She was now sitting in a chair at the side of the room.

"I'm not really consciously aware of what I'm drawing when I'm drawing it. It's only afterwards that I realize how gruesome it is."

"Regardless, it still has to be jarring."

Paige nodded, not saying anything further. Brett knew for a fact what a toll it took on her, at least physically. The fact that she hadn't ever looked back through these pictures attested to the toll it took on her emotionally. How could it not?

She looked exhausted. He moved over to her and kissed her on her forehead. "I'll take you home soon, okay? We've got the identity of these women and that's what we needed to do in stealth. The rest Alex and I can work on without you here."

"I'm all right. Let's see if we can spot a pattern. I'm good with patterns."

Brett knew he would need to get her out of the station in the next couple hours just to make sure no one came in early and spotted her. It was better to keep Paige out of everyone's line of sight as much as possible.

The three of them took a "before" picture of each of the women and placed them on a whiteboard in the conference room, ending with Teresa Cavasos. Underneath, they put the date of death, the cause of death, and the location of death.

Pertinent details about each woman –age, marital status, height and weight– followed underneath.

Then they all leaned back against the conference room table and studied the white board.

"Let's start with the obvious," Brett said. "All women, between the ages of 25 and 35, all relatively similar in stature and weight."

Alex nodded. "But different colored hair, and really not similar in appearance. Although I agree, they are all pretty small. Probably wouldn't be able to put up as much of a fight."

Paige's petite stature also met that requisite, but Brett didn't say anything to that effect.

"They're all unmarried," Paige said softly. "None of them had children. I'm not sure if that's important or not."

"Let's assume everything is important right now," Brett said.

"And, actually, that's an important distinction and goes towards proving Brett's theory that this is all the same guy. It's not impossible, but eight women killed, all who are that age and not married nor have kids? That goes a little further than coincidence."

"They all lived in west coast states. Three in California, three here in Oregon, and two were in Washington State." Brett knew that didn't necessarily mean anything conclusive.

"The reason it doesn't fit as a serial killer pattern is because of the different causes of death." Alex pointed out.

"That's what Ameling said too." Brett nodded as he sighed. He looked over at Paige. "Killers tend to stick with one MO when it comes to killing. Don't tend to deviate from that method. The same killer probably wouldn't jump between strangulation," – he pointed to the picture of the third victim – "stabbing, and burning."

"Different causes of death but they were all severely beaten before they were killed," Alex offered.

Brett saw Paige wince from the corner of his eye. This couldn't be easy for her.

"They were killed on different days of the week," Paige said.

"Yeah, but look, all the dates are somewhat similar," Alex offered. "Not exactly the same but close. Five were towards the end of the month, two are on the 15th, and one is on the 13th."

Alex's words reminded Brett of why he had thought about this case being similar in the first place.

"Paydays," he murmured. "I need a calendar." While Brett brought one up on his phone, Alex looked more closely at the date of each murder.

"You could be right," he said. "Look up April 13 of last year. Was that a Friday?"

Brett found it and turned to Alex. "Yes. So on that month someone who got paid twice a month would've been paid on the 13th rather than the normal 15th, because the 15th fell on a Sunday."

Brett looked up the other dates. "They are definitely all paydays. The last day of the month, or closest Friday to it or the 15th of the month or the closest Friday to it."

"If it wasn't for the different methods of death, I would be in full support of your one killer theory. But serial killers are almost always consistent. We both know that. "

Paige stood up from where she'd been leaning against the table and began studying the whiteboard more closely. "He is consistent. So consistent he can't change his own pattern."

Brett stood too. "How so? He kills in three different ways."

She walked over to the wall and put her finger on the corner of the picture of the first victim. "Strangled." She touched the second. "Stabbed." She touched the third. "Burned."

Brett shook his head, walking over to stand with her at the pictures. "I already thought of this. Looked for a distinct pattern in the order of the killing methods."

Paige wrote out a list on the white board next to the pictures.

1) Strangled. 2) Stabbed. 3) Strangled. 4) Burned. 5) Strangled. 6) Stabbed. 7) Burned. 8) Strangled.

Brett nodded. "Yes, that's correct, but there's no pattern. Teresa Cavasos was the last and she was strangled."

Paige looked over at him. "According to the dates, I should've been victim number 3. I would've been his 'burn' victim. He planned to leave me in that burning building. That's how I got away. He'd already doused the building with gasoline and it caught on fire too early."

Alex studied what she'd written on the board. "Even if that was true, it still wouldn't make a consistent pattern in the killing methodology. Too many strangles."

"It would be consistent if he has OCD. If he killed Victim C, Alexandra Dobbs, the woman after me, by strangling her, only to realize that was unacceptable to his pattern."

Brett realized Paige was right. What looked like an inconsistency with the pattern might actually be the killer resetting it.

"You should've been burned. Then the *next* victim would've been strangled. But you got away so it messed him up."

Realization dawned in Alex's eyes. "So he strangled the next victim, but that didn't give him the closure he needed, so he had to go back and burn someone."

Paige nodded. "Exactly. The pattern is strangle, stab, burn."

They all studied the pictures. It made twisted sense and tied together all the killings in a more believable way.

"A serial killer whose MO is a pattern, not just a single way of killing," Brett murmured.

Alex nodded. "It's not even the craziest thing I've ever seen."

"I should've been dead."

Paige's words were so soft he almost didn't hear them. He stepped closer to put an arm around her. "Baby…"

She stepped back, arms wrapped around her middle. "I know you suggested it before, but I should've died."

Brett wouldn't let her close herself off. He wrapped his arms around her. "But you didn't. You survived. And thank God."

"If I had died, then one of those other women would still be alive."

"You can't think like that, Paige," Alex said. "There's only one person responsible for the death of these women. The killer."

She didn't look convinced. She untangled herself from Brett's arms and walked to the table picking up the "before" picture of the woman they hadn't identified yet. "If we're right about the pattern then this woman will be the next victim and she'll be stabbed."

The woman was young, maybe late twenties, small in stature like Paige. She had black hair that fell down to the middle of her back. In the drawing she was laughing, looking at someone or something to the side. She didn't seem to have a care in the world.

"We'll find her," Brett said.

Paige slid the other picture of the woman over to Brett. It was another picture of violence, another brutally beaten face. By process of elimination they had determined it was the same woman, because she certainly could not be matched by appearance.

"But will she look like that when you do?"

CHAPTER 24

"HEY." PAIGE FELT A FINGER graze down her cheek. She'd been sitting over at the end of the conference room table for a while now while Brett and Alex continued to talk about the case. The women.

Charlotte Winters, Heather Brown, Alexandra Dobbs, Teresa Cavasos... All these women who had just been horrible pictures in her portfolio now had names. Real identities.

Were all dead.

Paige should've been dead also.

Brett had spoken his suspicions to her before but until she had seen the pattern for herself she hadn't truly believed it.

The man who attacked her, the man with the aura so black, had meant to kill her in the most brutal of fashions.

And more than that, Paige was connected to him in some way. Every person she had drawn had been one of his victims.

Paige didn't know how to get rid of the panic building inside her.

She was seeing inside a killer's mind.

Her mind was seeing what his was projecting. Her eyes saw and her hands drew what was most important to him. It was almost unbearable to be connected to him in this way.

How did Adrienne get through it? How hard she worked with the FBI all these years – being connected to the depraved thoughts and actions of multiple evil people? Paige obviously wasn't as strong as her sister was.

"Hey. Paige."

She finally focused on Brett who was crouched in front of her chair. He had obviously tried to get her attention more than once.

"You're exhausted. I already called your security team and they're sending someone to come get you."

Paige wanted to argue. Wanted to stay and help figure out anything else if she could. But Brett was right.

She couldn't remember ever feeling this exhausted before.

She could blame it on the fact that she hadn't gotten much sleep last night, worried about what was going through Brett's mind, and now she was on her second night of no sleep.

Not because she was linked in some way with a sadistic killer.

She nodded. "Yes, I'm sort of tired."

She felt his fingers trail down her cheek again. "I don't blame you. Plus, we've got to get you out of here before the normal detective workforce makes their way in. That will start happening in an hour or two."

Paige glanced over at the photos again. "I'm glad you were able to piece it all together." Paige had to face another hard truth. "If I had come forward with the pictures earlier we might've been able to save some of their lives."

Brett shook his head. "You can't think that way. There would've been no way to identify them and you've already tasted firsthand how receptive law enforcement would've been to you showing them the pictures."

"Crazy at best. Criminal at worst."

Brett shrugged. "Sadly, yes. For people who don't know you, for you to just show up with what are obviously exact replicas of crime scene photos would throw you into a very suspicious light. I can't say that I would've reacted any differently in the same circumstances."

Paige wrapped her arms around herself. Despite the mild temperature in the room, she felt like she couldn't get warm. Felt like she might never be warm again.

"Hey," Brett said again. "We're going to get through this. Going to catch this guy. For what he did to these women and for what he did to you."

She watched as Brett slipped off his jacket and wrapped it around her. It helped. The warmth of the fabric; the smell of it so uniquely Brett.

It brought her back from the void she felt so close to stumbling into.

"How are you going to catch him? You can't use these pictures. Nobody else is going to believe them."

"The pictures give us a link," he said. "Alex and me. Now that we know where to look and who to look at, we'll find something else to prove they're all connected. We won't bring you into it."

Paige nodded.

"Our first line of business will be identifying the unknown woman in the last drawing. Once we find her we can not only put a protection detail around her, we can hopefully use her to figure out who the killer is. See who's following her."

"We're going to have to use some creative arguments to get protective detail around someone we *hope* could potentially be the next victim." Alex still stood staring at the pictures.

As she shuddered in the jacket, Brett reached and pulled her up against him so they were both standing. Now with his heat against her she almost felt warm.

"You're going to be the one who leads us to him, sweetheart. The one person who got away will be the one who brings him down," Brett said against her forehead, his hands moving in circles on her back.

Brett's phone chirped.

"Tom's outside." Brett's hand at the small of her back began to ease her towards the door. "The best thing you can do is get some rest."

Paige just nodded. Exhaustion weighed so heavy on her there was nothing else she could do.

"Hey," Alex called out before they made it to the conference room door. "We will get this guy, Paige. What you've done is amazing. Don't doubt that."

Paige gave him a weak smile but the doubts weighing down her mind were so great she hardly knew how to express them.

Doubts about her mental health. How could she be connected to a killer? Doubts about her courage. How could she have just put these pictures in a box and not delved into them further?

Doubts about her very sanity. The next time she drew a picture she would know exactly what it meant. Another person dead.

She wasn't sure she would ever be able to go to sleep again for fear she'd find a new picture on her easel when she awoke.

Her stomach filled with a twisting despair. She brought both of her fists to her belly in an effort to keep the despondency inside.

"Whatever it is you're thinking, stop. Right now." Brett halted their progress towards the front door and turned her to look at him. "You made the right choice with the information you had. Once you knew these were real women, real victims, you haven't shied away from it."

"But..."

"There is no 'but.' Thinking these drawings had stemmed from what happened to you was not only logical, but healthy. There's nothing you should've done differently."

She heard what Brett was saying and even acknowledged that it was probably true. It didn't change the fact that she'd been drawing these pictures for over two years and some of those women had been alive when Paige had drawn them.

She stepped a little closer to Brett and put her hands on his arms. "It's just hard. And I'm tired. And all this is... overwhelming."

His arm slipped around her and he pulled her against his chest. "I know. You just have to hang in there. Give yourself a chance to process it all."

They walked the rest of the way out the front door to where Tom had parked on the curb and held the car door open. The darkness seemed even more oppressive. Paige shuddered again, even with Brett's arm wrapped protectively around her.

"Maybe I should come with you," he said, concern clear in his eyes as he looked at her. "You can't discount the trauma it does to a psyche to see this much violence when you're not accustomed to it."

As they stepped outside Paige wanted to brush his comment off. To make a light or witty statement that would take the look out of his eyes, the concern that she was pretty close to losing it.

And she was.

This blackness that seemed to surround them now was more than just night. Whatever anyone wanted to call it –the darkness before the dawn– it was ripping at her. Clawing at her mind.

"I just need sleep." It was the only sentence she could get out. She knew he needed to stay here. Needed to find out who that other woman was. Needed to do something besides cater to her psychotic episodes.

Her cowardice had already cost women their lives. The least she could do now was let him go do his job to stop the killer.

"Are you sure? I know Tom will take you straight home and you'll be safe but will you be okay?"

"Yes." The word came out as a croak and she knew she wouldn't fool him much longer. She kissed him on the cheek. She just needed to hold on a few seconds longer until she could get inside the car and fall apart on her own.

She slid into the backseat and gave her best smile to Brett.

"I'll be over as soon as I can. Just rest. Even if you can't sleep, just rest." He gave her a hard kiss on the lips and then pulled back closing the door.

She could hear him saying something to Tom but she didn't even try to listen. All she could do was hold onto herself, hold onto her sanity, as the blackness around her seemed to push against her further.

Tom didn't try to talk to her all the way back to the house, which was good because Paige wasn't sure she could get a sentence through her lips right now.

She saw his concerned gaze in the rearview mirror a few times, but she didn't even have it in her to try to give him a reassuring smile.

She just wanted to go home and sleep. She prayed sleep would not elude her tonight because she wasn't sure how she would cope if it did. She would even take a pill if she needed to.

She tried to pull some strength around her. To tell herself that she was capable of handling this. But with the darkness surrounding her so heavily on all sides she was finding it difficult to do so.

When they pulled up at the house Paige sat looking at it out the window. She didn't want to go inside. Didn't want to have to go through the darkness to get to the door.

She knew she was being unreasonable. She had full-time security here. There was no sadistic killer here. He was just inside her mind.

Still, she wished she had asked Brett to come with her. She wouldn't have even had to ask. She just wished she had agreed when he offered.

"Are you ready to go inside Miss Jeffries?" Tom was looking at her with concern from the rearview mirror again.

"Tom, can you just walk in with me? I know it's probably an insult to your professionalism to ask you to check the house one more time. But would you--"

"Absolutely. And it doesn't insult me in anyway. You pay us very well to make sure you feel secure. Whatever that means is what we'll do."

"I know you have to feel like I'm slipping off the wagon. Especially after how Jacob just talked about no one being after me."

Of course that had been before she knew she was connected to a killer.

"I do know exhaustion can play a factor in how secure someone feels. So don't be hard on yourself. See how you're feeling in a few hours after you get some sleep. I bet you'll feel much better and ready to handle it. Whatever it may be."

Tom helped her out of the car and ushered her into the house. She walked with him as he checked every room, every closet, under every bed.

Anywhere where the boogie man could hide.

"Guess this proves I'm pretty psychotic."

The older man shook his head kindly. "Not at all. It's always better to feel secure than to let your pride get you into a situation where your imagination can run away with you. I'll be right out in the guard house if you need me."

"Thank you, Tom. For everything."

"Detective Wagner updated me with some of the information. You can trust that we're going to be on full alert."

He nodded at her once more and then left.

Exhaustion flooded Paige. She was relieved to feel it.

She was home. She was secure. She was out of the oppressive darkness that seemed to be following her since she stepped out of the police station.

Tom was right. Brett was right. She needed sleep, to give her body and mind a chance to regroup. As she walked by the room with the easel, she felt relief that the box of pictures was gone. They were in Brett's hands now, where good could finally be done. If these women couldn't be saved, at least he could find justice for them.

The black hole painting, with all its shades of darkness, still sat on the easel. Paige took it down and turned it backwards facing the wall. She'd had enough darkness for one night.

She left the room and went into her bedroom. She kicked off her shoes and fell onto her bed fully clothed.

She fell asleep with the women's names echoing over and over in her mind. *Charlotte Winters, Heather Brown, Alexandra Dobbs, Teresa Cavasos...*

CHAPTER 25

THANKS FOR COMING WITH ME."

The next evening Paige looked much better. Obviously a night of rest had done her well. Brett wished he could've been there with her, but he and Alex had stayed to work the case.

Plus she wouldn't have gotten as much sleep if he'd stayed.

"How often do you go into the gallery?"

She rolled her eyes. "If Hunter had his way, I would be there every single day. Shaking hands and kissing babies whenever people enter the studio. But most of the time he comes up to my house when we need to talk business. At least in the last couple of years." She turned to stare out the window.

Hunter Barnes was one of the first people Brett had investigated and then cleared once he realized Paige was tied to the killer. Found documented proof that the man had been out of the country during the time of at least two of the murders.

Brett didn't want her focused on her attacker. She'd had him in her head enough recently. "Hunter's a good agent?"

She smiled. "He'd be the first one to tell you that we've grown together. I know my name has brought in some bigger clients for him, but he took a chance on me before my career took off, so a fair trade."

And no matter how successful Paige became she wouldn't break ties with Hunter, even if someone else might make her an international superstar. Because she was loyal.

"So are you just here to kiss babies and shake hands?"

"No. Evidently the 3D centerpiece at the show was very well received. Hunter has had some more made and wants to get my opinion on whether we should try to go live with them."

"It was impressive."

She shrugged a single shoulder. "I liked it, but I want to make sure it's not too gimmicky."

The gallery was relatively crowded even in the evening and Brett had to park down the block. As they strolled together on the sidewalk he could feel Paige become more and more tense.

"You doing okay?" He asked. "I'm sure Hunter wouldn't mind if you do this another time."

"No, I'm fine. I sometimes get the heebie-jeebies when I leave my house. You just have to ignore me."

He slipped an arm around her and pulled her close, kissing the side of her head. "Heebie-jeebies look good on you."

She rolled her eyes. "You better hope so, as often as I get them."

He had hoped the jokes might help distract her, but by the time they were inside the gallery tension radiated through her small body. Her face was already more pale than it had been just a few minutes ago.

"Let's go home," he said as the door closed behind them. The gallery had a couple dozen people in it. Being around them was just going to make her more stressed.

"No, we're already here."

Hunter saw them from across the room. "Paige, honey. There you are." He walked to her and kissed her on both cheeks. Then turned to Brett. "Officer Handsome. Good to see you again."

"Mr. Barnes." Brett held out his hand to shake the other man's.

"Hunter, please." He turned back to Paige. "You're not looking so good, sweetheart. Feeling all right?"

She gave him a smile, but it wasn't fooling anyone. "I'm fine."

Hunter linked his arm with hers. "Let me show you what we're thinking, and then you can get back home." They began walking towards the offices in the back.

They were about five steps away from the door when Paige stopped and refused to go any further. She held her hand up to her eyes. "I can't. I'm sorry."

She took a shaky step towards Brett. "I can't," she said again. "The dark... it's too much."

Every bit of color had drained from her face and if he and Hunter weren't holding her arms, Brett was afraid she might fall.

He turned to Hunter. "She like this normally when she gets here?"

"No, never. I've never seen her like this, not since right after the attack."

"Do you have somewhere she can sit?"

Hunter nodded. "Sure, right inside the door."

Paige resisted, but Brett led her in through the office door. "Let's just sit down for a minute."

By the time she was in the chair she was shaking. Her eyes were open but she couldn't see. He crouched down beside her. "Does your head hurt, Paige?" Maybe a migraine?

She clutched his hand. "No. It's the dark. Just like before, when…"

She trailed off but Brett knew what she meant. When she'd been attacked.

He looked at Hunter. "He's here. The guy who attacked her. He's here."

"How do you know?"

"Because some sort of darkness hits her like this when he's around. The guy's black aura is all she can see. Do you have security? Can they lock the doors?"

"Yes, but it's going to cause some problems. People generally don't like being told they can't leave somewhere they entered of their own accord."

"Are you willing to do it if it means catching Paige's attacker?"

Hunter nodded and grabbed a walkie-talkie sitting on the desk. "I'd shut this entire place down for good if it meant catching her attacker."

The words were no sooner out of his mouth before the power blew. Brett muttered a curse.

"Don't worry, the emergency generator will kick on," Hunter said.

It didn't.

Now Hunter cursed. "My security team will have moved to the doors as soon as the power went out. Their primary focus right now will be to make sure no one is stealing any of the art."

"Tell them not to let anybody in or out." Hunter nodded as Brett grabbed his cell and called Alex.

"Hel--"

"Alex, it's Brett. I need you to get uniforms down to the Barnes Gallery on West 50th. The killer is here, Alex."

"Are you sure?"

"Yes. And he just cut the power."

"I'm on my way. ETA 10 minutes. Squad cars should be there even sooner."

Brett disconnected the call.

"Killer?" Hunter asked. "I thought he'd only attacked Paige."

"We think Paige was supposed to be a murder victim, but got very, very lucky."

Two gunshots fired in the main area of the gallery. Brett drew his weapon moving towards the door.

"Can you stay here with her? She's defenseless like this, Hunter."

The other man nodded. "I won't leave her, no matter what."

Brett eased the door open into the gallery. People were scared, panicking. Everyone had turned on the lights in their phones and it was causing a weird sort of strobe effect as they all rushed around, demanding to be let out. Security was keeping them from the door, the way they'd been trained to do. Brett looked for the shooter but couldn't see anyone with a gun.

But he was out there. Somewhere in the room.

This was going to turn ugly very quickly. Brett grimaced. They were going to need to let people out before someone got trampled in the panic. But that meant also letting out the killer.

He opened the door and looked back at Hunter, barely able to make him out in the darkness. Paige hadn't moved at all.

"Tell your guards to let people out the front door. They're panicking and someone's going to get hurt or worse. And if that gun goes off again it's going to get even uglier."

Hunter made the announcement into the walkie-talkie and Brett went out to help try to keep everyone calm as they exited, all the while searching through the dim for anyone who caught his attention.

That's when Brett saw him.

He was standing at the opposite side of the gallery, near another set of doors, calmly watching the scene around him. Every once in a while someone's light would catch him there.

That was the killer.

As casually as possible Brett made his way towards the man, but he was only halfway across the gallery when the guy realized what Brett was doing. He turned and exited through the door behind him.

Brett immediately took off in a sprint.

As soon as he opened the door the man had gone through, Brett knew this had all been planned. The door led into a high-ceilinged storage area with dozens of paths created out of tall shelves and cases.

It was the perfect escape route.

Whoever was in here had studied this building and had known what to do to both cut the power and escape.

It was impossible to see anything clearly in the dark. Brett was tempted to turn on the flashlight of his phone, but that would be a dead giveaway as to where he was located.

Brett didn't want to leave this doorway, in case the guy decided to double back to try to get to Paige. But if Brett stayed here, the man would just escape.

He closed his eyes and focused on sound.

There. He'd heard something just over to his left. As silently as possible he made his way down one aisle, turning at the end of it towards the noise he'd heard.

Weapon raised, he rounded the corner. But even in the thick darkness he could see no one was there. He immediately stopped again to listen, particularly for the door that might lead back into the regular gallery and to Paige.

He heard another noise, further this time. The guy was definitely going for the exit. Brett sped up, moving towards the back of the storage area. As long as he could keep the man corralled away from the front door, that was all Brett cared about.

Soon this whole place would be crawling with police. All Brett had to do was keep the guy in here until then.

He heard the slight creak of a door and knew the killer was trying to ease his way out. Forgetting silence, Brett sprinted towards the sound of the door.

When he reached the door it was already closed. Brett reached for the handle, weapon once again raised, and slowly opened it. The man couldn't have gotten far, but might be waiting outside with his own weapon ready.

By the time Brett heard the sound behind him it was too late. He had just enough time to throw his arm up as one of the heavy shelving units came towering down on him. The force of it knocked him to the ground, and something heavy falling off the edge grazed his head, causing the room to spin.

Brett pushed at the metal on top of him, trying to get a clear view of the man, but couldn't see enough to make out any features.

The slightest bit of light reflected off the man's gun. It was pointed right at Brett. There wasn't anything Brett could do to stop him.

But the shot didn't come.

"Can't you see?" the man's voice whispered. "I'm just trying to help you. Betray. Abandon. Steal. It has to stop."

Something else crashed down on the shelving trapping him further, as he heard the backdoor open and the man slip out. Brett was just crawling out from under it when Paige and Hunter rushed in.

Paige's voice was tight. "Brett, are you okay?"

"Yeah. Alive. He snuck back behind me then got away. Are *you* okay?"

Hunter handed him a cloth for the blood that was dripping down the side of his head. "She snapped out of it a couple of minutes ago. Security said you'd gone in here."

"Did you see him at all?" she asked.

"No, it was too dark."

She grimaced. "Sounds familiar. Thank God the rest of the police got here when they did or he would've killed you. Hunter said he had a gun."

"I don't think so. He said he was trying to help me." Brett had no idea what the guy was talking about, and could not care less. "But we're definitely getting you out of here. This was no random occurrence. He had scoped out this entire place. He knew about this back room and knew how to cut both the main and backup power supplies."

"If you hadn't come with me tonight, I would've been completely defenseless." Paige shuddered and he wrapped an arm around her.

Brett couldn't tell her she wasn't right. Between this and the market, it was twice Paige had gone out and twice something had happened.

The killer was watching her. Might have been ever since the attack. The fact that she'd been so reluctant to leave her house was probably what had kept her alive for the last two years.

Brett was more determined than ever to catch this guy. And they still had the advantage: the killer wasn't aware they knew about all his victims. Paige and her drawings were the key.

The one that got away would be the one who brought the killer down.

CHAPTER 26

T HE DARKNESS HID HIM FROM *their view once again just as it had the night before at the police station. His fingers gripped the steering wheel with bloodless knuckles.*

She was working with the police. But she couldn't have remembered his face after all this time. If so, he had no doubt it would be plastered all over the news.

He'd gotten what information he could about Paige Jeffries over the last twenty-four months. Found out that she couldn't remember his face and that the police didn't trust her for some reason.

That had worked to his advantage.

But it looked like they trusted her now. Or at least this new Detective Wagner did. He'd tried to explain that he was on Wagner's side, on every man's side, but he didn't think the detective understood.

He probably should've killed Wagner tonight, but that would've been completely against the code.

Paige Jeffries was at fault, not Wagner.

He was going to have to make a change. The thought burned like acid in his gut. Because of her he was going to have to change the pattern again. Going to have to make a move sooner than he wanted.

But he couldn't take the chance on her living much longer. He would kill the other woman, even though it wasn't time, so that the pattern would be back to where Paige Jeffries belonged. She would burn.

Strangled. Stabbed. Burned.

His pattern, simple yet elegant, and had worked for him for years.

Until Paige Jeffries.

She had caused him to break his pattern and nothing had really been right since.

He would break his pattern one more time for her. Then she would burn.

And the pattern would be whole once again. She would be number ten. The end of this pattern.

It should've been nine victims. Three sets of three kills. The perfect union.

But Paige Jeffries had ruined it all. So now there would be ten. And she would be the last in this pattern to die.

In the most painful way possible.

He knew this would change everything for him, but it was a price he was willing to pay. Two last kills to fulfill this pattern then he would have to run. Hide. For a long time.

Then he would find a new pattern in a new place and start once again.

Brett and Alex spent the entire next day poring over the files. Brett had left Paige in her security team's care and made sure they were completely aware that Paige was all but under siege.

Both physically and mentally.

Being connected to a killer and knowing that killer was coming after you? Not easy to handle.

He wanted to stay with her. Probably would've if she'd asked him to. But he was needed here. In the short run it might've comforted Paige more for him to go with her now, but in the long run, the only thing that was going to give her peace was to catch this guy.

And now that they were certain the cases were connected it was easier to see links between them.

Any possible remaining doubts melted away when Alex pulled up a map on the computer and plotted the locations of all the murders.

"Holy shit," Alex murmured.

"Seattle, Medford, Eugene, Olympia. They're all along I-5," Brett said. Lined up along the map like that, it was impossible to miss the pattern. "The killer must work on that Interstate."

Every murder had occurred in a town within two or three miles of it.

"Could be a trucker." Alex started a list of professions on a notepad by his computer.

"Yep. Or sales rep. Repair man."

"Whoever it is, has a route between Sacramento and Seattle."

Brett nodded. "Probably not a trucker then, right?"

"I doubt it. Just having that route over and over? That would be pretty unusual. But I'll definitely look into it."

"And now we have something we can take to Ameling. This is a pattern that he can't deny." Brett grinned. "He's going to wonder how we came up with this, you know. How we figured out to search these particular cases. I don't want to bring Paige into it. He's gunning for her hard enough as it is."

Alex winked at him. "Haven't you heard? We're brilliant detectives. Nothing slips by us. Plus, you let me talk to Captain Ameling. Just like you want to leave Paige out of it, I want to leave you out of it as much as possible. Easier for him to swallow that way.

Brett didn't care about getting credit, he just cared about stopping this killer. So whatever Alex had to do was fine with him. "I'm glad he won't be able to deny it, but coordinating this is going to be a bitch. Three different states? This is going to get turned over to the Feds."

Conner Perigo came to mind. The man probably wouldn't be given the case but it would still be one of the first calls Brett would make. But he didn't want to give up the case even to Perigo.

"We can't call anybody until we have Ameling's approval. He's out today and tomorrow for that conference. So let's get as much info as we can before presenting it to him and it being taken out of our hands."

"I'll work on identifying the woman in Paige's last picture if you want to keep working on who might be going up and down that I-5 route," Brett said.

They had taken down the pictures and info on the whiteboard in the conference room just after Paige left. Until they were ready to officially go to Ameling with their findings, they needed to keep it to themselves.

Brett had all the case files and pictures sitting on his desk. He looked through the victims again.

The unknown woman's picture was being run through the facial recognition data bank which was a testament to how good the picture Paige drew actually was.

Unfortunately, unless the woman was a known terrorist or had committed a crime, she probably wouldn't show up in facial recognition.

Brett took the key info on each victim –whatever information they'd been able to fit on one note card– and placed them all on his desk.

Single. White. Between twenty-five and thirty-five years old. They all were pretty, but none of them so strikingly beautiful it would draw attention to them. They all had longish hair. Past their shoulders.

"He investigates them before he chooses them for sure," he called out to Alex. "That's how he knows they are not married. Doesn't just randomly pick someone out."

Alex nodded. "Okay. Maybe a sales rep or a repair man is a better fit than a trucker. Someone who stays in one place a couple days at a time."

"Yes, would give him a chance to study them. To select who he wanted."

Alex turned back to his work and Brett turned back to the notecards. These women had more in common than just their age and marital status. But it wasn't something obvious.

Tox screens for all the victims had shown up negative, so none of them were on illegal drugs. Brett grabbed the files to see if there was a prescription medication link between the victims.

Maybe the perp was a pharmaceutical rep.

But there wasn't any medication all of them took. A couple weren't on any medications at all. So that was out.

Their professions were widespread. Paige was an artist, of course. Teresa Cavasos had worked here in Portland in the Nike office, in research and development.

One of the victims had been a nurse. Another a secretary at Boeing in Seattle. The woman from Medford had been a physical therapist.

Hell, one of them had been a toy designer in Sacramento.

Brett spent the rest of the day researching what each woman did for a living and couldn't find any connection between them all. He checked where they all worked out, where they ate –at least based on their credit card history– any clubs or activities they were involved in but nothing he could find linked them all.

Maybe the killer wasn't connected to the I-5 route by his job at all. Maybe the guy didn't even have a job. Just spent his time wandering up and down the interstate until he found his next victim. Maybe the women were totally random. Had nothing whatsoever to do with one another except for vague general appearances. He just found one he liked, checked to see if she was married or had kids, and then waited until the next payday to kill her.

But he didn't kill every payday. Why was that? There didn't seem to be any exact measure of time between the kills. The shortest time between kills had been two weeks the longest time had been seven months.

Was that deliberate? A way of throwing law enforcement off of his trail?

Because detecting skills didn't matter if the guy chose women completely at random off the street and had no timetable in which he killed. They'd never be able to anticipate his moves.

Hell, if they didn't have the pictures from someone who drew in her sleep, they still wouldn't have any proof of a serial killer at all.

"Any luck with anything, man?" Alex asked from his desk.

"Is less than nothing possible?" Brett rubbed his fingers over his eyes. Going all night last night without sleep was catching up to him. "I've got eight victims, nine if you count Paige. I can't find a single thing that ties them together. They all have vastly different careers, from a secretary to a nurse to an artist. They all have vastly different interests and activities."

"So except for the fact that they were killed somewhere near I-5 and are in one of Paige's drawings, there's nothing tying them together."

"Except for being dead."

Alex let out a sigh. "Nothing much on my end either. I was looking up companies that did repairs or sales in a three state area, but like you said, without knowing what sort of field we're looking at it's impossible to narrow. Checked trucking companies too, found one possibility, but it was a woman who ran the route."

They knew for a fact the attacker was a man. Paige had known that much.

"Knowing one person killed all these women doesn't actually put us any closer to catching him." Brett said.

"Well, we know we've got at least ten days before he'll strike again. He's never deviated from the payday dates. And he doesn't know we're onto him. Doesn't know we now know it's one person responsible for all these murders and are working that angle. So we're still a step ahead."

"We've got to catch him soon, Alex. Paige is starting to crack under the pressure."

Alex nodded. "It's a lot for anyone to handle. Especially someone not used to this sort of violence. And to be so closely linked to it. Most people would crack. I'm surprised she hasn't before now."

Because she was strong. She'd done what she needed to in order to survive. That had meant shutting herself away, cutting herself off from the rest of the world. But she'd survived.

"Turning this over to the FBI is probably the best bet." Alex shook his head. "I hate to cut us out of a huge case, but they have resources we don't. Manpower we don't."

Brett agreed. "Yeah, I don't like it either. As soon as the captain is back I think we need to go to him and get this passed along to the right hands."

Brett still hadn't called Conner Perigo, but he would tomorrow as soon as they turned it over to the captain. Maybe Conner could at least keep him and Alex in the loop.

Brett's phone rang and he answered immediately when he saw it was Tom, part of Paige's security team.

"Tom? Everything okay?"

"Security wise, we are secure."

"Is Paige all right?"

"She went to sleep almost as soon as we got home. Had me double check the house, which was probably good for her peace of mind and mine."

"Sounds good. What's the problem?"

Because there was a problem. Brett knew it in his gut. The other man wouldn't have called otherwise.

"She just woke up not long ago. Jacob went in there to check on her before I headed out. There's something wrong, Brett."

Brett had never heard the other man call him by his first name. His grip tightened on the phone.

"What's going on?"

"She's just sitting on her couch, staring out the window. She won't talk to either of us at all. Won't look at us or move or do anything."

"Has this ever happened before?"

"No, never. She's never been like this. Something has happened. It's like she can't even see us."

But something similar had happened at the gallery yesterday, and it had been the killer. "Are you sure the premises are secure? One hundred percent sure?"

"Yes. But I'll send someone to triple check."

Brett was already headed towards the door. "I'm on my way."

CHAPTER 27

TOM MET BRETT AS HE parked his car in front of Paige's house.

"Any change?" He asked as he ripped the keys out of the car and moved quickly towards her front door.

"No, sir. She's been sitting in the living room staring out the window. It's almost like she's in a coma, but her eyes are open. We checked the house and grounds again. There is no one here except you, her and the team."

Brett felt a sort of panic clench his gut. He shouldn't have left her alone. All those pictures she'd drawn, figuring out she was somehow connected to the mind of a killer, that was too much for anyone to handle. Then what had happened at the gallery.

Paige had already been through so much. Maybe something inside her had snapped.

Brett rushed in the door and ran to the living room. He found Paige just as they had reported.

If it wasn't for her eerie stillness, he would think she was just enjoying the view out her window. She sat straight, exactly in the middle of the couch, with her hands in her lap.

Her eyes were open.

Brett came and crouched down right in front of her, cupping her face with his hands.

"Paige, honey, can you hear me?" He said the words softly, keeping his voice as even as possible.

She didn't flinch, didn't blink, didn't do anything.

He trailed his fingers up and down her cheek, and said her name again, but still received no response.

He looked over at Tom who was studying Paige with a worried expression. "So you said she's never done anything like this before?"

"No. When I first started working here, which would've been just a few weeks after the attack, she used to sit here a lot. Zone out. But never anything we couldn't bring her back from."

Brett wasn't sure what he should do. Was this her brain's way of protecting her? Should he just give her the peace she needed to work through what was going on in her mind?

"And this morning, when she got home, there were no problems? She wasn't crying? Upset?"

He tried calling Paige's name again, even clapping his hands in front of her face to startle her.

No response.

Tom shook his head. "She wanted me to double check the house, but she didn't seem hysterical or anything. Although she did look exhausted."

"She was exhausted. She was helping us with a case –a series of cases– at the station. We might've pushed her too hard."

"She's not great at asking for help."

Brett ran a finger down her cheek again. "Paige, can you come back to me, baby? I'm right here. I won't leave you to deal with this on your own."

She still didn't respond. No change in breathing, no change in her blank gaze out the window.

Her eyes were empty.

Brett glanced over at Tom. "I'm going to try something a little less gentle, okay? Trust me, no one wants to hurt her less than me."

Tom nodded, lips grim.

Brett grabbed Paige by the shoulders and shook her. Hard.

"Paige." He said in a much louder voice than he had been using. "Wake up, right now."

He hated the sound of his own voice, but if it brought her back from wherever she was –whatever place she was where he couldn't reach her– Brett would do it.

"Do you hear me, Paige? You're needed here right now. Let's go." He shook her again before tapping her on the cheek gently and then a little harder.

Nothing. She wasn't responding to harder words and touches any more than she was the softer ones. Brett couldn't bring himself to yell anymore.

He looked back over at Tom. "I had to try."

The other man nodded. "I wasn't sure if we should call an ambulance. I don't think she's in any pain, but…"

"It's almost like a form of PTSD." Brett said. "Like she's in shock."

Tom nodded. "I know she wouldn't want to come to and be in the hospital. That's why we didn't call 911."

"I agree. I think she would want to stay here. Do you mind if I try to talk to her alone, Tom?"

Tom nodded. "I'll just wait right outside the door."

Brett waited until the door closed behind Tom, then took Paige's hand and entwined their fingers together.

"Paige, sweetheart, it's just me. It's okay to come back. The killer can't hurt you, and we're going to catch him." He shifted so he was a little bit closer. "None of this is your fault, baby. So just come back and everything will be alright, I promise. I won't leave you alone to deal with this anymore. I'm so sorry. I shouldn't have let you go this morning."

Brett kept rubbing his hands up and down her arms hoping that it would make some sort of difference, even tried kissing her. But nothing worked.

Paige was lost somewhere inside her own mind. Maybe Tom was right and they were going to have to call in medical professionals.

Then she began shivering violently. Her body temperature seemed to drop right under his hand.

"Tom!" Brett called. "There's something not right." The other man rushed in and could immediately see Paige's physical distress.

She was still sitting straight up with her hands in her lap staring straight ahead except now her arms were covered with goosebumps and every once in a while a shudder would overwhelm her small body.

"This is definitely shock," Tom said. "I saw this sort of stuff when I was in the service. It didn't necessarily have to do with the temperature around the person."

"We don't have any choice now, whether she would want it or not, we need to at least get a doctor over here."

"Paige has a regular one that she sees. I'll get in touch with her. See if she would be willing to make a house call. That will at least be less jarring for Paige when she wakes up."

As Tom left the room, Brett grabbed the blanket off of the wingback chair and sat back on the couch. Paige's shudders were becoming bad enough to truly frighten him so he picked her up and set her on his lap wrapping the blanket tightly around her. Even though he moved her position her blank stare still gazed outward.

It was like she couldn't feel him at all.

He remembered what she had told him about why she couldn't remember her attacker's face. Blackness so thick she couldn't see anything else. That was almost like what was happening now. Like her mind was lost in blackness she couldn't find her way out.

"Paige." Aware the words would sound crazy to anyone else who heard them, he whispered them in her ear. "I know it's dark, but you have to find your way out. Just find my voice, can you do that? Can you listen to my voice and locate it? You have to find your way back to me. To us."

Paige couldn't see anything. Couldn't hear anything. The darkness drenched everything, not just blinding her, but deafening her in its thickness.

She couldn't escape from it, couldn't figure out where it had even come from.

The only other time this ever happened had been during her attack.

Oh God, was she being attacked now? She couldn't feel any pain like she had then, but that didn't mean it wouldn't be coming.

Or was she asleep? She always slept with a light on because the darkness frightened her so. Could she just be in her bedroom in the dark?

She tried to reach out her hands, to make her feet move so she could stand, but found she couldn't. It was like her brain wasn't controlling her body.

From within the darkness Paige closed her eyes. She had to think. Had to figure this out or she would be trapped here forever.

The thought of it sent a shiver coursing through her. Shudders.

Something that happened. Something had happened and that's why she was in the darkness now. What was it?

Her brain didn't want to go back to that point that had hurled her into the black. But she knew deep in the thickest part of the darkness encased by shadows was the answer. She forced her mind to walk towards it. She had to know what it was.

As she moved closer to that epicenter of darkness, she could feel violent tremors grip her. Her whole body shuddered now as her mind attempted to shy away from what had caused the blackness.

Paige let out a silent scream, pain shredding her brain, as she reached the point where the darkness was the blackest.

And she remembered.

The drawing. That was what had hurled her in here. When she had woken up this morning the agony in her muscles, the sickness in her stomach, the throbbing of her head, it all suggested that she had drawn another victim.

And she had.

She had drawn herself. Dead.

The tremors were overwhelming her now, exhausting her. Paige knew she wasn't going to survive it. She knew she wasn't going to make it out of the darkness in one piece.

The blackness was too thick. She was too cold. She would never find her way.

She wanted to fight, knew she should fight, but didn't know how. She felt her entire body seize as the cold washed over her again.

She had to try. Her mind began to crawl –walking was impossible– but she didn't know which way to go.

And then she saw it off in the distance. The slightest hint of colors, almost overshadowed by the blackness, but trying to shine through. Blues and teals, simmering. So faint. So far.

The shivering made it nearly impossible but she began to move her body towards the colors.

They seemed to fade in and out for the longest time, and Paige didn't know if she was imagining them completely.

But still she kept going.

She heard a sound all around her in the darkness. Almost like a voice, but through so many panes of glass it could not be understood. But the teals and blues were getting brighter. Not enough to illuminate the darkness but just enough to give her a direction to move towards.

And then she saw the purple at the center of the other colors. Brett.

These were Brett's colors. Was he in the darkness with her?

"Paige, baby, follow my voice. Come back to me."

He was here with her. Brett would protect her from the darkness, would help her get out.

She could hear him saying other things, but couldn't quite make out the words. She just kept dragging her exhausted mind towards his voice. Towards his colors.

Towards him.

She reached him just as the last of her mental strength failed her. She made one last desperate dive towards the very center of the deep purples and blues and teals.

And the darkness disappeared.

"Brett?" Her voice sounded rusty and unused even to her own ears.

"Paige. Oh thank God."

She felt his lips all over her face and hair. Felt how his arms wrapped around her holding her tightly against him.

She was back. He was with her. The darkness was gone. That's all that mattered. She was still so cold but at least now could feel the warmth he was trying to envelop her in.

Which was good because she couldn't move now anyway. Brett didn't seem to expect her to.

She had no idea how long they sat there with him continuously cradling her and rubbing his hands up and down her arms and back and hips.

She was vaguely aware that she was in her living room –she had no idea how she had gotten there– and that Brett would talk to Tom every once in a while.

Both of them had twin looks of concern on their faces, although the longer she stayed awake and coherent the more relieved their faces became. She finally stopped shivering and tried to sit up from Brett.

He pulled her back to him. "Do me a favor, okay? Just let me hold you for a little while. You scared the hell out of me. Out of Tom too."

Paige didn't want anything different so she didn't argue. She buried her face in Brett's neck. "I'm sorry."

Brett didn't say anything for long minutes. After a while Tom brought in a cup of her favorite hot tea.

"When you woke up I canceled the doctor we had about to come," Tom said, "but I can get Dr. Whitaker back out here if you want. She said she would come. That might be a good idea."

Paige knew she needed to explain what happened. At least to Brett.

"No, that's not necessary. I think it was just a mixture of exhaustion and shock."

She felt Brett nod against her hair. "I never should've brought you in to help with the cases. It was too much. You're not trained for it and it obviously adversely affected your psyche."

She lay back so that she could see his brown eyes. His face was haggard, residual fear etched in his features.

"Yes, I was definitely exhausted. But it was more than that. I need to show you something."

If anything his face got a little more haggard. "What?"

"I drew in my sleep last night."

She couldn't bring herself to admit that it was her own face and body –her own *dead* face and body– that she'd drawn.

He framed her face with both hands. "Show me."

CHAPTER 28

BRETT FOLLOWED PAIGE DOWN THE hallway to the sleep-drawing room. He wasn't sure exactly what he thought she was going to show him that triggered her episode this morning, but what he found was much, much worse.

It was *Paige*.

He swallowed his panic at seeing her features drawn in such striking realism. In the picture she was lying at an awkward angle at the bottom of a set of stairs. Blood dripped from her nose, a piece of jagged wood clenched in one fist, the other curled loosely by her face. Her eyes stared out into nothingness.

She was very obviously dead.

A vile curse slipped from Brett's lips as he walked closer to the image.

Closer didn't make him feel any better.

Paige stood in the corner, about as far as she could get from the drawing and still be in the room.

"You okay?" he asked. The last thing she needed was another repeat of her waking coma. Although now he understood why her brain had shut down to such a degree. Her mind had been protecting itself from the most traumatic drawing yet.

"Yeah, I'm just keeping my distance from it."

Brett didn't blame her. He wanted to keep his distance from it too. From the picture itself and everything it signified.

He turned and faced Paige. "That," —he jerked his thumb towards the picture— "is *not* going to happen. Do you hear me?"

"All the other pictures did."

"Not all of them. I'm still in hopes that we're going to find the last lady alive. She isn't dead or we would've identified her like the other women. So, maybe everyone you draw isn't an actual victim. Maybe they're just people he thinks about."

But there could be no doubt Paige was connected with the killer.

"I hope so."

Brett walked over and wrapped her in his arms. "But you can believe I'm not going to let this guy get to you."

He felt her nod against his chest, but she didn't say anything.

"Also, we should take into account that you spent hours looking over your drawings last night. Poring over them in a way you'd never done before."

"So?" Her voice was small, not combative at all.

"So, maybe that got into your psyche. The fact that we spent time talking about how you should've been one of the victims. Maybe this is just your mind's way of expressing survivor's guilt."

"I guess."

Brett prayed that was true. But the way her mind had completely shut down —trapping Paige in the dark? Brett didn't think so.

Either way, Paige needed a break from all of this. She'd done what she could and now he needed to shield her from the rest. That he could and would do.

He and Alex, and probably the Feds, would figure out who the killer was. The man didn't know they were on to him, so didn't know to be more cautious. Plus, they had time. Another payday wasn't coming up for over a week.

A phone call from Alex a few minutes later proved Brett wrong.

"We've got another victim, Wagner."

"Is it—?" he didn't even get the full question out.

"The lady from Paige's drawings? Unfortunately, yes."

Brett tried to keep the conversation from Paige, but one glance at her face told him she was aware of what was going on. *Shit.*

"She was found in Salem. Name's Denise Rubio. High school science teacher."

"Was she stabbed?"

Brett could hear the tightness in Alex's voice. "Yes. Fits the pattern just like we were discussing."

Brett glanced at Paige again. She'd gone white and was leaning heavily against the wall. He didn't blame her. This now meant every single woman she'd drawn had ended up dead. He tightened his grip on the phone desperate to find a reason Paige wouldn't be next on the list.

"How long has Denise Rubio been dead?"

"Coroner says less than twenty-four hours. She already had a crap ton of people looking for her, especially when she didn't show up for work today."

"But it's not a payday."

"I don't know why he deviated, man. All I know is that this is definitely the same woman, same position, same brutality as what Paige drew. It's the same guy."

Brett knew it. "I'm with Paige right now. I can't leave her. She's having some… issues." There was no way in hell he was leaving her without knowing for sure the blackness wasn't going to drag her back under.

He felt her hand on his back.

"I'll be okay," she whispered.

He wrapped the arm not holding the phone around her, pulling her to him.

"No," he said simply. He wasn't leaving her. Not tonight.

"That's fine," Alex responded. "We have an appointment with the Salem detectives tomorrow. They were pretty surprised to hear from me since they thought it was just an isolated incident."

"Ameling is going to skin us alive if we mention this theory to Salem PD."

"Let's see how far we can get without mentioning it. Because if we have to bring up Paige's pictures this is all going to get ugly real fast."

That was the damn truth. "It's not an option."

"It may be our *only* option, Brett. We can't keep letting women die. What happens when Paige draws another picture?"

He didn't want to have this conversation in front of her. "We'll talk about this tomorrow. I'll be in first thing."

"Work with her on alibis. Make sure she knows where she was on the dates of the deaths. It will go a long way if she has to be brought in for questioning again. And tell her to keep that lawyer's number handy."

Brett didn't want Paige anywhere near the station. Her mental state was fragile enough. But he knew there might not be any way around it.

Like it or not, she was their only link to the killer.

CHAPTER 29

THEY WERE ABLE TO KEEP Paige's drawings out of the conversation with the Salem police detectives. At least the murder had occurred within state lines, only about forty-five miles south of Portland, making Brett and Alex's interest a little less questionable. If the murder had occurred over state lines, working with the detectives would've required official permission.

But within state lines didn't make Denise Rubio any less dead.

She'd been beaten, like all the women before her. Then she'd been stabbed.

"Hell of a way to go," Detective Ramon Gil said. "According to the coroner, victim was already nearly dead before the perp even stabbed her. Seems like overkill."

Brett glanced at Alex. They'd thought the very same thing with some of the other victims.

"Anything unusual about Miss Rubio that you've found?" Alex asked. "Do you have any direction in particular you're looking?"

Detective Gil shrugged, a weary frown dragging his whole face. "Honestly, we're still trying to wrap our heads around it. We're smaller than Portland PD, don't get a lot vicious murders. I've seen a few drive-bys, domestic dispute murders, but nothing like this."

Brett nodded. "Any known enemies? Fights?" Even if she had, Brett was willing to bet it wasn't the person that murdered her.

"Nothing as far as we can tell. Miss Rubio was well liked at the school by both students and faculty. Not married. No kids. Lived here for five years since she graduated from college."

"We're going to talk to the principal next. See if we can find out anything."

Gil nodded, then studied them more carefully. "Why are you here anyway? No offense intended. This definitely isn't a pissing contest. If you've got some insight to offer, I'm all ears."

Alex's eyes shot to Brett. "We had a murder a few days ago. Lady was strangled, not stabbed, but she was beaten severely beforehand. Enough similarities that we thought we would see if there might be any connection."

The other detective looked like he would press the point further, but then just shrugged again. "I'd appreciate it if information could flow both ways."

"If we find out the cases are definitely connected, we'll let you know," Brett told him.

Not long after speaking with Gil they were on their way to the high school where Denise Rubio worked. Brett drove. He'd hoped to get a call in to Paige. She'd been asleep when he'd left her early this morning, exhausted from the tension and constant fear of falling asleep, worried that if she did she might draw again. It wouldn't matter if it was another unknown woman or herself, it would still be the same: death.

She'd tried to keep her terror from him as he lay in the bed next to her. She hadn't complained or talked or tossed and turned. But her body had radiated tension to such a degree that Brett couldn't help but know what was going on.

He'd pulled her into his arms, hoping the contact would help her, knowing she needed rest after what she'd already been through. She'd relaxed into his embrace, but it wasn't long before the tension had returned.

"Every time I close my eyes, all I see is darkness," she whispered, when he'd tried rubbing the tension out of the muscles in her shoulders.

It was an odd statement. One would expect to see darkness when closing eyes, but Brett knew what she meant. Not the darkness of a restful sleep, the overpowering blackness of the killer and her link with him.

"I won't let him get you," Brett had murmured back. "I won't let you get lost in the dark."

But his words hadn't made a difference. Finally, deep in the night, he'd pulled her body underneath him and made love to her, slowly, thoroughly, bringing her to climax first with his hand, then his mouth, and finally his body, until she couldn't fight the exhaustion any longer.

Brett kept his word, watching over her as she slept, on the lookout for any nightmares, or worse — a pull from the bed towards that damn easel.

Not on his watch.

When he left her this morning the sun had been shining brightly into all the windows. She'd made it through the night.

He'd still like to make sure she was okay. To hear her voice.

Brett wasn't sure how the hell she'd come to mean so much to him in such a short time, but he couldn't question it. Catching the killer went way beyond getting justice for Paige now. He wanted this guy off the street so whatever connection her subconscious had with him could be severed.

Otherwise, Brett was afraid he'd lose her. She'd lose herself.

"What does a science teacher, physical therapist, Nike R&D executive, nurse and a receptionist have in common?" Alex was looking at the notepad he always kept with him as they now drove towards the high school where Denise Rubio taught. "And an artist?"

"Besides the start of a 'walks into a bar' joke?" The professions of the women who'd been killed didn't seem to have any link whatsoever.

Neither did their gyms, shopping habits, political affiliations, or social media patterns.

A few of them were part of online dating sites, but not all. Some had attended religious services, but others didn't.

They hadn't found a single link between all the women except for Paige's drawings. Although there was. There had to be. They just hadn't found it yet.

Denise Rubio's principal, Lisa Haneberg, didn't provide much further insight. She confirmed, like Detective Gil had said, that the young teacher had been popular among students and colleagues alike. The school was obviously reeling after what had happened to her.

The principal took Brett and Alex to the teacher's lounge where Denise had been last seen. They spoke briefly to the English teacher who had been Denise's friend and was obviously distraught at her death.

No, Denise Rubio didn't have any enemies. No, she hadn't mentioned anything unusual or suspicious before her death.

The same answer that had been true about all the other victims. The only thing different about Denise was that she hadn't been killed on a payday, and she hadn't been held for as long as the other women had been.

This killer liked to toy with his victims. Let their beatings heal just slightly before he killed them. Brett's hands clenched into fists when he thought again of how close Paige had come to death.

Principal Haneberg took them to Denise's classroom. It wasn't anything unexpected. Instead of desks, the classroom had lab tables, wooden with solid black tops and small sinks in the middle. Various high school science equipment sat on the tables: microscopes, Bunsen burners, and beakers of various sizes.

"Students really responded to Denise," Principal Haneberg said softly. "Especially the girls. She had such a passion for encouraging them to pursue STEM degrees. Science, Mathematics, Engineering."

"Has anyone looked through Miss Rubio's work emails?" Alex asked as he looked around the teacher's desk. Brett walked further into the classroom.

Haneberg nodded. "Yes. I gave Detective Gil access right away. Nothing suspicious was found."

Of course not. Nothing suspicious had been found in the emails or phones of any of the victims. No "long lost friends" emailing wanting to meet for coffee, nor an "emergency" car breakdown text from a friend that would draw them out.

Whoever had killed them had watched them. Knew patterns about each of them.

Brett walked towards the back of the classroom, looking at a machine that stood there.

"That's a 3D printer," Haneberg said. "Denise was so proud when she got the grant award to buy it. It only just arrived a couple of weeks ago. Kids were so excited to get to use it."

This one had to be much smaller than the one used to make the huge centerpiece at Paige's art show.

"What would a science teacher want with a 3D printer?" he asked. He could understand why an art studio would want one, but not a science teacher.

Haneburg joined him at the back of the room. "I can show you Denise's whole proposal if you want. But basically she argued that it could be used to interest students in a number of different aspects of science. Architects and engineers use them on a regular basis now. Any company developing prototypes for just about anything. Medical fields use them for making prosthetic limbs and I'm sure other things."

Brett spun around at Haneburg's words. "Physical therapists would use these? Nurses?"

Haneburg shrugged. "Maybe. They might not use the printer themselves, but would definitely come in contact with what the printers can produce. Especially if it involved prosthetics."

Brett glanced at Alex before looking back at Haneburg. He was listening now also. "And a Nike Research and Development executive?"

She nodded. "Without a doubt. A company like Nike would probably own multiple high end 3D printers for prototypes of shoes and other products. Like I said, Denise made a very compelling case for having one to teach students what sort of STEM jobs were out there. That's what got her the grant. The printers aren't cheap."

Alex joined them, his thinking now exactly where Brett's was. "Boeing would also use one."

The fifth victim had been a receptionist for Boeing.

"Absolutely. Why?" the Principal asked.

They didn't provide her with any details, just got the name of the company who had sold and set up the 3D printer for the school. They were rushing back out to their car less than ten minutes later, on their way to FormLabs3D back in Portland.

The link between all the victims was found. And once they saw it, it couldn't be denied.

The northwest division of FormLabs3D, part of a much larger company, sold or serviced printers connected to the workplace of each victim, including the art studio connected to Paige. Charles Sevier, FormLabs3D's manager, was able to immediately confirm this.

"Boyd Anderson is the regional salesman for northern California, Oregon and Washington State. He's one of our best sales people, has an excellent record. He would've been at all those locations."

Brett gave Alex a grim smile. "Is Anderson on the road right now? We'll need his home address."

"What's this all about? Is Boyd in trouble?"

"We just need to talk to him about a case we're working on. He might have some pertinent information." Alex was careful not to leak anything important. The last thing they wanted was for the manager to let Anderson know they were looking for him in connection to the murders. He would take to ground.

"Boyd is out two weeks at a time on sales and service routes, then has one week off."

"Where is he now?" Brett asked. "On the road?"

Charles shifted uneasily on his feet. "He should've been here this morning. Normally he would've come here to check in before going back out on his route. Actually he should've been here yesterday, but I thought maybe I had his schedule confused. Boyd has never missed a day, so I honestly hadn't checked yet."

"But he didn't come in?" Alex asked.

"No. Like I said, it's the first time in the eight years he's worked for us that he hasn't shown up. I know he made it back to Portland last week. Turned in his normal files and receipts — he's meticulous about that. Everything is always in perfect order and he follows the rules to a T. But I haven't heard or seen anything since then. Here's his address."

"Do you pay your employees on a two-week pay schedule?" Brett asked as they turned to leave.

"Yeah. The first and fifteenth of each month. Why?"

"Anything particular about paydays that you remember with Anderson?"

"Not that I recall. He has direct deposit like everyone else." Charles shifted some papers around on his desk. "Although I will say, the only time I ever saw Boyd get angry was about four years ago when I told him about the notice I'd received that the federal government would be garnishing his wages to pay alimony he owed his ex-wife. Not that I could blame him. They'd already been divorced a while."

Payday. A constant reminder of his ex-wife taking advantage of him. Definitely enough to trigger something.

Alex was already getting out his phone. "I'll see where she's located and have her brought in if she's local."

They were out the door and running back towards the car. Time was of the essence now. Charles Sevier would begin to try to contact Boyd Anderson, if only to spread the gossip that detectives were looking for him. Anderson would run.

Of course, they had to face the fact that Denise Rubio's death happening on a non-payday date and Anderson's absence from his normal work pattern meant the man might already be gone.

CHAPTER 30

B OYD ANDERSON'S HOUSE ON THE outer suburbs
of Portland was empty. Frustration pooled through
Brett as they had to wait to get a warrant to enter the
premises. But given the tie they now had between the dates
and locations the women were killed and Anderson's itinerary,
the warrant didn't take very long.

It also meant that Captain Ameling was going to know
for certain what they'd been doing today when he'd expressly
told them not to pursue this.

Brett didn't give a rat's ass. All he cared about was
capturing this killer and breaking whatever psychic link he
had with Paige.

Brett called her while they were waiting.

"Hi." As much as he wanted to arrest Anderson right at
this moment, just hearing Paige's voice, husky and soft, had
him wishing he could be back there with her.

"How are you feeling?"

"Much better. No reoccurrences of crazy. Sleep really
helped, once I was... exhausted enough to actually fall
asleep." He could almost hear her blush.

Brett opened the car door and got out, not wanting to have
this entire conversation in front of Alex. "I'm happy to help
with the exhaustion option any time I'm needed."

"Is that part of the Portland PD detective job description?"

He smiled. "Just doing what I can to protect and to serve."

"Thanks. As long as you're not offering that to every citizen who calls you."

"Only the beautiful ones with impressive artistic talents." She sounded so relaxed, he hated to stop their light banter, but he wanted to see if she recognized Boyd Anderson. "I'm sending you a photo. Do you recognize this guy?"

A few moments later Paige responded. "Yes. Vaguely. I feel like I met him at the studio. Would that be right? Is he an agent or a buyer? I can't remember his name or anything about him."

There wasn't anything particularly memorable about the man. Brown hair, cut pretty close to his head. Brown eyes with soft jaw and cheeks. Nothing that screamed serial killer.

"He works for a 3D printer company. Probably sold your art studio the printer they used for your art shows."

Tension pooled in her voice. "Brett, is he…"

"We don't know for sure. We just know that he was in the areas at the right times. He's the connection we've been looking for."

He heard her shuddery release of breath. "I should remember him. If he's the man who attacked me… I should recognize him."

"Hey. Don't beat yourself up. You can't force your mind to see what it refuses to."

"Just be careful, Brett. He's dangerous."

"I will. We're going to get him, Paige. And once he's in jail, the only thing you're going to be drawing in your sleep is me. Naked."

Her laugh was small, but at least it was there. "Deal."

"I'll call you when I have more info."

Alex got out of the car and tilted his phone back and forth at Brett.

They had their warrant.

Brett said his goodbyes to Paige and they entered the premises, using force to open the front door, weapons drawn.

Once they established no one was inside they began to look around. The house was ordinary in almost every way. Relatively tidy, two bedrooms and two baths. No evidence of anyone else living or visiting other than one male individual.

Dude washed his dishes. Did his laundry. Lived a pretty ordinary life. Highly organized. Nothing to suggest he was a killer.

Alex searched the bedroom, Brett took the home office.

The first thing he noticed was the weight and exercise machine in the corner. Obviously used often.

"We've got a pretty high end home gym here," Brett called out, grimacing.

He heard Alex's ugly curse from the other room at that news. They both knew why Anderson would be working out. It took strength and endurance to overpower and batter women the way he did. Obviously he wanted to be up to the task.

Fury burned in the back of Brett's throat. These women —*Paige*— were all so petite. Subduing them wouldn't be a problem for almost any man. Anderson made himself stronger because he wanted to be able to cause them more damage.

Brett forced himself away from the workout equipment and turned towards the computer desk in the other half of the room. He found nothing in any of the drawers. The computer itself was password protected. Brett looked around to see if the password was written anywhere —amazing how often that happened— but couldn't find anything. They would need to bring in the department experts to get them in through some sort of back door.

"You got anything, Alex?"

"Nothing here. Guy is a neat freak. Closet is pretty standard. Bathroom is the same."

They both knew that didn't mean anything. Rarely did a serial killer keep vials of blood on their bathroom shelves just in case cops came by looking for proof to arrest them.

But it ended up Anderson did the next best thing.

"I've got it, Alex."

Alex came rushing in. Brett began pulling files from the filing cabinet.

"Nike. Boeing. Matthews High School."

There was a file for the company of every victim. And inside each file was the "before" picture of each woman, obviously taken by Anderson with his own camera. If Brett hadn't known the women were dead, he would've just taken it as contact info from a thorough salesman.

Alex blew out a whistle though his teeth. "Holy shit. These candid photos are exact replicas of Paige's drawings of each woman."

Brett nodded. "Or, more accurately, vice versa." Paige had drawn every woman just like Anderson had taken their picture. "She's connected to his mind in some way, Alex. I don't know how and I don't know why. I just know it's true."

"It's damn spooky."

"Evidently her sister has worked for the FBI as a profiler. She gets some sort of reading off objects a criminal has touched."

"They both have non-traditional abilities?" Alex's eyebrow raised.

"I've seen some of the Bureau case files. Like you said, damn spooky, but undeniable. Third sister has some type of mental talent too, but I'm not sure what. They're triplets."

"Born under a full moon, I'm sure."

Brett chuckled. "No doubt."

Alex took it in stride. "Let's get this stuff back to the station. We need to get an APB out on Boyd Anderson and a warning to any other places he has on his route. See what info we have about his ex-wife also."

Back at the station they were met by Captain Ameling's glare of death. Alex took the lead with him and Brett let him, knowing anything he said to the older man was just going to make the situation worse.

Once they showed him Boyd Anderson's files, the pictures of the dead women found in his house and the dates he'd been in each city, Ameling not only backed down, he gave them free rein of any resources they needed. He even stopped glowering at Brett.

Information about Anderson's ex-wife came in. Alex called her as Brett recreated the timeline they'd created with Paige two days ago. This time they didn't have to use her drawings as their only clues. They had Anderson's pictures.

"Kimberly Anderson lives in Atlanta," Alex told Brett as he got off the phone. "They were married two years and have been divorced for five. Ugly divorce —said Anderson is quote 'beyond obsessive compulsive'— but there's no history of abuse. She hasn't seen him in at least three years. She wasn't very forthcoming about answering questions about alimony."

Brett nodded. "I'll see what I can dig up about the divorce settlement."

Alex reached over to print a picture of Kimberly that she'd sent.

Thirty-five, overweight, brown hair in a short, pixie cut.

Brett grimaced. "Not what I was expecting."

"Me either. But look at this."

He printed another picture, a wedding photo. In this one, Kimberly was younger, thinner, and her hair was longer, reaching just past her shoulders.

Just like all of Anderson's victims.

Brett whistled through his teeth. "Now that is more what I was expecting."

"So let's assume they divorced, Boyd got the shaft. Now every time payday comes around he's reminded of his ex and how she screwed him."

Alex nodded, leaning back in his chair. "And he's smart enough to know that he couldn't hurt or kill her because he'd be a prime suspect."

"So he finds women who look vaguely like her. Same build, hair. Maybe that's close enough for him. Provides the sense of power he lost in the divorce settlement."

Brett scrubbed a hand over his face. "I've known of motives that made less sense than that."

"APB is out for his arrest in Oregon, California and Washington."

A text came through on Brett's phone from Tom, Paige's head of security.

Double checking that you will have Paige for the rest of the evening.

Paige was coming here? Why? He called Tom.

"Tom? It's Brett. I didn't understand your text. Are you bringing Paige here?" That wasn't necessarily a good plan, but maybe she had taken a turn for the worse after he'd talked to her on the phone.

There was a short silence from the other man. "I dropped her off at the station ten minutes ago."

Brett stood. "Why didn't you call me? I would've met her at the door." Brett began walking towards the reception area. The officer there wouldn't have just let her back unaccompanied. "Is she okay? Why did she want to come here rather than stay at home?"

"We came here because she got a call from you asking her to come." Brett's shoulders grew tense at the man's words.

"What?"

"Not you, but an associate from the station. She was told you had arrested the man you believed responsible for these attacks and you needed her at the station for her opinion of the guy."

Brett began to run. "We haven't arrested him, Tom. I didn't have anyone make a call."

"The person said to drop her off by the back entrance where you were the other night so that it wouldn't draw a lot of attention to her presence."

Brett made a sharp turn towards the back of the building but didn't stop running.

Tom's tone was full of tension. "I dropped her off and watched until she made it to the door, then had to leave because there was no parking."

As Brett reached the back doorway into the station, he looked up and down the hall. No one was there. He yanked the door open and looked around, fear sinking into him, sick and slimy.

Paige was nowhere to be seen.

CHAPTER 31

THE BLACKNESS WAS BACK. EVEN worse than before. Not only could Paige not make her mind move this time, she couldn't make her body move either.

She looked around her for a hint of color —Brett's colors— how they'd drawn her back last time, but she couldn't see anything.

Couldn't feel anything but coldness.

Fear crawled all over her body and she couldn't get rid of it. Her heart hammered against her ribs.

She struggled to concentrate. What had triggered this? Last time the darkness had been caused by seeing the drawing of her dead self. But that hadn't been what happened this time.

She'd gotten the call from the station. Brett needed her to come down. Had arrested Boyd Anderson and needed her opinion about something. Tom had driven her. Dropped her off.

The blackness had encroached as she approached the building. She'd thought it had been because of Anderson's presence inside. By the time she'd reached the rear door she'd been dizzy, the darkness swamping her.

By then it had been too late to make her way back to Tom. She'd just hoped someone would get her to Brett.

Then Paige remembered the voice.

Let me help you, Miss Jeffries. I've been waiting a long time.

She'd felt the sting in her neck, some sort of injection, before the blackness had claimed her.

The darkness wasn't just in her mind. She'd been given some sort of tranquilizer. It reassured her for a moment until she realized there was only one reason she could think of that someone would sedate her.

Boyd Anderson had come back to finish the job.

A different sort of fear assailed her. But at least the darkness wasn't inside her mind. She needed to wake up.

Her eyelids fluttered and she tried to move, but this time felt the restraints around her hands. She couldn't free herself, but at least she had control of her body.

"Finally waking up, Miss Jeffries?"

Paige opened her eyes, but still couldn't see. But knew this black. Anderson's aura. So ugly and opaque. She'd painted it just a few days ago.

But if she didn't look straight at him, the dark didn't overwhelm her. She glanced down at the ground where she was lying. Rough, wooden floors. She looked to the sides and realized Anderson had brought her back to the same rundown warehouse where he'd tried to kill her before.

He dropped a piece of paper on the ground in front of her. "What is this?"

It was the drawing of herself. She'd brought it with her to the station when Brett had called.

"It's a drawing of me."

He reached out and grabbed her hair by the roots, forcing her face closer to it. "It's a drawing of you in this building wearing the same clothes you are now. And you're dead in the picture."

Paige winced at the pain. What was she supposed to say?

Fortunately Anderson didn't seem to want an actual answer.

"You destroyed my pattern, you know. You ruined everything when you got away."

Out of the corner of her eye Paige saw his booted foot reach back to kick her. She turned quickly to the side so he hit her shoulder rather than her ribs. Agony still burst through her but at least she wasn't dealing with broken ribs.

He grabbed her hair again, yanking Paige upright. She closed her eyes rather than look at the sickly blackness that covered him. "My pattern was perfect until you. I tried to reset it, but I couldn't. It was never the same." He threw her back to the ground.

Paige pushed away from him, towards the stairs. Anderson just laughed, letting her crawl a few feet before grabbing her ankle and yanking her forcibly back towards him. This time when he yanked her up by the hair, it was his fist that sent her crashing back down.

The pain. Paige remembered the pain. She wouldn't survive it again.

She wanted to believe that Brett would come for her, but knew she couldn't. He probably didn't even know she'd been at the station in the first place if it had been Anderson who'd called her. It might be hours before Brett realized she wasn't at home where she was supposed to be. Even then he wouldn't know where to look.

They were back at the place where Anderson had attacked her before. What was left of it after it had burned. It was the last place they would look.

Nobody was coming to rescue her.

And besides, Paige already knew how this ended. The picture was right there in front of her, lying on the ground. None of her other drawings had been wrong, so why should she think this one was, just because it was her?

She was going to die in this warehouse today.

Fear closed around Brett's throat, merciless hands that choked him until he couldn't breathe. They were waiting for the footage from the back door security camera to be sent to their email.

Anderson had Paige. He'd been one step ahead of them the whole time. He'd been watching her.

"She told me she saw the darkness here at the station when she left the other morning," Brett said, pacing back and forth in front of his desk. "I chalked it up to stress. But if darkness is what she sees every time Anderson is near her…"

"She mentioned the same at the art show," Tom grimaced, holding his phone away from him for a second. "She didn't press it, of course, because she always felt embarrassed when she would get nervous."

Tom put his cheek back to his phone, was making calls to whatever private contacts he had that might be able to help.

Brett would take whatever help he could get.

He had no idea how long Anderson had been following Paige, but had a gut wrenching suspicion it had been since the beginning.

"He never let her go," Brett said to Alex. "It's like Anderson's ex-wife said about him being so obsessive compulsive. Paige was a part of his pattern and he needed to kill her to complete it."

"Maybe. But for two years?" Alex's shoulder raised in a half shrug. "That's a hell of a long time to not make a move."

Brett sat down in his office chair but then jumped right back up. He couldn't sit now. It was all he could do to keep from hitting a wall. "She never went out unaccompanied, so he couldn't get to her. But that didn't mean he wasn't watching."

Tom leaned away from the phone again. "That's true. She never went anywhere without part of the security detail right at her side. Rarely left the house at all to be honest. I was happy when the two of you started seeing each other. I thought it might encourage her to get out more."

All three of the men grimaced. Evidently Anderson had just been biding his time.

"At least now we know why he killed Denise Rubio even though it wasn't a payday." Brett ran a hand through his hair. "He saw Paige leave here the other night so he knew she'd been working with us. Maybe he thought she could identify him."

"He was trying to finish his strangled, stabbed, burned pattern," Alex finished the thought for Brett.

"Paige fits his needs twofold. First he gets back the prey that got away. And if Denise Rubio was stabbed, then Paige will be…"

Burned. Brett couldn't even bring himself to say it.

"That's not going to happen," Alex said softly.

Brett looked at Tom. "You know what caused her to go all comatose yesterday? She drew this." He grabbed his phone to show Tom and Alex the picture of Paige.

Both of them muttered low, rough words.

"She drew her own death. Just like she drew all those other women dead."

Tom, to his credit, didn't press for details about how or why Paige had been drawing dead women. Brett couldn't stop staring at the picture.

"Footage from the doorway just arrived via email." Alex brought up the images on his computer. It didn't take them long to rewind to twenty minutes ago.

"There." Brett pointed to Paige as she came into the frame. The camera didn't cover all the way back to the road where Tom had been stopped. Paige turned and gave a short wave to Tom.

"That's when I left," he muttered.

Her face was a pasty white and it was obvious she was struggling to stay on her feet.

"Anderson was nearby." Brett leaned to observe more closely. "That's why she's so unsteady. All she can see is blackness around him."

Anderson had never been inside the building. He stepped out from a darkened corner and slid an arm around Paige just as she reached the door.

"Shit. He injected her with something," Alex said.

They watched as Paige collapsed against him. He kept her upright by draping her arm around his neck and keeping his arm brutally wrapped around her body and clamped to her upper arm. A moment later they were both out of range of the camera. No way to tell which direction Anderson had taken her once he'd gotten her to the vehicle.

Brett slammed his fist down on the desk.

"Her shirt was red," Tom said. "It's black in the drawing she did of herself. Not red."

Brett felt a little bit of hope but then shook his head. "Rewind it to just before they stepped out from under the overhang."

In front of them Anderson drugged Paige again and then stepped out into the rain. They were only in frame for a couple of seconds but in that time Paige's shirt was already getting wet, turning the red into a much darker color.

"By the time he got her to his vehicle her shirt would be black with rain," Brett said.

And if her drawing held true, unless Anderson was keeping her out in the open somewhere, she'd be dead before it dried.

Captain Ameling joined them, already aware of the situation. For once he wasn't combative. "We've got APBs out on both of them. I've made sure everyone knows to get the details of Boyd Anderson's car out to every official and unofficial contact we have. I even called Chief Pickett personally to see if he could get the governor to get us more resources, since Paige Jeffries is friends with his wife."

That call couldn't have been easy to make, given Ameling's feelings about Brett and the chief. "Thank you," Brett said.

Ameling shrugged. "You tried to tell me there was a link, but I didn't want to believe it. It looks like this guy is a serial killer. I don't want to lose another woman."

"Captain, Brett, I think you need to look at this." Alex had taken the electronic copy of the picture Paige had drawn and enlarged it on his computer screen.

"What am I looking at?" Ameling asked. "Besides Paige Jeffries."

"Sir, you probably don't want to know," Brett told him. He didn't want to get into all the drawings right now.

Ameling rolled his eyes. "Fine." He studied the picture longer. "She looks pretty dead."

"Look at the detail around the stairs, Captain," Alex said. "I think this might be the same place Anderson held her before."

For the first time the slightest smidgen of hope lit Brett's chest. "I thought that place burned down. A warehouse, right?"

"She got away because of a fire, but the building didn't completely burn down."

"And it could make sense that he would take her there, given his obsessiveness with patterns. He'd want to finish what he'd started."

"You two go," Ameling said. "It's worth a shot. If anything comes in here, I'll let you know immediately."

Brett and Alex were already running out the door.

CHAPTER 32

"YOU RUINED EVERYTHING." ANDERSON ACCENTUATED his words with an open blow to Paige's face. He once again held her up by her collar. "My pattern would've been perfect if not for you. You betray. You abandon. You steal. I'm doing future men a favor by killing you. By killing you all."

Paige could feel his hot breath on her cheek as he held her pulled up to her knees. She still didn't look at him. Kept her gaze down, away from the darkness.

"I never knew why you didn't identify me." His touch was almost gentle when he stroked some hair away from her face. "I thought your brain had just blocked it out or something. But that wasn't it, was it? Your eyes don't work right or something."

His gentle fingers trailing down her cheek were almost worse than his fists. "I can't see you because of all the black. All your evil."

He snickered and released her arm, dropping her back to the ground. "I read about you. Before and after our first... meeting. I read how some critic said your paintings are the colors of people's souls. I thought it was a load of crap, if you don't mind me saying so." He grabbed her chin with his hand, forcing her to look up at him. Paige kept her view to the side. "But maybe it was true."

He squeezed her jaw so tightly she could feel her teeth grind against the inside of her cheek and tasted blood.

"But you know what? It doesn't matter if you can identify me or not because you're not going to be alive to tell anyone about me."

Paige couldn't help herself, she whimpered.

"You ruined my pattern. I tried to start over but it wasn't the same. I've waited to get to you for two years. Two years." He threw her back down again. She could make out his shoes from where he stood in front of her. "So I'm going to finish you off today. Burn you until there's nothing left. Today I save another man —probably that handsome detective— from making the mistake of taking someone like you as a wife. Someone who will just use him. Betray, abandon, steal."

His foot flew out again, but this time she couldn't turn away fast enough. He caught her in the ribs. Agony blasted through her as she fell to the side, gasping for air. A second later another kick caught her in the hip. Paige huddled into a ball trying to protect herself. She waited for another brutal blow, but it didn't come.

Instead a few moments later liquid poured down on her.

Gasoline.

It soaked her hair and shirt. Breathing became nearly impossible through the fumes.

"I won't make the same mistake as last time. This time when the building burns, you burn with it."

She heard the sickening sound of a lighter being flicked on and off, as he opened and closed it with a snapping motion of one hand. She sat up, struggling to get air through both the gasoline and the agony in her ribs.

"It's your fault I must leave and start my pattern again. And I will, you know." His shoes began to pace back and forth in front of the stairs. "I'll just begin the pattern somewhere else. But this time I won't let anyone ruin it."

Paige shifted to try to get some relief for her ribs and felt the drawing of herself under her hand. The gasoline had dripped down onto it and blurred the image.

Paige crumpled the picture, ignoring Anderson as he continued to monologue about… whatever the hell reason he had for torturing and killing women. She didn't care anymore.

She wasn't going to cower in front of him any longer. If she was going to die here, so be it.

But that didn't mean she couldn't take this bastard with her.

Using the last of her strength she burst up from the ground and propelled herself at the darkness that was Anderson. She heard his curse as she slammed into him, flinging them both down the stairs. She grabbed at the banister to catch herself, but it broke off in her hand. Anderson's scream echoed in her ears and she knew this was the end —that these were the steps where she'd meet her death— as she hit the bottom and everything went dark.

All the pain disappeared.

But a few moments later it was back. Darkness still surrounded her. Somehow she wasn't dead.

"It's amazing." Anderson's voice was right over her. "Look at you. You're lying exactly as you were in that drawing. You drew yourself dead before it even happened." He gave a sickening chuckle.

But she wasn't dead. How was it possible she wasn't dead? She could feel the jagged piece of wood in her hand, just like the picture. Could feel the bend of her leg at the angle she'd drawn it, draped over the stairs.

But she wasn't dead.

Maybe this time, this *one* time, instead of drawing the moment of the victim's death, she'd drawn the moment the victim determined to *live*.

"I don't care if you're dead, you're still going to burn," Anderson said. She heard the lighter flick again.

"Not today." She forced the words past her battered lips. Heard his gasp.

Calling on her last bit of strength, Paige brought the wood from the banister still resting in her grip and slammed it with every bit of force she could muster into Anderson's head. He fell over, moaning and she twisted herself up, bringing the club of wood down against his head again.

This time he fell over for good, his neck landing at a sickening angle. The darkness surrounding Anderson disappeared and Paige could finally see him. His aura was gone.

Boyd Anderson was dead.

Paige crumpled back onto the steps, completely spent.

She watched as the lighter fell out of his hand and onto the floor, still flaming. The gasoline that had been dripping off her body was now almost to the open flame. She forced herself to move, sobbing in agony as she tried to pull herself back up the stairs, but realized that with the gasoline still dripping off her clothes the flame would chase her no matter where she went.

It seemed like she couldn't outrun death after all.

Paige closed her eyes wishing she could do more. Her breathing was becoming more and more labored, air harder to pull into her lungs. Anderson's kicks followed by the fall down the stairs had done some pretty serious damage. Even if the fire didn't get her, she wasn't going to make it out of here alive.

She just wished she could see Brett one more time.

And then as if her thoughts had conjured him, he was there, weapon drawn, stomping the line of flames snaking its way towards her. Alex was right behind him. She could see relief on Brett's face as their eyes met, before it was swallowed by concern.

Brett turned and muttered something to Alex who pulled out his phone. Paige couldn't hear them. Nothing seemed to be working right. She couldn't even get up from the stairs.

"Hey, sweetheart." Brett crouched right in front of her, his purples and blues such a refreshing change from the black. He brushed her hair back from her forehead, gently. Sweetly. "We've got an ambulance coming."

"My drawing was wrong," she murmured. "I didn't die."

"Damn right you didn't."

"I don't want to draw any more. Never again. I'll stick to painting." Breathing was becoming more difficult.

"Don't talk sweetie, okay?" She could see gray starting to overtake Brett's other colors. His fear. Worry for her.

"I'm just going to rest."

"Paige, no baby. No resting. Not yet. Open those gorgeous blue eyes, okay? If you do, I'll tell you about how I thought your eyes were so gorgeous even in high school…"

She tried to open her eyes, she really did. Wanted to know if he was telling the truth. And she'd had enough of darkness, even the normal kind that came from closing one's eyes. But she couldn't keep them open.

The darkness pulled her under once again.

It was the longest two days of Brett's life.

By the time the paramedics arrived Paige's breathing was shallow. Panic had Brett's heart hammering against his ribs. The danger had not died with Boyd Anderson.

Paige's internal injuries had been severe. One lung punctured, the other completely collapsed. Concussion, dislocated shoulder.

They'd kept her in a medically induced coma to give her body a chance to heal. Brett had refused to leave her side, informing the hospital that he was Paige's fiancé.

Hell, it had worked in a movie once, so it had been worth a try. Anything to be able to stay with her.

Then Paige's sisters, Adrienne and Chloe, showed up a few hours later. They spent a long time talking to the doctors to find out Paige's exact status and seemed reassured when they were told she would be waking up soon.

More importantly he'd been glad they hadn't had him thrown out.

"Fiancé?" Chloe asked.

Brett shrugged. "Worked in *While You Were Sleeping*."

Chloe grinned. "That's true."

Adrienne, obviously in her third trimester of pregnancy, had brought her husband Conner. After talking to the doctors, she'd asked her husband to leave before Brett could even talk to him.

Brett found it interesting that Conner Perigo rolled his eyes, but did it.

"You've got five minutes," he said to Adrienne on his way out the door. "I'm not leaving you here unshielded any longer than that."

She blew him a kiss. "I only need three."

Brett gave the two women a confused look. "I have no idea what's going on."

"Adrienne wants to make sure you're a good guy. Not going to hurt Paige. She can't do that if Conner's around."

Chloe shrugged. She turned to her sister. "I could still read Brett, Adrienne. You didn't have to make Conner leave."

"What do you mean, *read me?*" Brett asked.

Chloe ignored him. "He's got no thoughts but whether Paige is going to be alright and if he's going to pull his badge if we try to kick him out of the room."

Brett nearly choked on his shock. Those were the exact things he'd been thinking.

"I need to know for myself. He's who Paige has chosen." Adrienne's voice was softer, more like Paige's and less like Chloe's more animated one. Her face was already pinched.

"I'm not really her fiancé," Brett said. "I just want to make sure you know that."

Adrienne nodded. "But you're still who she's chosen."

He reached out to Adrienne who was looking paler than she had a minute ago. "Are you okay?"

She smiled, although it still looked a little pained. "I was going to ask if I could touch your arm, but I don't have to. It's nice to meet such a clear good guy."

Brett looked back and forth between the two women. "Okay, I seriously don't understand what's happening."

Chloe and Adrienne both just smiled at him. There was no doubt these women were Paige's sisters. They weren't identical —Adrienne's hair was short and brown, Chloe's was longer with red highlights— but they had the same elegant bone structure, crystalline blue eyes and lush mouths.

And these women obviously loved and wanted to protect Paige.

Even if it was by using some sort of woo-woo power.

A moment later Conner Perigo walked back into the room. Adrienne immediately began looking stronger, less pale. Conner slipped his arm around her. "I knew five minutes would be too long. It's too crowded here."

Adrienne kissed him. "You're around me so much now. I forget how loud it is without you."

Chloe jumped up from the chair she'd taken and patted Brett on the shoulder. "Conner blocks all the mental noise for Adrienne. Keeps the bad guys out of her head. Handy."

"And you?" Brett asked. "Does someone help you block… whatever it is you do?"

She grinned and winked at him. "Nah. I can turn down the volume myself. I don't take things quite as seriously as my two big sisters."

"You're the writer, right? For that zombie vampire paranormal show?"

"Yep." She popped the p. "Amazing how hearing the thoughts of everyone around me gives me good ideas. Reality is stranger than…"

Chloe turned away from him and moved toward Paige. She walked over so she was standing right by Paige's head.

"That's right, sister." Chloe said softly into Paige's ear as they all watched. "We're all right here. You come on back to us when you're ready."

Chloe looked back at them. "Paige hears us. Likes to hear us all talking. Lets her know she's not trapped in the black." She touched Brett's arm. "You led her out of the darkness before. Evidently she's using your colors to lead her out again."

Brett reached down and kissed Paige on the forehead. "My colors are right here waiting for you."

CHAPTER 33

Six months later.

"OH MY GOSH, WAGNER, YOU have got to hold still. Where's that QB focus you're so famous for?"

Brett rolled his eyes and shifted slightly on the stool. "I'm damn sure I never did anything like this in my quarterback days."

"That's a shame because you probably could've distracted the other teams this way. Or at least all the females in the stands." Paige laughed, the pure, carefree sound of it so beautiful it took Brett's breath away. He would do anything to hear that sound from her as often as possible.

Even this.

The shadows were gone from her eyes. The wounds from Boyd Anderson's attack completely faded. She was happy, no longer afraid the darkness would overtake her.

"Besides, you were the one who gave me this idea." He couldn't see her now but could hear the smile in her voice.

"I know, don't remind me. *I know*," he grumbled. "No good deed goes unpunished."

"And this is for a grade. I'm almost done. So hold still, Wagner!"

Brett shifted again on the stool. "You make millions of dollars every year selling your paintings. Why on earth do you need to take a drawing class?"

He knew why. Her brain obviously knew how to draw with eerie realism, but she'd never been able to do it consciously. She thought taking a drawing class would help. Maybe trigger something subconsciously. Brett had thought it was a great idea.

Right up until a couple of hours ago when she pointed out that he'd once offered, actually *demanded*, that if she wanted to draw something that it would be him.

Naked.

So now his bare ass was on a stool in the middle of the room that used to hold such bad memories for her. He hoped to God this helped her let the fear and ugliness of the other drawings go.

"This isn't ever going to get around the station, is it?"

"Of course not, honey," she said from behind the easel, not even poking her head out to look at him. "I would make much more money selling it to your ex-cheerleaders."

Brett groaned. The little minx might even do it too.

"Well hurry up. I actually ordered some paints and they came in today." He pointed at the bag sitting on the couch. "I was hoping you could help me use them."

Now she looked at him from behind the easel. "Really?" Her smile beamed at him. "You want to try painting? You didn't have to order any paints. You could've used some from my studio."

These were a very special kind of paints. Ones he was quite sure she didn't have even in her extensive collection. He barely refrained from waggling his eyebrows.

"I know. But I didn't want to use yours. So hurry so we can get to my painting."

She put down the pencil. "I'm done. I've just been torturing you by making you sit there. I like looking at you naked."

"Pervert." He grinned. "Can I see it?"

She sighed. "Yeah. Bring your paints. That way I can give you a lesson in painting and won't feel so bad. We can both compare our lack of talent."

He grabbed the bag and came to stand behind her at the easel. When he saw the drawing she'd done, he burst out laughing.

It was terrible. Nowhere near the detail of the drawings she had done in her sleep. No one would ever recognize him from the paper on her easel right now.

She elbowed him in the stomach. "Don't laugh." But she joined him. "It is pretty bad. I'm going to have to start with something more basic, not the human body."

"Why don't you just stick to painting? I think that will be just fine."

She turned around and he began unbuttoning the shirt of his she was wearing. Kissed her as he slid it off her shoulders.

"I thought I was giving you a painting lesson."

He reached down and grabbed the special paint he ordered, holding it out in front of her.

Edible body paint.

"Actually, I'm going to give you a painting lesson."

Her eyes widened and a wicked smile moved over her lips. "You know the best paintings take time. Hours. And lots and lots of lessons."

He cupped the back of her neck and pulled her to him. "I can be a slow learner. I'm probably going to need lessons for the next fifty years or so."

"I think I can manage that." She barely got the words out before his mouth devoured hers and he smeared paint across her shoulders before slowly licking it off.

It was definitely better than the art class they'd had in high school.

ABOUT THE AUTHOR

"Passion that leaps right off the page." - Romantic Times Book Reviews

Winner of the Golden Quill Award for Best Romantic Suspense, and a finalist in multiple other Romance literary awards, Janie Crouch loves to read - almost exclusively romance - and has been doing so since middle school. She cut her teeth on Harlequin (Mills & Boon) Romances when she lived in Wales, UK as a preteen, then moved on to a passion for romantic suspense as an adult.

Janie recently relocated with her husband and four children to Germany (due to her husband's job as support for the U.S. Military), after living in Virginia for nearly 20 years.

When she's not listening to the voices in her head (and even when she is), she enjoys traveling, long-distance running, movie-watching, knitting and adventure (obstacle) racing. Janie completed an Ironman Triathlon in 2014 and is prepping for another one in 2017.

Her favorite quote: "Life is a daring adventure or nothing." - Helen Keller.

www.janiecrouch.com

Made in the USA
Middletown, DE
29 January 2024

48764750R00139